Praise for
For the Good of the Realm

"This lighthearted, female-led fantasy adventure from Moore (*The Weave*) follows a pair of Queen's Guards—staid, circumspect Anna and feisty, impulsive Asamir—as they become embroiled in the machinations of the rulers of Grande Terre. As the threat of war looms and a sinister undercurrent of forbidden magic becomes harder for Anna to ignore, the two women must out-fight and out-think the enemies of the realm in a series of duels and cloak-and-dagger intrigues.... With a principal cast of mostly women, this is sure to appeal to readers looking for stories of empowered female characters that go beyond simply giving them swords."

—*Publishers Weekly*, June 2021

"*For the Good of the Realm* is a sparkling tournament of a novel, full of thrills as well as feats of storytelling bravado. Moore has invented a feminist medieval otherworld that is egalitarian in its sword and sorcery, yet political intrigue ultimately rules as Anna, a stalwart member of the Queen's Guard, collaborates with a range of surprising characters to foil the nefarious plots of a power-hungry Hierofante. Spirited and funny, this is a great read."

—Lesley Wheeler, author of *Unbecoming*

"*For the Good of the Realm* is a splendid, swashbuckling romp that captures the very spirit of the Musketeers. The author weaves palace intrigue, swordplay, romance, and divided loyalties into a deeply satisfying fantasy adventure with women at the center of the narrative, wielding and negotiating power."

—Tansy Rayner Roberts, author of *Musketeer Space* and The Creature Court Trilogy

For the Good of the Realm

For the Good of the Realm

by

Nancy Jane Moore

Aqueduct Press

Aqueduct Press
PO Box 95787
Seattle, Washington 98145-2787
www.aqueductpress.com

Library of Congress Control Number: 2021936037

ISBN: 978-1-61976-187-2

First Edition, First Printing, June 2021

10 9 8 7 6 5 4 3 2 1

Cover illustration courtesy Ruby Rae Jones
www.rubyraejones.com, @ruby.rae
Book design by Kathryn Wilham

Printed in the USA by McNaughton & Gunn

Acknowledgments

This book owes its biggest debt to Alexandre Dumas. At the end of the 20th century, I binge-read Dumas's Musketeer books, not just *The Three Musketeers*, but also the sequels that detailed d'Artagnan's later career. I love a good adventure story, and Dumas wrote some of the best, but the women in his stories left a lot to be desired. I always hated the "Milady" story and Dumas's Queen is a weepy mess (or perhaps I am remembering the way Geraldine Chaplin played her in my favorite movie version, the one in which a young Michael York played d'Artagnan).

I doubt Dumas would appreciate where I have taken his story. But perhaps he might forgive me a bit if I suggest that Roland de Barthes in this story bears some physical resemblance to him.

This book started in 1999, when I wrote the first draft of a short story about Anna and the rest during a writing retreat in Sainte-Anne-de-Beaupre, Quebec, with my Clarion West classmates Therese Pieczynski, Robert Wexler, and the late (and deeply missed) Kate Major. That story, "A Mere Scutcheon," was published in my PS Publishing collection *Conscientious Inconsistencies*. It was PS editor Nick Gevers who first suggested to me that it should become a novel.

The idea stayed in the back of my mind, but it took me quite a few years to get around to it. Events of the past few years convinced me that spending time in a world where the political intrigue and crises did not resemble our own would provide me with respite and might appeal to readers as well.

Our local writing group, the Flying Kerrs (named in honor of member Katharine Kerr), read an early draft. I am particularly grateful to Madeleine E. Robins who suggested at one point that the character who became the Hierofante could be a woman. Once again I discovered the value in shifting genders.

My sweetheart Jim Lutz and my sister, poet Katrinka Moore, both provided useful and encouraging advice when it was most needed. And as always, I greatly appreciate the editing at Aqueduct by L. Timmel Duchamp and Kath Wilham.

The late Vonda N. McIntyre read and commented on a late draft. Her encouragement and advice made this a better book. I wish she could be here to read the final version.

All errors and shortcomings are, of course, my own.

Dedication

In memory of Vonda N. McIntyre

Chapter 1

"OUR CREDIT SHOULD still be good at the Café Maudite," Asamir said, leaning toward the mirror to rearrange her blonde curls for the third time. She pinched her pale white cheeks to give them a hint of color.

Anna d'Gart waited—with resignation rather than patience—while her fellow guardswoman primped. She had casually tied back her thick chestnut hair after training, but she was accustomed to Asamir's vanity. "The King's Guardsmen frequent the Maudite," she said. "We might find some trouble there."

"Do you have funds for dinner?" Asamir asked.

"No."

"Well then." Asamir gave her hair a final pat and smoothed out the front of her blue velvet tunic trimmed in real gold. Anna's tunic—like those worn by the rest of the Queen's Guard—was made of blue wool embroidered with dyed thread. Not as elegant as Asamir's, perhaps, but much easier to care for.

Indeed, Anna's prediction proved correct, for men in the red and gold of the King's Guard filled the Maudite. But the host greeted the women fondly and gave them a good table against the back wall. They ordered bread and cheese, and a little wine. And all went well until a young guardsman began to pester Asamir.

The man was not known to them—a new member of the Guard, no doubt recently come from some province where he had made a name in battle. Handsome enough, with shiny straight black hair and a warm tan complexion, he might have piqued

Asamir's interest but for the fact that he had already reached the obnoxious stage of drunkenness.

At first he tried to entice Asamir to spend the evening with him, for the fact that he served the King and she the Queen did not seem to affect his romantic desires. Nor, Anna knew, would that alone have affected Asamir's, had she been interested.

But Asamir declined his advances—Anna suspected she had an engagement with the Marquis de _____, whose wife was said to be in the country this week—and the young man took offense.

He insulted the Queen's virtue, and Asamir told him to behave himself. Then he insulted the virtue of the Queen's Guard, and that of Asamir in particular, and Asamir put her hand on the hilt of her sword and suggested he watch his tongue.

And then he insulted the fighting ability of the Queen's Guard. Asamir stood up, saying, "You have gone too far, sir." Anna sighed, but also stood.

A couple of the King's men nearby egged him on, but another who had been sitting with him pulled him back. "He is only jesting, my friends," the second man said, but the first shook free and stood up, showing himself to be a head shorter than Asamir.

"I am not. No woman can fight as well as a man, and I will be glad to prove it."

"Shall we step outside, then?" Asamir said.

Anna said, "Let him be. He is drunk."

"What? Let him get away with insulting us in public?" She started for the back door. Anna sighed once more, but she followed. Asamir would need a second.

The night was clear and the moon at three-quarters, providing a little light in the narrow alley behind the tavern. Several King's men had come out to see the show, and two of them had brought candles from the tables inside, increasing the illumination. The strong smell of piss near the door demonstrated that many customers did not bother going as far as the latrine across the way. Given the smells emanating from that location, their behavior was wise. The ground was dusty; there had been no rain in the past week.

In the dim light, Anna could see that the drunk had drawn his sword and was making fancy feints with it. Asamir drew her own and crossed swords with him.

The man who had pulled the drunk back also joined them in the alley. He met Anna's eyes. The two were of a height, both taller than his friend but shorter than Asamir. Honor demanded that they fight on behalf of their friends. He bowed. "Roland de Barthes, at your service, Madame."

Anna had heard the name. Rumor said he saved the King's life when the court had traveled to the provinces to view a battle on the Realm's frontiers during the last war with Foraoise. Legend had it that Roland had pushed the King over and yelled, "Down, you fool" to keep him from being shot.

A fine-looking man, with thick black curls that hung to his shoulders, skin a darker shade than Anna's own rich olive brown, and deep brown eyes that looked like they might be merry in other circumstances. "Anna d'Gart at yours, sir."

His eyes widened. "Ah, Jean-Paul has an unerring eye for formidable opponents. Everyone has heard of the honorable Anna d'Gart." But he drew his blade, and they began to parry and strike.

It took only a few moves for Anna to determine that Roland himself was as formidable as his reputation had indicated. She saw what should have been a fatal opening and lunged, but he parried easily and caught the edge of her sleeve with his return.

Out of the corner of her eye she could see that Jean-Paul was giving Asamir some trouble. He used his shorter stature to advantage, crouching and striking low, often a problem for taller fighters such as Asamir. Had he not been so drunk, he would have presented her with a real challenge. But Anna saw him stumble to a knee before Roland came in with a flurry of moves that commanded all of her attention.

She heard Jean-Paul cry out, followed by a triumphant yell from Asamir.

Roland pulled back, holding his sword in front of him, pointing it toward the sky. "Honor is satisfied," he said.

Anna yielded as well. "Best you take him out of here, before someone comes."

Blood stained Jean-Paul's chest. Roland half-dragged him down the alley. Anna took Asamir's arm, and they slipped out the other direction.

Asamir went off to keep her engagement with the Marquis, and Anna took a discreet way home. She thought someone might have reported them. And, indeed, when she reached her flat, she saw two soldiers attired in the Hierofante's white and gold loitering in her street. None lurked in the alley behind her building, however. She climbed to her lodgings using the solid chestnut that grew outside her rear window.

A girl wearing the finery of a Queen's page sat at her table. And the impertinent snip was drinking the last of her wine!

The girl jumped up. She gave Anna a deep curtsy, and said, "Madame, the Queen would like to see you forthwith."

"At this hour, child? Surely Her Majesty has gone to bed."

"Well, indeed, Madame, she wished to see you some hours earlier. But she said to bring you as soon as I found you, and I have found you." The girl broke from her formality to finish her wine. "Come, let us be gone," she said, moving toward the window.

Anna looked at her, somewhat surprised.

"The Queen did bid me be very discreet. And the Hierofante's soldiers wait in your street, as you must know."

The girl scrambled down the tree as easily as Anna, despite her fancy dress. Likely she would become a guardswoman rather than a lady-in-waiting when she grew older.

They used a back entrance at the palace as well. The Queen was pacing up and down her chamber when Anna was shown in.

"Your Majesty," Anna said, giving a deep bow.

"Oh, Madame, I am so glad you have come. I am in great need of your wise counsel and your strong arm."

"I am at your service, Your Majesty."

The Queen wrung her hands. Dark purplish circles under reddened eyes marked her light brown face. Her hairdresser would have bemoaned the state of her ebony curls, pulled this way and that.

"The King is giving a ball in two weeks."

Anna nodded. She had heard of the ball. She was among the members of the Queen's Guard who had been selected to attend.

"He has asked that I wear the sapphire necklace he gave to me at the first anniversary of our marriage."

Anna nodded again.

The Queen turned her back. "I have given it to the Countess of Beaufort." She buried her face in her hands.

Anna sighed, though not loudly enough for the Queen to hear. The Countess's estate lay far north of the Capital, a good four days' ride. With no complications, she would just be able to get there and back before the ball. And no gambler would bet on there being no complications.

"The King must not hear that I have sent you to the Countess, else he might suspect something amiss."

Anna rather thought the King already suspected something amiss, or he would not have made an issue about the necklace.

The marriage of the Queen to the King five years earlier had reunified the Realm. For the hundred and fifty years previous to that marriage, there had been two competing royal families, the Andrean line, which had produced the Queen, and the Meloran line, ancestors to the King. They had not officially divided the Realm between them, but only because when duels and even battles between the factions reached a peak and some began to press for a complete division, saner heads had prevailed, pointing out that complete severance would leave the Realm at the mercy of Foraoise on its northeast and Alhambra on its southwest borders,

5

not to mention several other nearby countries. And indeed, whenever the Realm had been threatened, the two sides joined forces in its defense, though if the truth be told, they squabbled quite a bit over how to do so as well.

The separation had meant the competing rulers usually made policy separately, decisions that not infrequently caused complications for the Realm as a whole. For example, the Meloran rulers often provoked difficulties with Foraoise over the Airgead mines, a major source of gold and other valuable metals located in the east on the border between the two realms. It was the Meloran contention that those mines belonged to the Realm, while the rulers of Foraoise were equally adamant about their ownership of the mines. The Andreans took no position on the mines, but from time to time disputed with the Alhambrans over the precise location of the southwestern border.

Control of the Church also passed back and forth between the two sides, since the Hierofante who led it was always appointed from among members of the royal family not destined to rule. At times, there were competing hierofantes as well as rulers.

The negotiations that led to the marriage of the current King and Queen also led to the installation of the King's aunt as Hierofante. There were those of the Andrean side who objected to this, but as the Andrean claimant to the position had recently died, leaving no high ranking bishop or even priest among that line, the Queen's family agreed to this compromise. While the Hierofante's preference for the King her nephew and the Meloran side were well known, the Andreans who agreed to the decision considered the Queen more than a match for the Hierofante.

And indeed, the marriage had up to this point brought about a more peaceful time within the Realm, for the ongoing skirmishes between the Andrean and Meloran armies had been reduced to duels between the elite Queen's and King's Guards. These duels were numerous, since the initial members of the Queen's Guard had been part of the Andrean forces, while the

King's had been staffed exclusively with Melorans, but they were rarely fatal. Since both guards added new members from time to time, this distinction had faded, but the politics of it still held sway. The members of most of the other forces—with the major exception of the Hierofante's Guard—had been combined into a national army, with a number of separate guard troops; this unification had gone more smoothly than the other compromises, in part because of a short war with Foraoise that, while it resolved very little between the two countries, allowed the members of the new army to develop esprit de corps. It rained excessively throughout that war, and the soldiers had united in cursing both the mud and those who led them into an impossible conflict.

Upon their marriage, the Queen and King had moved into the royal palace in the Capital, a building that had been vacant for a century and a half, except for the brief occasions when the two sides had come together to fight outside attack. It promised to be a new era for the Realm, if they could manage to work together. Their heir—should they ever get around to producing one—would rule without the division. But since it was a marriage made for political reasons, not for love, both parties had an incentive to seek love elsewhere. Such behavior was usually ignored so long as no evidence of it was produced. But the absence of the necklace threatened that détente.

Certainly the Hierofante would take advantage of the situation. She had manipulated the King his entire life. Her Majesty, though religious, was not easily swayed by the Hierofante's words, particularly when the religious leader opined on issues not related to God and worship. The two were often at odds, with the Queen usually prevailing on matters of state. Should the Queen be discredited...

Her Majesty did not impress in this moment of personal need. Her behavior had been foolish in the extreme. Taking a lover was one thing, but giving gifts that could be traced quite another. However, Anna had also seen the Queen meet with generals and make hard decisions of state, and at those times she acquitted herself well. Better, in fact, than her husband, who was not noted for his ability to understand the details of affairs foreign and domestic. In fact, many whispered that the King's father had sought the marriage and reunification because he knew his son was incapable of ruling on his own.

And even had Anna not respected the abilities of the Queen, she was sworn to protect and defend her. If that meant a hell-for-leather ride to retrieve a gift that should never have been given, so be it. Honor demanded it.

"I dare not give you any written message for the Countess," the Queen said. "You will have to persuade her of your bona fides."

"Perhaps a word shared between the two of you that no one else might know would establish my good faith," Anna said.

"Yes, of course." The Queen hesitated, then leaned forward to whisper in Anna's ear. "Tell her that her Royal Honey needs her help." Her Majesty blushed as she said it.

Anna managed to control her impulse to smile. She backed up and bowed, but did not turn to leave.

"Please hurry, Madame. We have not much time."

"My lady, I will need supplies and a horse."

"Oh, yes, of course." The Queen motioned to the nearest lady-in-waiting, who handed Anna a purse. "Please leave as soon as you can."

"Of course, Your Majesty." She gave her best bow.

Anna spent the remainder of the night in a tavern where she was unknown. In the early morning, she set out for the Queen's Guard headquarters to get permission from the Captain for a few days' leave.

At the gate of the barracks she met Asamir. "The Captain wants to see us," Asamir said.

"Someone did turn us in for dueling, then."

And, indeed, the gate guard confirmed it. "An emissary from the Hierofante came earlier."

Asamir touched her head and then her heart, a gesture used by the religious to seek holy protection. "If the Hierofante has heard of this, I will never be allowed to take holy orders."

Anna gave her a look. She did not believe in Asamir's oft-repeated plan to take vows. The vow of chastity might not cause much of a problem—it was but lightly honored by most of the clergy—but the idea that Asamir would cover the hair she fussed over and dress in black wool was frankly ludicrous. However, all she said was, "I told you not to fight a drunken man. If you had not run him through, we would not be in all this trouble."

"He besmirched my honor—our honor," Asamir said. "How could I allow such disrespect? Besides, we followed the proper rules of dueling. The fight was fair."

"That will not keep us from being hanged for dueling," Anna said.

"Oh, they will not hang us," Asamir said confidently as they went in. "The Captain will protect us."

Inside the gate was a large compound, with training grounds, barracks, and other facilities scattered about. In the center, a three-story building overlooked the entire area. The first floor was an open space used for meetings and large dinners; the second consisted of offices, with the captain's being the largest. The captain herself lived on the third floor. She had chosen this arrangement, she said, because when she reached the point where she found it too hard to climb the stairs, she would know it was time to retire.

Anna and Asamir reached the landing that led to the captain's office. The captain's squire started to say something but her words were lost as the Captain flung open the door of her office and said, "Have they arrived yet?"

The squire indicated the two guardswomen. The Captain, a large woman, her gray hair cut close to her scalp, had a sharp-angled face that looked to be carved from the heart of a mahogany tree. She gave them a look that spoke volumes—unpleasant

9

volumes. They crossed the landing and entered her office without waiting for another word. Anna noticed that Asamir now appeared less confident.

Both women stood at attention while the Captain paced up and down her office. "What am I going to do with you?" she said. "You know that dueling is outlawed—and you further know that it is outlawed precisely to keep members of our Guard from dueling with the King's men. And yet you persist not only in challenging others, but in doing it in public taverns so that the whole world hears about it."

"But, Captain," Asamir started.

"Be quiet. I do not wish to hear your excuses. I am sure they involve declarations of honor. Anyway, I know you have no sense. But you," she said to Anna, "you do know better than to participate in such ludicrous behavior. Why were you there?"

Anna said nothing.

"I know, I know," the Captain said. "Everyone praises the honor of Anna d'Gart. You would not abandon your friend. And you should not. But your friend should pick her causes more carefully." She paused. "The Hierofante is demanding that I do something about the behavior of my guardswomen. She suggested prison." She gave them a hard stare. "The idea has its merits."

Anna prayed silently to her patron saint—for even a casual believer takes refuge in prayer in times of crisis—and trod on Asamir's toe to keep her from saying anything.

"Fortunately, you did not kill the man. He is only slightly wounded."

Asamir looked disappointed.

"And I am sure the King's men contributed to the disturbance, but the Hierofante does not seem to take the same interest in their misdeeds."

Anna knew the Hierofante's favoritism toward the King's Guard was a sore point with the Captain. She offered more prayers.

The Captain sighed. "As it happens, I am owed some few favors. Why I protect the two of you I do not know. Perhaps God does. Hide yourselves for a week. Leave the Capital."

"Yes, Captain," Anna said.

"Return in time for the King's Ball. Despite your behavior, I shall still need you in attendance. Too many things can go wrong." She waved her arms at them. "Go, go. Get out of here before I change my mind. And do not expect to draw your pay for that week."

They both pivoted sharply and left. Neither spoke until they had exited through the main gate of the barracks.

Asamir sighed. "A week's exile, and no money to spend. I shall have to go to a convent or I will starve."

"I can offer you both sufficient funds and entertainment," Anna said, and she told her about the Queen's mission.

Asamir rubbed her hands together with glee. Nothing pleased her more than a chance for adventure, except on occasion a handsome man. "Just the sort of thing we need. But why did you not tell the Captain? Do you not trust her?"

"With my life. But this is the Queen's secret, and honor demands that we not share it."

Chapter 2

ANNA AND ASAMIR left in the afternoon through the southern gate. They took the high road until dusk, and then, with no others in sight, set off cross-country around the Capital on the western side and circled back toward the northern route.

"This giving of tokens to a lover is very foolish," said Asamir as they made their way among the trees, moving slowly to give their horses a chance to pick safe footing in the dark. "A lover should be satisfied that he or she has the other's heart and ask for nothing more. The Queen should give tokens to her husband, so that he will believe she is his alone."

"Do you never give tokens to your lovers?"

"They give tokens to me," Asamir said. "It is enough for them that they have the friendship of someone in the Queen's Guard. And I sell the objects as soon as I can, for a ring may be evidence, but gold can belong to anyone."

"Perhaps the Queen cares more for her lovers than you," Anna said.

"Certainly not. I am madly, passionately in love with the Marquis de...with an outstanding gentleman, and the Queen cannot love the Countess of Beaufort half as much as I love him. The Queen is just sentimental."

They slept a bit in the darkest hours of the night, but by daybreak they were some distance north and west of the Capital. Riding east, they joined the high northern road just before it crossed the Adabarean River, which flowed across the Realm from the northwest to the southeast, where it emptied into the larger river that formed the border with Foraoise. The river was high with the snow melt of winter, though it had retreated from its highest point. Now that it was spring, when rains tended to be light in the northwestern portion of the Realm, the river would continue to drop until the downpours of summer refilled it.

They breakfasted at an inn just north of the river. The round-about trip had been to keep them from being followed out of the city, but the time allotted for this venture was too short for them to avoid taking the main road from here on out even though they might be seen and recognized.

In the late afternoon they came to Querville, a market village that needed no gates, being well-protected by an ancient oak forest, and stopped at an inn on the edge of town not far off the high road. The innkeeper greeted them effusively—they were well-known to her from earlier travels.

"Ah, my good ladies, it is a great pleasure to see you again. The omens told me that someone important would be traveling through, and I butchered a lamb to be ready." She beckoned to one of her children. "Here, take these ladies' horses—they look as if they've been ridden for days. Come in, come in. The wine from the harvest four years previous has just reached perfection. Let me set before you a feast."

"Good hostess," Anna said, "We have been thinking of your fine cuisine for many miles. But could you serve us in a private chamber? There may be other travelers on the road whom we would prefer not to meet." She held a few coins from the Queen's purse in her hand.

"Nothing could be simpler, my ladies. I will have my son stable your horses with my own. And the chamber on the second floor is available. Quite well-appointed, and with a balcony that commands a view of the front of the inn."

"Excellent," said Anna.

And, indeed, excellent also applied to the food, while the wine proved to be as good as the best to be found in the Capital.

As they lingered over one last glass of wine, they heard voices in the courtyard. New arrivals. Slipping quietly onto the balcony, they observed two men in the uniform of the King's Guard. The hostess was greeting them graciously. In response to a question Anna could not hear, the innkeeper said, "No, I have seen no other soldiers on the road tonight. I have only some church elders, and they have already retired for the evening."

"You spent the Queen's gold well," Asamir observed. "One of those men I know slightly, but the other I have not seen before."

"Roland de Barthes," Anna said. "I fought him as your second when you challenged that young guardsman."

"Was he any good?"

"Very. An honorable man. Handsome, too."

"If you like them dark, thin, and wiry," Asamir said.

"The question is, how do they come to be here, looking for soldiers?"

"I suppose they might have followed us." Asamir's voice made it clear she found that unlikely.

Anna shook her head firmly. "No one followed us."

"The King might have a spy in the Queen's chamber."

"Possible. Or perhaps he merely has strong suspicions about the Countess of Beaufort and is sending men this way on speculation."

"So what shall we do?"

"Sleep now—and leave well before the dawn."

The two men enjoyed the innkeeper's hospitality until rather late, and Anna heard them snoring when she and Asamir crept out of the inn before the sun rose. They saddled their horses and were off, though not before Anna had slipped into the main stable and let out the guardsmen's horses.

"They will know we were here," Asamir said.

"It will take them some time to round up the horses, and there are no others here that will serve their needs."

"The innkeeper will be angry."

"I left her more gold for her trouble."

"I hope the Queen's purse proves bottomless, the way you spend it."

Indeed, they gained a great deal on their pursuers, for they did not see the men again on the road. They reached the Countess's estates without further incident.

The Countess paled when she learned of the Queen's predicament. Since she was fair-skinned to begin with, she looked like her own ghost. She brought them the necklace at once.

"Please hurry back to your great lady, and tell her how sorry I am that she has suffered all this trouble. I would ask you to stay the night, but you must hurry. And my husband..."

Anna mentioned that they would need fresh horses, and the Countess parted with a small purse.

They left the Countess's palace with five days remaining before the ball.

"This mission is going quite well," Asamir said. "We shall be back in sufficient time for the ball. Just as well, because I have the matter of my attire to attend to."

Anna and Asamir were prepared for anyone they could outfight, outwit, or outcharm, depending on the circumstances. But given the time of year, they were not prepared for heavy rain.

It started a few hours after they left the Countess. Torrents of rain that dug great holes into the road and made it impossible to consider traveling cross country, the kind of rain that if it kept up too long would drown the seeds just planted and force the rivers outside of their banks.

The first day, they rode through it, soaking themselves to the skin. They finally camped for the night in an abandoned shepherd's hut, though they could find no dry wood for a fire. The rain pounded on the roof of the hut as they sat shivering inside. There was little room, since they had brought the horses in as well. "I do not like this rain," Anna said.

Asamir was trying to shake the water out of her hair. "I think I shall never be dry again," she said, "though in truth the storm is no worse than that during the Battle of Seges. You remember how we sank in mud to our knees."

"That was in the winter," Anna said, "when it rains like this when it does not snow. Something about this rain is not natural." She heard a brief rustle and knew that Asamir had put her cupped fingers to her forehead and then her heart, making the religious gesture to protect herself against the mention of things forbidden by the Church. The Church condemned magic.

"Why think you so?"

"It should not rain so this time of year," Anna said. She knew the answer was unsatisfactory, and yet she had no better one.

Asamir laughed and said, "Oh, now you understand the weather."

"My family's homestead is in this region. Rains this time of year are usually gentle. Something is not right." Anna shivered with more than cold.

"Holy Mother protect us," Asamir said, her laughter gone.

As tired as she was, Anna found it impossible to sleep. She spent the night trying to convince herself that out-of-season weather could happen without uncanny interference. Her efforts were unsuccessful.

They rode through the downpour the second day as well, but at a slower pace, letting their horses pick their footing. That night they begged hospitality of a farmwife. In return for some of their coin, she gave them a dry shed and grain for the horses. A few additional coins bought them the farmwife's bed, which they shared with an assortment of animals. But they stayed blessedly dry, though Anna woke frequently to listen to the storm.

The sun appeared the next morning, and they were cheered. Both they and their horses were the better for a dry and warm night's rest. But the farmwife eyed the agitation of her animals, and sniffed the air. "The weather looks poor, my ladies."

"Surely the rain has ended," Anna said. "It is not usual to have so much this time of year."

"Were you country-raised then, my lady?" the farmwife said. And, at Anna's nod, she added, "Then you should know that this is no natural rain."

Anna felt as if her heart had dropped into her stomach. She had let the sun convince her that she was worrying for naught, but now she could no longer take that refuge.

Asamir made the gesture, and the woman laughed. "Fat lot of good that will do you."

Conscious of the necessity of arriving soon in the Capital, they eschewed her advice to stay. After about an hour, the rain came again, this time accompanied by thunder and lightning. When they reached a small village, they took refuge in an inn, along with a large crush of people and animals who had come to town for market day.

"The Adabarean must be overflowing its banks," Anna said as they sat shivering by the fire after having made sure their horses were dried off and under cover.

The innkeeper's daughter, who was bringing them steaming mugs, said, "Ah, my lady, if this keeps up even the great bridges will soon wash away."

Anna looked at Asamir, and they both sighed. If the bridge on the high road washed out, and the water stayed at flood stage, they would not reach the Capital before the ball. Anna eyed the girl. She seemed to be a person of more than usual resourcefulness. "I have heard it said that this is not a natural rain," Anna said in a low voice.

Asamir gave a sharp intake of breath and looked around to make sure no one else was listening to their conversation.

The girl raised an eyebrow, but did not look frightened. "Some of the travelers have observed that it is only raining along the high road, the one that leads to the Capital. And it should not be raining so hard, this time of year."

Anna took a coin from the purse, laid it casually on the table. "I wonder," she said, as if to Asamir, "if there might be a village wisewoman nearby who could advise me on this rain." For country people, Anna knew, would pray of a Sunday but follow the older ways should the occasion arise.

The girl looked at the coin, then at Anna, then back at the coin, considering. "They say, my lady, that the old woman who lives out on the edge of the forest knows her herbs and such. Perhaps she could advise you."

Anna pushed the coin along so that it was easily in the girl's reach. The girl shoved it quickly down into her pocket.

Asamir said in an undertone, "You cannot be seriously considering this course."

"Shall we wait until the bridge washes away, taking our mission with it?"

"But affairs of, of magic"—Asamir barely breathed the word—"are an abomination. You threaten your immortal soul."

"Then why is the Hierofante dealing in them? Does she not fear for her immortal soul?"

"You do not know the Hierofante brought on these rains."

"Who else? The King?"

Asamir had to concede that was unlikely. "I suppose one of the Hierofante's aides might go so far as to consult someone."

"Without the Hierofante's knowledge?"

Asamir made a face.

Anna stood. "You can wait for me here, if you are afraid."

Asamir picked up her sword, as Anna had known she would. "I cannot let you take such risk alone."

In the crush of people, no one but the young girl saw them leave.

They did not speak as they rode through the driving rain, but when they reached the forest's edge, Asamir laid her hand on Anna's reins, and said, "Are you truly certain of this course? To imperil our souls?"

While Anna, like every person in the Realm, was nominally a member of the Church, she had long since moved away from taking its pronouncements at face value. Having grown up in the country, where it was not unusual for the local midwife or herbalist to use other powers when the priest's back was turned, she knew that magic was not the unqualified evil that religious leaders preached. On the other hand, magic that could change the weather was a great deal more frightening than a spell that made herbal remedies more potent. She was afraid, but as she could see no other solution to their present difficulty and because she did not want to make Asamir more nervous than she already was, she said, "Would God want us to stand quietly by and let others use such powers against Her Majesty?"

Asamir sighed loudly enough to be heard over the storm, made the religious gesture, and spurred her horse. "I am with you."

The directions were incomplete, and it was difficult to follow the path in the downpour, but despite all that, they soon arrived at a clearing in which sat a cottage and some outbuildings. As they moved from the path onto the homestead, the rain seemed to let up a little. They dismounted, leaving their horses in an open shed covered by a thatched roof, and walked toward the cottage. Anna had the sudden feeling that she had done this before: ridden a horse to this stead, left it in the shed, and walked to the cottage. She could not recall any such experience in her life, but the feeling was so overpowering that it took her deepest reserves of courage to put one foot in front of the other. Even just before a battle sure to be brutal, that time when the awareness one could die was at its zenith, she had never been so afraid.

But she walked forward and rapped loudly on the door. The eaves of the roof dripped on the guardswomen's heads as they stood there, though they were so soaked through they scarcely noticed. When an old woman finally opened the door, she did not invite them in.

"Good dame," said Anna, "Could you not let two travelers caught in the storm dry themselves before your fire?"

"Travelers do not pass this way by chance, guardswoman. What want you here?"

Asamir, bristling at the remark, laid a hand on her sword.

The woman laughed, as Anna reached out to calm Asamir. "I should cooperate or you will take what I have, is that it?" Her open mouth showed she still had most of her teeth.

"No," said Anna. "We do not take. We ask, and we pay for services rendered." She took out her purse.

"Well, then, come in," the old woman said. She stepped back from the door, took a look at the purse, as if deciding how much gold it might contain, and then stepped over to put another log on the fire.

Once inside, Anna got a good look at the woman for the first time. The witch was tall and lean, with deep brown skin weathered by years and life outside. Her head was uncovered, showing a mass of silver and black curls. She looked directly at Anna and smiled as if in recognition.

Anna did not know the woman, or, at least, did not think she knew her, but there was something familiar about her, perhaps related to the earlier feeling of déjà vu. Was she being manipulated by the witch, or was there a simpler explanation? She took a deep breath to keep her fear at bay.

The witch gave her another smile, one that did not answer Anna's uncertainty but rather left it in the air between them. She waved her hand toward a low bench in front of the fire.

The guardswomen sat, though they were so wet that Anna thought they would not likely dry out even if they should sit in front of a good fire for a week. She said, trying for a casual tone to hide her disquiet, "It is a hard rain out there. Some have suggested that it might not be, well, a natural rain."

The old woman said, "Oh, come. Please do not waste my time being coy and careful. You've come because you think I can stop the rain, have you not?"

Anna threw caution to the wind and said, "Yes, we have."

Asamir made the gesture.

The woman snorted. "Will you pay to stop it?"

"Can you do it?"

"If you can make it worth my while. It is, as you say, not a natural rain. And only a fool meddles in the unnatural without fair compensation, particularly when she will also be meddling in the affairs of princes."

Asamir said, "Princes? Mean you the King?"

"Ah, guardswoman, there are all kinds of princes in the world. Princes of the realm, and princes of the church. Princesses as well. And all of them dangerous to any who might stand between them and their desires, be it queens, or soldiers, or witches."

The witch's words did not sound like a speech to drum up business, but rather like the matter-of-fact statement of someone who knew quite well what she was dealing with. Anna opened her purse and pulled out a gold coin, laying it on the bench beside her.

The woman smiled, but said nothing.

Anna took out a second, putting it on the first. And then, when no reaction came, she added a third.

"One more, my lady. One more, and the rain will plague you no more."

"And the bridge will be standing when we reach it?"

"Ah, yes," the woman said. "The bridge will be there." She laughed as she scooped up the coins.

Anna and Asamir made no move to go. The old woman said, "Well, now, you've made your request. Be off."

"But it is still raining."

"It will stop. Do you really want to watch what I do?" She looked straight at Asamir as she said this, and Asamir again made the religious gesture. "Go on, get on your way."

They found themselves back out in the downpour. By the time they got back to the high road, though, the rain had slackened off considerably, and it stopped completely by the time night fell. They found a simple inn—really only a home with an extra room for guests and a shed for their mounts—and took refuge for the night.

As they sat over bowls of vegetable soup, bought with the last of the Countess's money, Anna said, "We have no choice but to take the high road directly to the Capital tomorrow. We certainly will not be able to ford anywhere."

"And I suspect we will not travel the main road alone," said Asamir.

Chapter 3

THE NEXT DAY did dawn clear, as if the rain had washed all the dirt and evil from the world. Asamir looked out at it and made the religious gesture. "The Hierofante will know we have stopped the rain."

"Perhaps. But what can she do, unless she admits she knew how it began?"

They set out, clean, rested, in clothes that were almost dry, and had not gone more than a league when they saw a flutter of white off in the distance. Anna took up her spyglass for a better look. "Hierofante's guards. Six of them."

"Perhaps they have other business and are not here for us," Asamir said.

"That would be too much to hope for. The whole situation reeks of the Hierofante. The King would never have thought of the necklace on his own anymore than he would have dared to have someone affect the weather. Besides, they have dismounted and blocked the road."

"What shall we do?"

"Pray, my lady the abbess-to-be."

"And fight," said Asamir. "Though our horses are rested. Perhaps we can gallop through them."

"Were we on our own mounts, we could try it. But these horses are not bred for battle. They are likely to shy at the wrong moment, especially if there is blood. We should dismount and try reason first."

"And then fight," Asamir said. "They have not sent out six for a parlay."

The Hierofante's soldiers had drawn no weapons. Anna and Asamir kept their swords sheathed as well.

"Well met, mesdames," said their leader, a man called Lefevre. Like Anna and Asamir, he was a senior member of his Guard. "We have heard that some among the Queen's Guard might be in danger from the storms and have come to give you assistance."

"And yet, as you see, we were not harmed by the storm," Anna said. "We thank you, kind ladies and gentlemen, for your offer, but have no need of your aid."

"Nevertheless, we will escort you back to the Capital," Lefevre said.

"We must decline."

"We must insist," he said, his hand on his hilt. His soldiers followed his lead.

Anna and Asamir also reached for their swords.

"You are outnumbered, mesdames. It would not be dishonorable to surrender to us."

"We have orders that make that impossible, sir," Anna said.

"Your captain said you were on leave, Madame."

"Perhaps she thought my orders were none of your affair, sir. Do you intend to attack all at once, or will you fight us one at a time, as honorable officers?"

"Madame, I would prefer to fight you individually, but I, too, have orders." And the soldiers attacked.

The Hierofante's troops had counted on their numbers to overwhelm the Queen's women, for they came in directly, with little strategy. However, Anna and Asamir—who had fought jointly in many a battle, not to mention more than a few brawls—kept together, so that Anna's left was protected by Asamir and Asamir's right by Anna. While this might have appeared to leave Asamir at a disadvantage, with her left presented to the soldiers, Anna knew that the abbess-manqué could fight equally well with either hand. In the end, the Hierofante's soldiers were forced to come at them one at a time, for they could not reach them otherwise.

A scream told Anna that Asamir had quickly cut her first opponent—for those who lack experience with left-handed fighters suffer from a significant disadvantage. Anna made short work of the young woman who attacked her as well, disarming her with a quick flick of her sword and cutting her wrist as she moved past her to face her next opponent. With the sound of Asamir's sword ringing behind her, Anna ducked under a sword blow to the head, cutting her opponent under his upper arm as she passed. He, too, dropped his sword, and now she faced Lefevre. Although she had exchanged sharp words with him on more than one occasion, they had never dueled before, due to Her Eminence's strict orders to her guards to avoid street brawling.

If he attacked, she had many options. But he did not. He stood several feet from her, sword held forward pointing directly at her throat. He was a large man, both taller and wider than she, and it was a heavy sword; he was waiting for her to attack and counting on his strength to hold his sword against any strike she made. But Anna, having removed the threat of the first two opponents and ascertaining from the noise behind her that Asamir was having little trouble with her fights, felt no urgency to attack. She held her own sword in front of her, low, and waited.

Her patience exceeded his. With a roar, he raised his sword above his head and rushed toward her. She moved slightly off the line once he was committed, and raised her own sword to his throat. It cut him slightly as he fought to regain control. She pressed harder, and he dropped his blade in surrender.

"Tell the others to yield," she said.

He gave an order.

Anna kept her sword at his throat. The only person remaining uninjured let his sword fall to his side, and the injured stopped trying to pick themselves back up for another fight.

"We will be traveling on, alone. Your word as an officer and a gentlemen that you will not trouble us further."

"My word," Lefevre said. "Theirs as well."

Anna backed off slightly, but still kept her sword up. Lefevre had given his word, but he was too much the Hierofante's man for her to completely trust him. All guards should be honorable when it came to giving their word, but this was a matter of politics, and the man's orders might outrank his honor. "You," she said to the uninjured man. "Fetch our horses."

"Do it," Lefevre said.

The two women mounted quickly and rode off before the others could regroup. They ran their horses fast until their attackers were well out of sight. "I do not think they can follow us, given the damage we did," Anna said when at last they pulled up for a rest. "But we should continue to hurry. They might decide to do something desperate to avoid the Hierofante's wrath."

After another hour of riding, they crested a hill and looked down at the river valley before them. The great bridge stood open.

"The old woman was right. The bridge was not washed out," Anna said. "We should ride hard. The Queen will be beside herself with worry until we arrive."

Asamir swore suddenly and pulled out her spyglass. She took a long look. "I think we may be delayed." She passed the glass to Anna.

Four horsemen had positioned themselves in front of the bridge. Even at that distance the red tunics of the King's Guard shone like a banner.

"After we have defeated six, what are four?" Anna said. "But they have remained mounted, and since they are close to the Capital, their horses may be battle-trained. How shall we approach them?" She touched her side, to make certain that the necklace, which lay in a purse under her tunic, was secure.

Asamir watched her move, and then smiled. "Let us ride down. I have a plan." She explained her idea to Anna, who joined her in the smile.

"Though you may be at risk if they all follow you."

"Bah. If it gets too bad, I will surrender. I do not have the necklace."

They cantered down the hill.

"Mesdames." Roland de Barthes inclined his head in a hint at formal greeting. "We have been sent to escort you to the King."

"Our apologies to His Majesty, but we have other orders that take precedence," Anna replied.

Jean-Paul was next to Roland. He did not appear hampered by his injury from the previous week's duel. He smiled at Asamir — the smile of a man who has looked forward to a rematch. The other two sat on their horses quietly. Anna had dueled with both and knew them to be worthy opponents.

"I am afraid we must insist," Roland said.

Asamir was moving away from her. Anna saw her pat her side, as if she were checking to see if she still carried something there. The gesture did not go unnoticed by Jean-Paul.

"I am afraid we must decline," Anna said.

Roland drew his sword, and Anna drew hers almost as quickly. And, at that moment, when the other three guardsmen were watching Roland and Anna to see what might happen next, Asamir spurred her horse straight ahead across the bridge.

"She carries the necklace," Jean-Paul shouted, turning his horse and taking off in pursuit. And before Roland could stop them, the other two followed behind him.

Roland remained. "I doubt that she does," he said to Anna. "I do not think she would have run if she did, for her chances of escaping all three seem small, and she is not a fool. Will you surrender to me now, Madame?"

"If I would not surrender to four, why should I surrender to one?" She dismounted quickly, sword in hand.

Roland leapt lightly from his own mount, and they crossed swords.

Anna had found Roland a worthy opponent in their first encounter, when neither she nor he had truly wanted to fight. Now that they met in earnest, she saw that he equaled her in skill. Or even perhaps surpassed her. Every opening she found was blocked against her, as if it had been shown only to draw her in. Every cut she made missed by a hair's breadth.

At last she saw his arm go up and thought sure she would stab him. But as she came in, he shifted slightly, so that her sword met air. She stumbled a bit. His blade cut across her tunic, sliced open the purse underneath, and the necklace came tumbling out.

Roland dropped to the ground, holding his sword high to keep Anna back, and grabbed for the necklace with his left hand. But he had taken his eyes off Anna when he reached out, making it easy for her to knock his sword off line. She stepped on his hand and the necklace.

He grimaced, but did not cry out, and tried to pull free, but Anna ground her boot more firmly into his hand. He could do nothing with his blade from his awkward position on the ground.

"Do you yield, sir?"

Roland let his sword drop to the ground. "I yield."

Anna took her foot from his hand, and knelt to retrieve the necklace, keeping her eye and her sword on him as she did so. She tucked the jewels away. "You must forget that you have seen that," she said.

"Madame, I cannot do that."

"Come, you yielded. Give me your word, sir."

"I yielded to your mercy, and I remain at it, Madame, but I must tell the King what I have seen. I am sworn to him, and to do less would be to betray my oath. Honor demands it."

"Then I will be forced to kill you, for my honor demands that I take this to the Queen, without the King's knowledge."

"So be it, then." His face showed no trace of fear.

Anna raised her sword, then let it fall. "Pick up your sword. I will not kill you like this."

He picked it up. "I have no desire to kill you either, but I suppose that only one of us can leave here alive. I am sworn to the King, and you to the Queen."

"And both of us to the Realm," Anna said suddenly.

"Indeed, both of us to the Realm."

"And that will resolve our situation. For we both have duty to the Realm."

"What do you mean?"

"Sir, the King and Queen were married to unite the Realm, not their hearts, were they not?"

"Indeed, so I understand."

"So a flirtation by one or the other means little. That the Queen may have given her heart to another is of no true importance to the King."

"Ah, but the evidence of it humiliates him," Roland said.

"Yes, if he is forced to take notice of it, and if others know. But if the truth remains unknown to all..."

"But he has sent me to discover it, and honor demands that I follow my orders."

"Honor be damned," said Anna d'Gart. "We speak too much of honor."

Roland's eyes opened wide.

"You and I have fought twice because of honor, when we had no quarrel of our own. And would it be honorable to divide the Realm again because we both must keep our honor?

"What happens if the Queen is dishonored, sir? At best, she is pushed aside, removed from power. And who fills the space that she leaves—for we both know that the King cannot rule alone, without aid. Who, I ask you?"

"The Hierofante," Roland said slowly. "And it was Her Eminence who told the King of the Countess of Beaufort."

"In the best of circumstances, we shall be ruled by the Hierofante. But surely you know the followers of the Queen will not countenance such an outcome. I, for one, will fight to regain her honor, and I will not be alone. The Realm will once again divide, and this time we are likely to end up in civil war."

"That would be a great evil," said Roland.

"So we must choose between our personal honor and the greater good of the Realm," Anna said. "Forget you saw this bauble—tell the King you met me on the road and found no evidence that I had done aught but travel outside of the Capital, as my Captain will tell you."

He hesitated. "'Tis very difficult, to sacrifice my honor."

"My God, man. I am asking you to sacrifice it for your duty. 'Twould be more dishonorable if you and I hold onto our personal honor and failed in our duty to the Realm."

"So it would. My word then, Madame. And may I escort you back to the Capital?"

"I would be honored, sir."

"What of your friend? My men may have captured her. Or worse."

"She will say nothing, and has no evidence. And Asamir can take care of herself. I hope some of your men remain alive."

The Queen looked ravishing at the Ball, wearing her new gown of the palest blue, with the sapphires glowing around her neck. The King cut a splendid image in red, wearing a gold chain given him by Her Majesty. For once they flirted only with each other and gave every indication of being a couple truly in love.

"Perhaps," said the Captain of the Queen's Guard to her counterpart of the King's, "we will get an heir at last."

Anna, standing near the Queen, missed none of this. She eyed the room as the others danced.

Asamir wore a tunic of the finest silk, so well-cut that it resembled a fine ball gown despite the sword at her waist. The sling on her arm was also made of silk and did not detract overmuch from her appearance. Jean-Paul, with whom she was dancing, sported a black eye.

Anna wondered about Asamir's Marquis, but saw him standing with his wife. He looked less happy than the average guest as he watched Asamir and Jean-Paul.

"Will you dance, Madame?" Roland de Barthes made her a deep bow.

"With pleasure, sir. Though since I have duty here, we must keep near to the Queen."

"That will be easy. I must keep near to the King, and for once they stand together."

"And we caused that to happen. We have saved the Realm, sir."

"Enough of that," said Roland, and he kissed her.

Chapter 4

THE REALM LIES in a central location. To its southwest is Alhambra, and beyond that are roads to countries farther south, whence come spices and dyes and a variety of plants and animals that developed in warmer climates. On the northwest a coastline fronts on a small sea; a similar coast stretches along one southeast edge. Both give the Realm access to the great oceans and thence to those who come from far off places in all the directions of the compass. Cold lands lie due north, offering leathers and furs and wooly animals. Beyond Foraoise on the east lie many other places, sources of very different goods that are not made or do not grow nearby.

For centuries, people from all over have traveled through the Realm to trade with each other. Some of those who came tired of the travel and set up as innkeepers and merchants, and eventually as farmers and artisans. They joined the people who had lived there since time immemorial—that is, going back before the time anyone kept records more complex than long stories—marrying among them and establishing families. As the Realm developed, with some households gaining power and declaring themselves as lords, and one house in particular deciding it should be the overlord and proclaiming itself royal, it grew a population that came in all shades of humanity, with all the differences of hair and size and eye color that come with that. And since such things did not interfere with marriages and other partnerships, the variety of human appearance in the Realm was unusually broad. Only the neighboring realm of Foraoise included similar diversity; perhaps it was no accident that Foraoise was the Realm's greatest rival.

The century-and-a-half divide in the Realm came about after two young women of the royal line claimed the throne as sister queens. The machinations of their uncle, who thought that he, though not himself in the line of succession—being, in fact, the brother of their father, who was prince consort and not king—should make the key decisions on how the Realm should proceed caused the division.

The Queen of the Realm had given birth to twins, two little girls so identical that the only person who was ever able to tell them apart was their nurse. Even their parents were never sure which was which, and the girls learned by the age of three to take advantage of this confusion. By the time they had grown into young women, their nurse had passed on, which meant that no one but they themselves knew which was which, and therefore no one but they knew which was the elder and entitled to the throne. And, as they pointed out when asked to address this question, while they knew who they were individually, they did not remember which of them was born first and had only the word of others as to what name went with the birth order. Which is to say, they declined to tell anyone and took on the new names of Andrea and Melora, which gave no information to anyone else.

They were inseparable, and they intended to rule together. Their elders, and particularly their uncle, had other ideas, but the two young women were a match for most of the intrigues that came along.

They were, of course, beautiful (because all young women are beautiful) with flowing light-brown hair, hazel eyes, and skin that darkened quickly in sun to a warm color that complemented their hair. And they were much beloved by the people, which is not something that even royal families can afford to sneeze at.

Eventually, their uncle, who (not by chance) was also chancellor, introduced them to two equally beautiful young men (because all young men are also beautiful—youth is like spring flowers; it just cannot help being beautiful). They were tall and very blonde, with pale skin and bright blue eyes, and while they were not twins or even brothers, they were cousins, close in age, and said to be devoted to each other. They came of good noble, almost royal, lineage, though from a realm in the far north.

Melora took an immediate liking to one of the cousins, a sweet young man named Artur who was devoted to philosophical speculation and frequently forgot to come to dinner or formal affairs if not reminded by aides. But Andrea rejected the other. Instead, she announced that she would take as her prince consort—for since the twins planned to rule together as joint queens, there would be no kings—another beautiful young man from the southwesterly realm of Alhambra. Roth was well-proportioned, if not as tall as the two cousins, with skin the color of obsidian, and highly regarded for his studies in natural philosophy. Their shared interest in scholarship made Roth and Artur fast friends, Melora approved of her sister's choice, and both young men were admired by the people. The twins considered the matter settled and began to make wedding plans.

However, some of the royal family, particularly the chancellor uncle, as well as a few among the higher nobility, objected to the marriage on the grounds that while Roth came of good lineage, he was not of noble birth. His mother had risen to high rank in the military, and his father held a key secretary post in the diplomatic corps—they were important people but not of the highest rank.

In presenting her choice to her mother, uncle, and the others of the court, Andrea, who was wise in the way of political affairs even in her youth, did not make it an issue of personal preference. Instead, she emphasized the importance of an alliance with a southern realm as well as one with the northern. Because there were two of them, the twins could reach in more than one direction and build ties that would strengthen their Realm. The trade routes across the Realm that had served to make it wealthy and to build its diverse population also made it vulnerable to disputes with all those other countries. Diplomacy through royal marriage was the time-honored way of dealing with such disputes without war.

In private discussions with Melora—and with no one else—Andrea gave out a second reason. There was something unsettling about the other cousin, a man called Edgar. Part of him was always closed off. Her intuition said that he was dangerous, and she refused to align herself with him. Melora, who had indeed noticed some of the same signs that gave Andrea pause, agreed with her evaluation.

Their mother—who was planning to abdicate in favor of the twins once they were married and settled, since she was still grieving the loss of her husband and prince consort and wished to take holy orders and live the remainder of her years in contemplation—approved Andrea's choice, and the remainder of the court agreed, for that is what nobles do when royals make decisions.

But while their uncle acquiesced to this decision in public, being a savvy courtier, he continued to make other plans in private. He knew something unknown to anyone else, since it would bring about his ruin if it were ever revealed: Edgar was a sorcerer. The official position of the Church of the Realm was condemnation of magic, with excommunication for anyone who advocated it or spoke in its favor even mildly, and far greater penalties for anyone who made use of it. Although the uncle and chancellor scoffed at the church in private while appearing devout in public (a practice shared by much of the nobility), he knew that even his power was not enough to save him should he be caught using supernatural means to gain his ends. He would be exiled, if not executed. It was, however, a risk he was willing to take, for he despaired of the direction the Realm might go under the leadership of the two strong-minded young women, and he wanted no part of anything that even smelled of an alliance with their southwestern neighbor.

Artur was aware of his cousin's power; it was not an uncommon thing in their realm and was, in fact, considered of great value. He had some slight powers himself. But for all his otherworldly aspect, he was well aware that it was dangerous to even hint at such things in the Realm. This was a political marriage, even though he had quickly come to love Melora, and he approved of the political ends. Further, he loved his cousin and did not suspect him of evil intentions. So he did not mention Edgar's skill to her or to anyone, especially after the cousins took baptism in the Church. Edgar had decided to remain in the Realm rather than to return to his home, claiming devotion to his cousin, so he had also accepted the Church. He soon found a spouse of his own, the heir to an important duchy who was serving as one of the ladies in waiting to Andrea and Melora.

The twins would have preferred to send Edgar back north, for though they did not know of his powers, they were suspicious of his intentions and of their uncle's. But his decision to accept the Church and his choice of bride, coupled with Artur's fondness for him, made that impossible. They had noticed at an early age that their mother did not trust their uncle. As young teenagers, they had assumed his continued authority to be a failure on the part of their mother and asserted to each other that they would remove him from office as soon as they had the power. But as they grew older, they realized that their mother would have dismissed and banned him but for the strength of his support within the nobility, even though he was roundly disliked by the people. It was their first lesson in the reality that absolute power is far from absolute, and they applied it in their dealings with Edgar. They allowed him to stay, but they did not make the mistake of giving him any authority.

For a time, all went well. The twins were married in an elaborate joint ceremony presided over by the Hierofante of the Realm and a year later—for even a wealthy and established Realm should not hold all of its formal celebrations too close to each other—the Queen stepped down and Andrea and Melora were crowned.

The first few years of their joint reign begat a flowering of the Realm never before seen. The scholarly appetites of the two prince consorts brought many philosophers to the Capital. A university was established from what had originally been a college of religious studies, and both princes endowed chairs and recruited others to support scholarship. Some great treatises were begun, books that would provide guidance for centuries to come for those studying the natural world and to those contemplating the proper lives of human beings.

Artists and poets also flocked to the Capital. The rulers were beautiful, and the best painters on the continent vied with each other for commissions to do official portraits. And the love of the sisters for each other, as well as their love for their consorts, provided an underpinning for both romantic poetry and epic tales. Musicians, too, traveled across the Realm and to other countries, expanding the repertoire of the locals.

Those years proved unusually peaceful. All was quiet on the Alhambra border due to Andrea's consort, and while things were slightly less stable with their northwest neighbor of Foraoise—Melora's husband having come from a country farther north—a settlement over the mines of Airgead was negotiated that, while it left the mines under Foraoisian control, provided the Realm with more than enough gold and silver to satisfy its needs. Though the Realm maintained an army, with the Royal Guard the most elite of forces, its services were rarely needed.

Peace, of course, makes trade easier. The furs and leathers so common in the far north became luxury items for the nobles, while the spices, herbs, and dyes from the exotic plants of Alhambra made their way to other countries through the Realm. Different varieties of sheep, goats, pigs, and horses were traded across borders, laying the groundwork for some new hybrids.

Andrea gave birth to a daughter, and, as the sisters had agreed, the child, as the first-born, was set to become the heir to the throne. Not long after, Melora gave birth to a son, cementing the future of the Realm, for it is always better to have others in the line of succession. For some time thereafter things continued to go well.

Perhaps it was the decision of the sister Queens to remove their uncle from his position as chancellor that brought about the end of this magical time, though perhaps it would have happened in any case. They had discovered their uncle's efforts to provoke a war with Foraoise—the settlement over the mines had cost him money—and used that to give them sufficient reason to replace him with a duchess well-known for her propriety and common sense. He left without showing rancor, but it was not long afterwards that things began to go wrong.

Edgar, while well-trained in all aspects of sorcery, had intended to use his skills only to protect the interests of his own family and country. He had never sought to use them for personal gain (he had charmed his wife without them) or to promote the political ends of others. During his time in the Realm, he had rarely engaged in any significant sorcery, except on occasion to aid healers (in ways they would not notice) so that people recovered from serious illness more often than was typical. But the now-deposed chancellor sought him out and threatened him with exposure if he did not act to disrupt matters in the Realm. He thought of leaving, but by then he had two children and a wife who was now a ruling duchess. He loved his family, but he could not take them with him. Further, the deposed chancellor also threatened to expose his cousin Artur, which would have caused great scandal for all that his magic was paltry.

The easiest magic to do unnoticed is that which affects the health of others, for little is known about the causes and cures of disease—village wisewomen notwithstanding—and people are mortal. Given the risks inherent in childbirth both to the mother and the future baby, interfering at that time was perhaps the easiest magic of all. And while both Queens had given birth to heirs, they were sufficiently aware of the vagaries of life to want to have more children, just in case. Royal power is only as strong as its line of succession.

He began with an attack on Andrea, now pregnant with her second child. She went from a joyous pregnancy to lying in bed all day, scarcely able to move. But Edgar had not counted on her consort. Alhambra did not abjure sorcery as the Realm did, and Roth, suspecting something unnatural, sent to his home for the midwife who had attended his mother and sisters, a woman he knew to be more than a simple herbalist. She countered the effects of Edgar's actions, allowing Andrea to give birth to a son. She also was able to discern who had introduced the evil magic. But the condemnation of magic in the Realm meant that Roth could not call Edgar out directly, or even explain the situation to Andrea, without bringing suspicion upon himself. He said nothing.

Edgar then turned reluctantly to an attack on Melora. Of course, Artur saw immediately what was happening and confronted his cousin. Despite Edgar's protestations that he was trying to protect them both, Artur refused to go along. The two fought, and Edgar killed Artur. By dint of sorcery, he managed to blame this death on someone else. Grief made Melora sicker, and she died before her second child could be born.

The uncle took advantage of the confusion and despair resulting from these matters and snatched Melora's first born. He declared that the joint rulership had always been a fraud and that this son, for whom he proposed to be regent, was the real ruler of the Realm. Andrea, of course, rejected this, and demanded that he return her nephew to her for proper raising, but the uncle had enough following among the Guard and in the Church—the then Hierofante was his daughter—that he brought the Realm to civil war.

But the uncle was unable to ride out that war to ultimate victory. Edgar, broken-hearted in his own grief over the death of Artur and what he had done, used sorcerous means to tangle things up so that for the next century and a half, the Realm operated with two claimants to the throne but not a full scale civil war. Once Edgar was certain he had succeeded in blocking the uncle's claim, he took his own life. Students of history who know the full story—of which there are only a few, and those few rarely willing to admit to what they know—sometimes opine in hushed conversations with those they trust absolutely that he would have done better to kill the deposed chancellor. A few have speculated—even more privately—that the chancellor had other sorcerers at his disposal and used them to destroy Edgar. But this has never been proven.

Despite the split in the royal family and the rulership of the Realm, the Church remained whole. It had been founded within the Realm in ancient times—well, several hundred years back— by a duke who claimed he had been visited by holy beings while walking in the wilderness abutting his lands. After his revelation, he wandered through the Realm, preaching the word of One God, the Holy Mother of Us All. Though many of his peers among the nobility opined that the man was often disassociated from his right mind, his charismatic speech endeared him to both country people and the more cynical inhabitants of the larger towns and even the Capital. Belief in the all-powerful Mother led people to build houses of worship. By the time the duke passed on—an old man in his bed, attended by a family relieved to see him gone as well as newly minted priests who had taken up his teaching—his religion was well on its way to becoming the Church of the Realm.

The duke—enshrined in lore as a saint, the Holy Fool—had never spoken against magic nor criticized the old ways that circulated among the common folk, particularly in the country. Because of this, many country people accepted the new alongside the old. Some observers thought the choice of a Holy Mother as opposed to the father gods worshipped in Foraoise and Alhambra was a brilliant stroke, for it smoothed the path between the old ways, which were often female-centric, and the new one. New religions had started to appear in other countries as well, and while some did a good job of incorporating traditional ways, others did not. A few people went so far as to think perhaps the duke was not a Holy Fool at all, but a man who had seen a tool for unifying the Realm and been willing to play the fool to get it. But those who held such opinions were not such fools as to share them widely.

The decision of the Church to forbid many of the old ways, particularly the practice of magic, came later, under the rule of a Hierofante who abhorred the peasantry and anything that smacked of it. It came after the then King—brother to that Hierofante—had brutally suppressed a famine-inspired revolt in the countryside. The two of them staged raids on those suspected of witchcraft throughout their years of power. While many were killed, the attacks did not succeed in wiping out magic within the Realm, though the witches and others who understood it did withdraw from public view. Most common people, along with some in the nobility who lived far from the Capital, never completely gave up the old ways, though they also remained loyal to the Church because of the memory of the Holy Fool.

While the Church continued to preach against magic and to excommunicate those it associated with the old ways, the split in the Realm made it impossible for the hierofantes during that period to obtain sufficient support from the rulers to send out raiders against witches. The rulers officially forbade magic, but as each used the excuse of magic to stir up trouble against the other, any action against the old ways became a struggle between them. During the split, those with magical talent both small and large built a quiet network. And while they, along with most others, supported reunification, they waited in the shadows to see whether a united Realm would reopen attacks on witches.

Chapter 5

FOR A TIME, it did appear that Anna and Roland had truly saved the Realm. The King and Queen were often seen together, not only on official business, but also on walks about the palace grounds or sitting in the royal box watching the Symphony of the Realm—most unusual since the King was known for his dislike of music. A month of this went by, then two, then three. Then in early summer came rumors the Queen had asked the royal dressmaker to let out her seams. Her face glowed as she and the King took their by now daily walk.

"Ah," said the courtiers and the servants and the merchants—and the men and women of the Guards—"we will get an heir at last."

The happy circumstances of the King and Queen lessened the usual tensions between their respective guards. Dueling still went on, of course, but most of the fights were friendly contests, without serious outcomes. Anna and Roland took advantage of the détente to become better acquainted. They trained together from time to time, went for walks in the countryside, shared food and drink, and—eventually—a bed. Anna took great care to avoid the Queen's fate, for while an heir is important for royalty, it is an encumbrance for a soldier. Her mother had taught her the country ways of protecting oneself, and she applied them.

Asamir and Jean-Paul also became better acquainted, but their friendship proved more tumultuous. Asamir refused to give up her marquis, who was, after all, a wealthy man, while Jean-Paul had only his meagre guard wages. Whenever Jean-

Paul pressed her too much, she threatened to take vows religious, which made him even wilder. Anna was often on the receiving end of Asamir's complaints, and Roland found himself listening to Jean-Paul on far too many occasions.

"They will resolve things," Roland told Anna one evening as they shared a bottle in the Café Maudite.

"They will not," she replied. "They will vex us with their absurdities forever."

"They do seem to enjoy the turmoil they produce."

"Oh, they are meant for each other, right enough."

Her deepening relationship with Roland surprised Anna. While she had ventured into romantic flings from time to time, affairs of the heart were not a common feature of her life. Unlike Asamir, she was not inclined to bed every likely person who came along, and few of the people she encountered struck her as worth her time, even when she felt the stirrings of lust. But Roland differed from the rest. Their earlier misadventures had given her a sense of his standards of honor and duty, but as they became better acquainted she also discovered that he never drank to excess, a practice that she shared, and rarely initiated duels, though he was not averse to a friendly training bout. Most guards were content with lives that revolved around duels for fun, warfare when required, drinking into the night, and grabbing pleasure where they found it. But while Roland did not eschew the necessary fight or pass up opportunities to celebrate any more than he failed to do his duty as he saw it, he did those things with moderation and thought. Though he had not been long in the King's Guard and held no official position, it was clear from the missions he was assigned that his captain thought highly of him.

His background remained mysterious to Anna. A few hints from his language and behavior led her to believe that he came from a noble family, but he never spoke of it. She was, in fact, not entirely sure whether his loyalties before the wedding of the Queen and King had been on the Andrean or the Meloran side — an issue that could have caused difficulties between them had they met at an earlier time. That issue, at least, was resolved one day when they shared an early supper at the Maudite after training for several hours. The sun still shone, for the days were getting long, and the usual crowd had not yet descended.

"Why," Roland asked as they enjoyed a soup made from the vegetables now available in abundance, "when the negotiations for the Royal Wedding were made was it decided that the Queen's Guard would be all women and the King's all men? Surely both the Andrean and Meloran Guards were not so divided."

"It was decided at a higher level than my own," said Anna, "since I was but a junior member of the Andrean. The rationale was that it would be parallel to the way that the courtiers in attendance on Her Majesty are all women while those for His Majesty are men, but I know that more than one person suspected that Her Eminence suggested the plan. At the time, the current captains of both guards held those positions, so it did not mean a change in leadership, though I know for my part that the men of the Andrean Guard were angered by the plan and our captain did not endorse it."

"But the Hierofante's Guard has always included everyone. It seems odd that she would advocate separation."

"I suspect she thought it would weaken both guards, leaving the Hierofante's people in a position of greater power. Many good people had to find other positions. However, over the years both Guards have been able to recruit sufficiently to repair any lacks. We have taken in a number of women who were once Melorans, and I am sure that your Guard has made similar decisions."

"Indeed, though I was never in the Andrean Guard myself, my sympathies were more on that side when things were divided," Roland said. "I might well have opted for the Queen's Guard had it been an option."

"A family loyalty?"

"A matter of enmity with some who professed Meloran sympathies," he replied. "But the real question is why should we keep this state of affairs?"

"It is already tradition, though perhaps one that should be done away with before it is so well-established that no one will consider it."

"Ah, well. It is perhaps more important that the two guards are no longer divided along outdated political lines, if we wish to ensure the continued healthiness of the Realm. For united is stronger than divided, and matters that date back so many years should not define our future."

"A wise thought. It is most important that the Realm not fracture again."

They toasted peace and unity, and their conversation moved on to other matters. Roland never explained who might be his enemies among the former Melorans. But Anna was gratified to have learned at least that much about him.

Alas, peace was not the natural state of the Realm any more than it was the natural state between Asamir and Jean-Paul. Nor were friendly relations between the Queen and King and their respective soldiers in the interest of the Hierofante, or so it seemed from the rumors that floated throughout the Capital, for things began to go wrong. Little things at first. The Queen and King were seen to walk together less often. The Hierofante's Guard patrolled with unnecessary aggression, bringing charges for dueling against those who engaged in friendly bouts, albeit friendly bouts with money riding on the outcome.

The captain cautioned Anna and Asamir to be more circumspect in their friendships with members of the King's Guard. Roland seemed pensive when he and Anna were together. As time went on, the two of them had difficulty finding times to meet. Nothing was ever said between them, but they stopped spending nights together. Something had gone amiss.

One warm night in the middle of summer, Anna came home after a party with fellow guardswomen celebrating various promotions to once again find a Queen's page sitting in her rooms. The same page as before, a muscular young woman with tan skin whose straight black hair was coming undone from the elaborate style worn by courtiers. She took a last swallow of Anna's best wine, stood, hiccupped, and gave a deep curtsy. "Madame, Her Majesty wishes to see you at once."

"And again it is late for visiting the palace."

"And again you have come home late, no doubt from ribald excesses. But I am to bring you as soon as you are to be found."

Anna sighed for her bed, but duty called. She turned toward the door.

"We should climb down the back way," the girl said.

"There are no soldiers in my street tonight, child."

"These are troubled times, Madame. There are no soldiers, true, but there might be spies. It is better that we not be seen on this journey." She hitched up her skirts and opened the window. "And besides, it is much more fun to go this way." She climbed out and grabbed a branch.

"Girl, why are you serving as a page when you so obviously belong in a soldiers' school?" Anna asked in a quiet voice as she followed the girl down the old tree.

"My father thinks learning palace intrigue will prove more useful to me than learning the art of the sword. He has visions of my becoming a famous diplomat or perhaps foreign minister, not a soldier. Though I do not see why he will not let me learn both." She jumped the last several feet and landed silently.

Anna joined her. "Your abilities at leaving by the back entrance would stand you in good stead for both careers."

"Both my father and Her Majesty have old-fashioned ideas about the proper behavior of young women of good families. Not wishing to offend either of them, I must often make use of alternative means of entrance and egress." She paused. "Though I think the Queen must be aware of my behavior, since she always sends me when she needs someone who will not be seen."

"Discretion is a useful tool for diplomats and ladies-in-waiting," Anna said as they made their way through dark alleys and lightly traveled streets.

"Perhaps. But they spend their days standing around in their best clothes and pretending they are not bored to tears."

"Should you like to learn the sword, then?"

"With all my heart."

"Perhaps Her Majesty would allow you to study with me."

The girl stopped suddenly. "Oh, that would be quite wonderful," she said, still keeping her voice down. "But perhaps we should not tell the Queen exactly what it is I would study."

"Perhaps you are right."

The last time Anna had been called to a late-night meeting with the Queen, she had found the woman distraught. On this evening, though, Her Majesty was seated at a table with the Minister for Foreign Affairs, who, despite the fact that she wore the robes of one in holy orders, was known to not take the part of the Hierofante. Others at the table included two women dressed in the elaborate fashion of high-placed courtiers, their sop to custom, for they were among the Queen's most trusted advisors. The Queen's midwife made up the final member of the party. Her Majesty was taking no chances with this pregnancy.

Anna bowed deeply. "Your Majesty. My ladies."

The Queen waved a hand. "Please take a seat, Guardswoman. We have matters to discuss with you."

Anna had never before been asked to sit in the presence of the Queen. She did so, stiffly, on the edge of a chair.

"We are given to understand that you have a friend among the King's Guard," the foreign minister said.

Anna and Roland had done their best to be discreet, but secrets have a way of seeping out, particularly secrets that might generate licentious gossip.

"I do have good relations with some among His Majesty's men," Anna said. She noticed a slight grin on the face of one of the courtiers.

"Might you be able to find out from him if the King is making any, um, unusual plans?" Her Majesty had not bothered with the pretense that Anna was on good terms with more than one guardsman.

Anna thought of saying that her friend was not so highly placed as to be in the know about such things, but she rejected that idea. The Queen's advisors clearly knew of Roland and likely were aware that his captain often called on him for advice. Indeed, Anna herself suspected that it was the press of the King's business and warnings from his captain that had caused Roland to draw back from their relationship of late.

"My friend is very loyal to the King," she said.

"But he is also known to be loyal to the Realm," the Minister said.

Anna wondered what the Minister knew. Neither she nor Roland had ever told anyone what had transpired between them on the road back to the Capital. Perhaps the Minister was simply skilled at reading between the lines, or perhaps she merely spoke of his reputation from the most recent war. Anna hoped for Roland's sake that it was the later.

"It is true that he thinks the current arrangement between Your Majesty and His Majesty is a good one," Anna said. "And that he supports a unified Realm. But he would not betray his duty to His Majesty. Perhaps you had best tell me what you think I might be able to learn from him."

The Queen looked at the Minister and the other two advisors, and then seemed to reach a decision. "His Majesty has been meeting with generals without my assistance—and without the assistance of Madame the Minister as well. When I inquired about the meetings, His Majesty said he did not like to disturb me while I was indisposed. He gave no explanation of why the minister was excluded."

"Soldiers have been sent to strengthen our garrisons on the Foraoise border, as well," said the Minister. "Her Eminence the Hierofante appears to be well-informed about these matters, despite the fact that neither Her Majesty nor I have been consulted."

Though both women had been formal and soft spoken, Anna could tell from their pinched lips and clipped words that they were quite angry. She shared their feelings. Clearly the Hierofante was once again trying to damage the relationship between their Majesties for her own purposes. She wondered if Her Eminence had ties with someone in Foraoise. Surely not; that would be treason. But she must have some larger reason to stir up war plans; it would make no sense to do something so drastic just to reduce the influence of Her Majesty.

Perhaps Anna's puzzlement showed on her face, for one of the courtiers said, "Her Eminence has long thought the Mines of Airgead should be under our control."

"And Her Majesty and I have opposed any efforts to gain that control through more warfare," the minister said. "Our last failure made that quite clear. Better we build up a strong alliance and trade relationship than fight a well-armed country over mines whose ownership has been in dispute for centuries."

Anna remembered well the last war with Foraoise. The conflict had not ended with the onset of winter weather—as was usual—and the soldiers had slogged through mud and snowdrifts for many weeks before the generals on both sides gave up and agreed to stop fighting. The Foraoisians had a strong army; she doubted any new adventures in that direction would have a better outcome.

Roland had not yet been a King's guardsman during that last war, but it was in one of those battles where he had made his name and gained his commission with His Majesty. Anna knew that he shared her opinion of the foolishness of the whole enterprise. Perhaps that would give her an opening to ask questions of him.

"I may be able to find a way to inquire without compromising my friend," she said. "But I shall have to be discreet."

The Minister nodded. "The entire matter must be handled with care. That is why Her Majesty suggested asking for your help. Your discretion is as well-known as your loyalty."

"I thank you." Anna rose to go, but before she bowed, she had another thought. "Your Majesty, perhaps it would help keep our discussions discreet if you were to send your page to me for training in an open manner. That way I could send messages to you, and you to me, without anyone noticing something out of the ordinary."

"What kind of training would you give her?" one of the courtiers asked.

But the Queen laughed. "In the art of the sword, of course. That child chafes whenever she is expected to act the part of a lady. I will send her to you on the morrow."

On her way back home, Anna thought about how to approach Roland. Perhaps she could inquire about his experiences in the last war with Foraoise. That might open the door for her to suggest she had heard a rumor. Still, Roland was as well-known for his discretion as she. A private discussion would be unlikely to lead to any secrets. But if Jean-Paul were present...

Chapter 6

"A PICNIC, I think," said Asamir in response to Anna's desire to meet with Roland and Jean-Paul in a way that might encourage some disclosures from the men. "People are always more careless when sitting on the ground on a lovely day, eating and drinking."

"It is the right time of year for a picnic," Anna said. "Such an invitation would not arouse suspicions." They were in the common room at Guard headquarters, relaxing after a morning of training. Or rather, Anna was relaxing with a cup of tea while Asamir primped before the mirror. The others with whom they had been training had left for luncheon, but Anna had relied on Asamir's beauty regimen to allow them some privacy.

"So the King is making plans without the Queen again. Foolish man. War plans, I suppose?"

Anna had been vague about her meeting with the Queen, but Asamir was too observant to have missed the increased chilliness in royal relations and too well-schooled in the Realm's intrigues not to have drawn conclusions. "I do not know all the details," Anna said.

"You need not betray the Queen's trust," Asamir said. "For purposes of eliciting information from Jean-Paul and Roland, it does not matter whether the King is deceiving her about matters of state or matters of the heart. We shall get them relaxed and take note of the things they say, and then put the facts together. Yes, a picnic. The Marquis will be in the country over the Sabbath. We could go to the Governor's Gardens in the early afternoon."

"Will you not be at services all day?" Anna asked, knowing full well that Asamir worshipped just often enough to avoid censure by the priests.

"One does not have to pray all day to show one's respect for God," Asamir said. "Perhaps you will come with me to the early service."

"Perhaps I will not," said Anna, who made no pretense of religious practice.

One of the junior guards appeared in the door. "There is a page from the Queen downstairs asking for Anna d'Gart."

"Royal emissaries now," said Asamir. "You are likely to become a state minister if you are not more careful."

"It is a much simpler matter than that. This particular page is causing the Queen no end of grief. Her Majesty thinks the girl will calm down if she is introduced to the rigors of sword training. Exhausting the young with physical training is known to be effective in keeping them home at night. Except, of course, in your case." Asamir's unsanctioned adventures had given her a certain notoriety back when the two of them studied at the soldiers' school of Saint Demetrius.

The page had dressed in tunic and pants rather than her usual court attire, and her hair was pulled back in a braid. "Madame, the Queen says I may train for an hour," she said, bowing formally to Anna.

"We will begin, then," said Anna, leading her charge to the training ground. Only a few of the junior guards remained on the field, two of them doing sword drills and a third running around the compound—whether for disciplinary reasons or her own training, Anna was unsure. Anna went to the rack of wooden swords and selected a two-handed style that she judged would soon feel too heavy to her charge. "By the way, child," she said as she handed it to her—formally, as if it were a real blade—what is your name?"

"Cecile," the girl said, taking the stick of wood in both hands. She bowed to Anna, and then took hold of the hilt, careful to avoid the blade even though it was not real.

Clearly she had observed how real swordswomen handled weapons, though her hands were not in the correct position. Anna placed the girl's right hand just under the guard, her left almost at the end of the hilt, and showed her how to grip with her little fingers to allow for the greatest flexibility while still controlling the weapon. Then she drew her own sword and demonstrated the most basic of cuts, from above the head straight down. After several tries, Cecile began to do a passable imitation.

"Good," said Anna. "Now do a thousand cuts. Count aloud while you do them."

The girl began with enthusiasm, but was starting to sag before she reached one hundred. But she said no word in complaint even as her hair began to come unraveled and sweat poured down her face. Anna kept an eye on her as she offered pointers to the women doing sword drills. The woman who had been running went inside, and was shortly followed by the other two. Anna walked over to Cecile, who was counting "three-hundred-twelve" in ragged breaths. Her shoulders were almost to her ears.

Anna put her hands on the girl's shoulders. "Relax," she said, giving her a brief massage. "It will be easier if you do not work so hard." And then, more quietly, "Do you have any message from the Queen?"

"She said to tell you," the child gasped for a breath, "that there was another meeting only this morning. Three-hundred-eighteen." Another gasp. "And she bids me ask whether you have made any progress. Three-hundred-nineteen."

"I hope to have some greater knowledge by the evening of the Holy Day."

"I will relay that to her. Three-hundred-twenty-three."

"Good. Pray continue," Anna said. She left the training ground. But once inside, she peered out through the window to see what the girl might do. She was pleased to note that, despite the absence of an overseer, Cecile continued with the cuts. She would make a swordswoman.

Asamir, who had finally reached a point of satisfaction with her appearance, joined Anna at the window. "Sadist," she said.

"The child has a lot of catching up to do. My mother had me doing a thousand cuts a day by the time I was five."

"So that is why you were already so good with the sword when you first came to Saint Demetrius. All this time I have thought you a prodigy, and now I find out it was only hard work."

Anna smiled. She knew she was being teased, not insulted. She also knew that the reason Asamir took so much time over her appearance after training was that when she trained, she worked quite as hard as Anna did, for all that she liked to pretend she simply skated by. She became as sweaty and disheveled as everyone else, but cared more abut repairing that than most. The two of them had figured each other out during Anna's first week at school.

The daughter of a pig farmer, Anna had brought with her the mannerisms of a country child and started a year behind her peers because she had been needed at home due to the birth of her youngest sister. The senior students had laughed at her carelessly braided hair, her outdated tunics, and her enthusiasm for school. In her first sword class, she had been paired with a very experienced student, who had tried to humiliate her by attacking fast and hard. Anna not only moved out of the way of the attack in time, but tripped the boy and ended the match with her training sword at his throat.

The next day at the break time an older girl had challenged her to spar empty handed. In short order, Anna threw her to the ground. By the end of her first week, Anna had fought a half a dozen highly skilled students and beaten every one. What none of the challengers knew until much later was that Anna's mother had served for ten years in the Andrean Guard, this being well-before the reunification of the Realm, before returning home to take over her family's pig farm. She had begun training Anna when the girl turned two.

Asamir had joined in the laughter at Anna's appearance when she first arrived, but she had stopped laughing after watching Anna fight. Or rather, she had started laughing at the foolish people who kept challenging her. They had not quite become friends, but loyalties had shifted. At the end of the first week, Asamir caught Anna sneaking out of their room in the girls' barracks.

"Where are you going?"

"I have been challenged to a duel."

"You know it is against the rules to sneak out at night."

Anna had also been observing Asamir's ways. "You do it."

Asamir did not bother to blush or deny. "I do not sneak out to fight duels. I go to have fun. Early to bed may be a silly rule, but the prohibition on fighting duels in private is a good one. Better to fight duels out in the open during break, so that no one can cheat."

Anna sighed. "I must show up. It would not be honorable if I did not go."

"Besides, it is certainly a trap," Asamir said. "You have embarrassed a lot of people this week. There will be at least half a dozen people waiting to jump you."

"That would be dishonorable." Anna was shocked.

"Not everyone here has your view of honor. But I have an idea. Wait here."

Anna waited impatiently and was on the verge of leaving anyway when Asamir returned. "I will be late," she said.

"We will be late together," Asamir said. When Anna gave her a look of surprise, she added, "I cannot let you face those bullies alone."

Asamir proved right about the trap, because when they arrived at the agreed upon space—a clearing in the woods just beyond the crumbling wall of the old fort—six boys and girls stood there, all armed with wooden swords, not the padded ones used for sparring.

"You are late," the leader said.

"I am here now," Anna said.

Before he could give the order to rush her, Asamir said, "And she is not alone."

The leader hesitated.

Then another voice said, "They are not alone."

A dozen girls emerged from the woods. Asamir said, "We have come to make certain the duel is fair. Anna is ready to fight you. The rest of us will watch to make certain no one else attacks. I have brought you a padded sword so that there will be no injuries."

The leader hesitated again, but nodded.

The fight was over in a matter of minutes. The leader was big and strong, but he held his sword too tightly. Anna struck once, twice, three times, and his sword went flying out of his hands.

The story became school legend. Anna and Asamir had been inseparable friends ever since.

Despite—or perhaps because of—Asamir's neglect of him in favor of her marquis, Jean-Paul responded with enthusiasm to the idea of a Sunday afternoon picnic. Anna was glad of it, since Roland's agreement to participate seemed to be the result of Jean-Paul's cajoling and pleading rather than any desire on his own part. They had not seen each other in a fortnight, and Roland had little to say as the four of them, eschewing the carriages favored by gentry as unsuitable to soldiers, rode through the streets to the Governor's Gardens.

Anna asked his opinion on the weather, which had been uncommonly fine.

"Very nice," Roland replied, and returned to silence.

She commented on the roses climbing over a nearby wall (providing a welcome aroma to offset the muck of the street), then on a passing carriage dripping with gilt (who might be within?), and again on a well-laid-out garden, all to grunts or one-word replies. Meanwhile, Asamir and Jean-Paul began their all-too-familiar quibbling.

"It is unconscionable that I have not seen you in more than a week. You must allow me more time with you."

"You must learn not to make such demands."

"But you return my passion. I know you do. You just prefer to toy with me, as if I were a...a puppy."

Asamir laughed at him.

Under the cover of that laugh, Anna said, "He is very like a puppy."

Roland also laughed, the first friendly sound she had heard from him all day. "He is at that. At the barracks, the captain is always saying 'Down, boy' to him. But of course, Asamir provokes him."

"She has found great success in the provocation of men."

Roland laughed again. "The two of them are entertaining, at least. Which must be why you and I put up with them."

They both looked up at a shout from Jean-Paul. Asamir had issued a challenge to race and spurred her horse. The two of them galloped full speed down the street, heedless of carriages, well-dressed gentry, small children, dogs, and chickens.

"Perhaps they will break their necks," said Anna.

"And deprive the Realm of two brave fighters? What a tragedy! I do hope they do not run over anyone important."

"Indeed. Hanging them would also deprive the Realm of soldiers, though it might provide relief to their friends."

"If they were not both such talented soldiers, one could almost wish for such a result."

The ice broken, they continued to engage in friendly — though inconsequential — conversation as they continued their slow pace to the park. The Governor's Gardens—the name of the governor who supposedly established them was lost to time—covered several dozen acres at the heart of the capital city. At a time when precisely pruned hedges and severely maintained flowering bushes were all the rage, it was instead a lightly maintained semi-wild area, crisscrossed by several creeks that fed small ponds used by the more adventurous for swimming. Anna's favorite area for outings was on the bank of one such pond, a small meadow reached by narrow trails through surrounding woods. Roland and Anna dismounted and led their horses down the path, moving slowly to enjoy the coolness of the shade and the mixed odors from the trees.

When they arrived at the picnic grounds, Jean-Paul was dusting himself off, having been dehorsed in his hell-for-leather ride down the trail, and protesting loudly that Asamir had cheated by knocking a branch back into him. Asamir, looking as impeccable as ever despite her own fast ride, was laughing at him.

"I fear you have over-shaken the wine," Anna said as she and Roland joined them.

"Nonsense. My horse gallops so smoothly that the bottles were barely disturbed," Asamir said. Though she did examine the bottles carefully as she removed them.

Roland shook out a blanket and laid it on the ground while Anna unpacked the delectables they had brought—a fine cheese, some fresh sausages, two loaves of bread, berries picked only that morning. They led their horses to the pond—reminding Asamir and Jean-Paul to care for their own mounts, which were more sorely in need of a drink—and then tied them loosely in the shade of an oak so old that their grandparents might have done the same. The horses began to nibble grass. Anna would have unsaddled her horse, but she noticed that Roland did not. *He is on alert*, she thought; *I best be the same.*

"Such perfect summer weather," Anna said, sitting on the blanket and bringing out a knife for the cheese. "I am astounded that we are enjoying the pleasures of the city at this time rather than on a campaign."

"But do you not find it dull to be at peace during such prime fighting weather?" said Asamir, catching the drift of her conversation.

"Oh, yes," said Jean-Paul. "It is absurd that we are lolling around when we are pressed on all sides and should be out advancing the interests of our Realm."

Roland gave him a sharp look, but Anna responded quickly. "I do not mind times of peace, so long as they do not mean that those who make these decisions will decide to take us to war when the weather grows colder. Remember the war with Foraoise?"

"Slogging through snow and mud," said Asamir.

"Never dry. Ever," said Jean-Paul.

"It was ill-timed," Roland said.

"And ultimately unsuccessful. The weather always draws the blame for the stalemate, but I think poor planning led to it. Had we waited until spring to invade..."

Anna was interrupted by Jean-Paul. "The weather would still have caused trouble. That was no natural winter." He made the religious gesture.

Asamir did the same.

Anna laughed. "Bad weather can happen without sorcery."

But Roland seemed more somber. "Perhaps. But starting a war at a time of uncertain weather can give sorcerers useful material for creating their magics. I have heard tell that it is easier to create wintry conditions when there is a hint of coolness and rain in the air."

"So you, too, think wars should only be fought in the summer, despite the fact that it would deprive us of such joys as this picnic?"

"Despite being a soldier, I am inclined to oppose wars being fought at any time."

Asamir and Jean-Paul both leaped in to protest. "But the glory of battle," said one. "The clash of steel, the roar of the cannon," said the other.

"The death of far too many for far too few reasons," said Roland.

For a moment they were all struck solemn. They knew those losses well. All soldiers do. And while they all loved to fight—for why else would they have taken up the sword?—they were not immune to the fear of death.

"Well," said Anna, pouring another round of wine, "let us toast the fact that we are not at war today and that no battles are imminent."

They all took a glass and raised it. Asamir and Jean-Paul immediately began a new quarrel over who had drunk first, but Anna could see that Roland looked troubled.

"Do you think," she asked in a quiet voice that endeavored to recreate the somberness of the discussion, "that despite the current peace there might be some risk of war in the future? Our neighbors have been peaceful of late, and despite Jean-Paul's belief that we should be aggressive, I see no need to expand our borders. But such things can change."

He shrugged. "I only know that those who make such decisions rarely listen to the advice of the people who will do the fighting."

She thought he wanted to say more, but his natural discretion held him back. Blast Asamir anyway. She and Jean-Paul were now racing around the park as if they were children, calling taunts. If they had been present for this conversation, perhaps Jean-Paul would have blurted something out.

The conversation turned to other matters. At least Roland appeared to enjoy her company. Perhaps they would be able to spend more time together, and she would have other opportunities to elicit some information. For now, though, all she had for the Queen were a few more speculations.

The ride home was quiet. Asamir and Jean-Paul appeared to have exhausted themselves and rode side by side, making fond noises at each other. Anna and Roland kept a more discreet distance apart, though Anna was hoping that he would join her in her chambers that evening. It had been far too long.

As they reached the high road, they were halted by soldiers wearing the Hierofante's white. "Make way, make way," a herald cried.

A convoy of closed carriages traveled down the road at a fast pace, each escorted by several soldiers. Anna caught the crest of the Realm of Foraoise on the side of one carriage. The carriages were followed by a troop of soldiers in Foraoisian black and gold, accompanied by a greater number of Hierofante's guards.

"Erick," Anna said, calling out to a Hierofante's guard known to her, "What is happening here?"

"The Foraoise ambassador and her party are leaving the Realm, and good riddance," Erick replied.

Anna whispered to Roland. "It appears that neither your guard nor mine were informed of this departure. I see naught but Hierofante's troops."

"Perhaps the ambassador only informed the Hierofante and asked for an escort."

"Or perhaps the Hierofante told them to leave. That is far more guards than would be required for a formal escort."

"But the Hierofante could not take such action on her own," Roland said.

"Could she not?"

"She should not." As the road cleared before them, Roland turned his horse in a new direction. "I must discuss this with my captain."

"And I with mine," Anna said, not without regret.

Asamir gave her a wave as Anna headed for Queen's Guard headquarters. "I will leave the reporting to you."

Anna resisted the temptation to demand that Asamir accompany her. It would add nothing to her report; she would only be doing it out of spite because she had been deprived of her evening with Roland. "Best that you report early tomorrow. I fear our peaceful sojourn is at an end."

As Anna started in the direction of the headquarters of the Queen's Guard, she heard a horse coming up behind her. She turned. It was Roland.

"Meet me later tonight at the Maudite," he said. "Perhaps around nine? I will send word if I cannot come due to duties."

"Agreed, though I may also have duties."

He waved a hand and galloped off.

Chapter 7

THE CAPTAIN WAS not pleased by the news. "The ambassador of Foraoise? And her entire retinue? Are you certain?"

"The carriages were closed," Anna said. "But the seal was on each one. And the Hierofante's guards asserted that it was the ambassador. I am certain that the troops that accompanied them were of Foraoise. I recognized several faces among them."

"Seals can be faked, and the Hierofante's guards can lie. But it is unlikely that Foraoisian soldiers would participate in a fraud. Still, if tensions between our rulers and theirs are in such disarray that ambassadors are returning home—or even being sent away—why have we heard nothing about it?"

"It appears," Anna said, "that the King's Guard knew nothing of it as well. I was in the company of a gentlemen of the Guard when I saw this procession, and he was as startled as I."

The captain gave her a sharp look, and Anna remembered that she had been cautioned about spending time with guardsmen. But all her superior officer said was, "If Roland de Barthes does not know of such a thing, it is unlikely that his captain does. The King's captain does not make many decisions without consulting your friend. But surely the King would have included the captain in his consultations." She paused. "In truth, surely the Queen would have consulted me. Do you suppose the Hierofante acted on her own?"

"I fear it." Now it was Anna who hesitated. The captain was not unaware that Anna was in the Queen's confidence, but Anna had made a point of not discussing her errands for the Queen with her superior. For the most part, that was because the Queen relied on Anna to handle affairs that might cause embarrassment to the captain or others in official positions. But the current situation was not one of those times. True, Anna had been asked to spy, which was not the kind of action that the Queen liked to ask of her Guard in an official manner. But the matter was fast escalating. The captain must know, she decided. "Madame, I have reason to believe that the Queen knows nothing of this." She told her of the meeting with Her Majesty.

The captain's frown deepened as she listened. "That man is such a fool."

Anna thought she referred to the King, though even in anger the captain was not so careless as to say so directly.

The captain was less careful in letting her opinion of the Hierofante be known. "This whole business does smell of Her Eminence's intrigues. May her God have mercy on us all if we end up at war with Foraoise in the winter again. Luck saved us last time, but luck is fickle."

"Surely the Hierofante knows the risk of going to war with a more northerly country during the worst of weather," Anna said. "She is not a foolish woman."

"Nor a careless one. And that means there is something more happening here. Ejecting the ambassador is tantamount to declaring war, but we have made no preparations for battle. And if the ambassador agreed to leave without demanding an audience with Their Majesties or otherwise protesting, she must have had compelling reasons. She is no fool either and not likely to be intimidated by Her Eminence unless there are other factors at play. Could something be going on in Foraoise?"

"And is Her Eminence involved in that as well?" Anna said it quietly. She and the captain were wont to talk frankly, but even though most members of the Queen's Guard were loyal to both their captain and their Queen to the point of fanaticism, it was risky to say too much about someone who had both the Church and royal birth on her side, even if she had done something that threatened the Realm.

The captain shook her head. "We need more information. It is an outrage that we must engage in espionage just to do the job entrusted to us by the Realm, but it would be foolish of us to pretend that such things are not necessary in desperate times. Do you not have a friend in Foraoise?"

Anna gave a hesitant nod. Sotha's father had been banished from Foraoise at one point and had brought his family to the Realm as refugees. Because of that, Sotha had trained at Saint Demetrius along with her and Asamir. They had become fast friends then. Since their time in school, the rulership in Foraoise had changed, Sotha's family had been welcomed home, and their friend—a better strategist than fighter—had returned to hold a key defense post. In the unfortunate winter war with Foraoise, Anna had recognized Sotha's hand in their enemy's strategy; in fact, her familiarity with his thinking had saved her troop at one point.

"I do not know if our bonds of friendship have survived the war, though I hope they have. For my part, I know that we were only opposed because of our loyalty to our respective realms, not out of any animosity between us. I doubt he or his father would take kindly to Her Eminence, if only because they are followers of their own religion. Of course, he may have been forced to deal with her for the benefit of his Queen. In intrigues for the benefit of rulers, personal feelings have no place."

The captain sighed. "You speak truth, but we might still benefit if you could speak with him. Let us keep that idea available, for we may need it. I understand you have arranged a simple way of communicating with Her Majesty."

The captain had not missed Cecile's presence on the training ground.

"Please let her know that we can make others of the Guard available to her—in a discreet manner—if it should become necessary."

"I may also be able to learn more of what the King's Guard knows," Anna said. "That is, unless you have other duties for me this evening."

"There is no task you could do tonight that would be more important. Go meet with your friend, and find out what you can."

The clock had not yet struck nine when Anna reached the Maudite, but Roland was there before her and had secured a table despite the crowd. He waved a hand at the server in a request for more wine as Anna joined him. Much as she wanted to, she did not reach out a hand to him. Though everyone who mattered in the Capital knew of their relationship, both still felt it unwise to display affection in public, even at the best of times. And this was not the best of times.

The table was in a corner of the room. Roland sat with his back to one wall, and the chair he had saved for Anna was against the other, allowing them to be aware of who was around them as they spoke. At the moment, the only people within earshot were several very drunk members of the King's Guard. Unlikely that those men would remember anything they might hear, and, given the rowdiness of their behavior, it was probable that they would hear nothing said in less than a bellow.

Roland responded politely as Anna asked after his health just as if they had not made plans to meet, but as his small talk was stilted and forced, she concluded that his experience had been no better than hers. Once the server had brought Anna a cup—and left the bottle—Roland said quietly, "I fear things are as bad as we suspected. I have been cautioned not to share too much with you, but my captain can see wisdom in discreet communication with yours. As far as we know, the King was not made aware of the departure of the ambassador until after it occurred. If he did know of it, he did not discuss it with my captain, which would be even worse. However, as I was leaving, a page came to summon the captain to the palace, so things may be changing as we speak. I have orders to return soon, in case he may need my advice."

Once again, intrigue has spoiled our opportunity for a pleasant evening, Anna thought. "The situation of my captain is similar, though she had not been summoned when I left. It does appear that...someone may have acted without royal permission." Even if no one could hear their quiet words, Anna did not want to mention the Hierofante by any name or title.

"That someone may have received permission after the fact," he said. Roland was loyal to the King, but he had few illusions about the man beneath the crown. "It is possible that someone has exceeded their authority, but someone is known to be very persuasive and such action may be overlooked. Or even praised."

"And perhaps there are uncanny means of persuasion available."

Roland sat up straight. "Oh, surely the Hier...someone... would not use such means in dealing with the highest authority. In fact, surely they would not do such a thing at all. It is strictly forbidden."

Anna thought Roland was trying to convince himself more than her. She had never told him of her suspicion that the Hierofante had dabbled in magic to prevent her trip back with the necklace, and she did not tell him now. Yet despite his words in protest, she had the feeling that the idea had crossed his mind. Had he seen the King behave as if had been spelled in some way? But all she said was, "I wish I were as certain."

They sat and drank in silence for a time. Then Roland said, "I must get back to my captain. But let us try to keep communications open between us, despite what orders we may be given. I fear that the good of the Realm may once again be in our hands." He surprised her by taking her hand and kissing it, as if she were a lady-in-waiting and not a guard and this were a formal drawing room and not a rowdy bar, before making his way to the door.

Anna found Cecile in her rooms when she returned home. "Madame, I fear this is a sadly mediocre vintage," the page said, indicating the bottle open in front of her.

"That is because you finished all of my good wines on your previous visits. Why are you here, child? Do you and Her Majesty not realize that the purpose of your coming to me for lessons is to reduce the chance you may be discovered coming to my abode?"

"I was not seen," Cecile said in the tone of one far too confident of her own skills. "And the Queen wishes to see you now, not tomorrow."

"Surely she needs to speak with my captain."

"And she has. But she now wishes to see you."

Anna followed the girl as they once again climbed down the old tree behind her quarters. She was beginning to fear that someone would discover that path, sooner or later. Cecile did not lack discretion, but she was very young, and the young make mistakes.

The Queen, sitting with several of her ladies when Anna and Cecile arrived, sent everyone but Anna away and motioned for her to sit.

"The ambassador from Foraoise left the city this afternoon," the Queen said.

"I saw her leave, Your Majesty. I reported it to my captain, who had heard nothing of such business."

"And she sent a messenger to me. Her message came before an official notice was received by the minister of foreign affairs. There is something very wrong afoot. Mishandled, it could lead to war. I need your help in finding the truth."

"Your majesty, I am sure the captain will be glad to do everything in her power. No one wants an unnecessary war."

"And I shall make use of the captain and the Guard. But what I need from you involves more discretion. I am told you have a friend in Foraoise."

Was her entire personal history known to everyone? Anna said, "I do not know that we are still friends, given the last war. But yes, I know Sotha of the Foraoisian Defense Ministry."

"I know of no one else reliable who might be able to discover what is happening in Foraoise. I want to send you there, to see if you can discover the truth. I will ask your captain to give you leave, but I wanted to make certain that you were willing to do this before asking her."

Anna was, indeed, more than a little reluctant to undertake this mission. Her skills did not lie in espionage. However, she would not—could not—refuse the Queen. The captain must have informed Her Majesty of Anna's connection with Sotha. It was obvious she had no choice. "As you wish."

"You should leave soon, though not so soon that all will immediately guess why you are gone. I fear others know of your connection to Foraoise."

Anna nodded. "May I take others with me?"

"If they can be discreet."

"They can. If I may presume, I believe that Cecile could be useful for this expedition." The beginnings of a disguise were starting to form in Anna's mind. She might have no talent for pretending to be someone she was not, but others did. If she brought them along, they could provide cover for her investigations.

"I am certain the child would be thrilled to accompany you, though her father would be horrified. But he lives in the far northwest and rarely comes to the Capital, so he need not find out. You must take good care of her, though, or he will haunt you, and me, forever. Make whatever arrangements would be suitable. I will provide you with sufficient funds for your trip."

⤙⤚

Asamir rubbed her hands in glee when Anna sketched out her plan for slipping into Foraoise. "Ah, intrigue. If we cannot fight a war, at least we can have an adventure. But do you think Sotha will be willing to meet with us? After the last war, will he still treat us as friends?"

"That is the reason for the intrigue. I do not want him to know we are there until we are in his company. If we entered as ourselves—even if we crossed the border by stealth—we might find him prepared for our visit. As for whether he still thinks of us as friends, I do not know. But I hope we share enough memories in common to at least get a reasonable audience with him."

They had met at Saint Demetrius in the year after Anna had arrived. Sotha, small for his size and clumsy in sword class, had been put in advanced classes in strategy and philosophy. He stood out there, and while it did not help him with the bullies who always targeted new students who seemed different—and as the child of a man who had been exiled from Foraoise, Sotha was more different than usual—it made Anna warm to him. She sought him out for help with her own studies and they became friends.

Asamir disdained him at first, but that changed after a shared adventure.

Anna had been sitting on the low stone wall alongside the exercise ground, rubbing beeswax into her wooden sword. It was the hour before dinner, a free period. She watched with envy as several senior students practiced forms with real swords, the metal glinting in the sun. There was nothing in life she wanted more than a true sword with a sharp blade, but it would be two more years before she was allowed to train with one.

A short girl and a tall, wiry boy began a sparring match, using sticks wrapped in leather so that they could fight seriously without injuring each other. Anna watched as they parried and blocked. After a few moves, the boy knocked the girl's training sword aside, moving in so that the tip of his weapon pointed at her throat from about six inches away. The girl looked as if she would yield, and then smacked the side of his blade with the palm of her hand, knocking it aside. Before he could respond, she hit him on the top of his head with her stick.

"Ow," he yelled, and the girl laughed.

Asamir sat down beside her on the wall. "Valen makes that same mistake every time," she said. "The whole school takes advantage of it. When will he learn to get close enough?"

Anna looked at her friend. Asamir's blond hair hung in perfect ringlets, and she had put on a fresh uniform. A bit of lace peeked out from under its dull brown wool. Asamir had spent half the break on her appearance.

Anna herself was still sweaty from training, and her hair was sticking to her neck where it had come loose from her braid.

Asamir said, "Are you going to spend your whole break working on that sword?"

"You heard the lecture this morning about taking care of your weapons. 'Take care of your sword as if your life depended on it—'"

"'Because it does,'" Asamir finished. "But that is only a piece of wood, not a real sword." She, too, looked with envy at those swinging actual blades.

Anna ran her cloth over the sword one last time and rose to go clean up for dinner. Asamir said, "I heard something about your boyfriend Sotha today."

"He is not my boyfriend," Anna said. "He is my friend, who happens to be a boy. There is a difference. You are the one with boyfriends."

"Whatever you say. Anyway, some of the older boys are planning to jump him tonight. Five or six of them, I heard."

"What? Why would they do that?"

"He is new, he is small, he is Foraoisian, he was put in advanced classes even though he is barely thirteen."

"It must be more than that," Anna said.

Asamir hesitated. "They believe Sotha's father is a sorcerer." She made the religious gesture, as she often did when conversations touched on practices forbidden by the Church. "They think if they attack Sotha, he might attack back with magic. The Hierofante would be very upset if she caught wind of that and her displeasure might cause the officials of the Realm on both sides to revoke his family's right to stay in the Realm."

"That is ridiculous," Anna said. "Sotha is no magician, and neither is his father."

"Are you sure?"

"Yes," Anna said, though she was not, not really. She had never seen any indication that Sotha knew magic, but she did not know his father. Sotha's father had come from Foraoise, where magic was common, after a change in power in that country left him out of favor, and he had become an aide to the Duke of Bosque. With his aid, the duke had become very skilled at balancing the interests of the Meloran and Andrean factions, giving him a great deal of influence in the Realm. Perhaps he had done that by magic. But she said, "They are just making things up. They pick on him because he is a foreigner."

Asamir shrugged. "Those boys do not need much reason to pick on someone." She nodded her head toward the wiry boy, who was still rubbing his head. "Valen is apparently the leader, and you know he likes to torment anyone he can."

"We have to help Sotha," Anna said.

"I told you so you could warn him."

"He would still be outnumbered. He needs our help."

"They plan to do this tonight, in the boys' barracks. How do we help him there?"

"We sneak in," Anna said. "Or we help him sneak out."

"You, the person who always follows the rules, you want to sneak into the boys' barracks?"

"Sometimes you have to break one rule to follow another. Taking care of our fellow soldiers is a rule, too. We cannot let our friend get hurt."

"He is your friend, not mine," Asamir said. "Anyway, how will you get into the boys' barracks?"

"I was expecting you to help me. You do it often, do you not?"

Another girl might have blushed, but Asamir just grinned. "What makes you think I will come along?"

"Surely you would not miss a chance to break a rule. Or have an adventure. Besides, you like a good fight too much," Anna added. "Come. We will warn Sotha and lay our plans."

As she had expected, Asamir came with her.

Sotha was shaken by their news. "I knew they hated me, but I never thought of anything like this."

"They are bullies," Asamir said. "And they think no one will help you."

"The other boys in my room certainly will not," Sotha said. "They do not like me much, either."

"We will help you," Anna said. "Can we hide in your room?"

He shook his head. "Not without my roommates knowing you were there. They would probably call for the dorm master."

"Outside the window, then," Asamir said.

But Anna disagreed. "We would be at a disadvantage as we came back in."

"What can three of us do against so many others? They are all older and stronger than we. My roommates might even help them."

Asamir drew herself up. "You may feel weak in their presence, but Anna and I do not. Odds of two to one do not concern us. Though your roommates could cause complications. Are you six to a room?"

He nodded.

"And none of them like you enough to fight for you?"

Sotha looked embarrassed. "I think they decided not to like me because the older students made fun of me."

Anna suspected it was also because he did so well in school work. But she said, "Then we must make them attack you somewhere else. Can you sneak out of your room, but leave a hint behind so your roommates can tell the bullies where you went?"

He thought for a minute. "If I got into an argument with one of the others after the dorm master comes by to put out the lanterns, I could let him win the argument and mock me. Then no one would be surprised if I went running off." He grinned. "I could even cry and mutter something about where I am going."

"Yes," said Anna. She was impressed with his idea. "Come over to the clump of trees near the girls' barracks. We can hide easily there. They will think you are alone."

"But will not the other girls or perhaps the dorm mother hear us if we fight near…" Sotha broke off in mid-sentence. "Oh. Of course they will." He grinned again.

"Perhaps we can even scare them away without a fight," Anna said.

"But why are you helping me?"

"You are my friend," Anna said. "And what they are doing is not honorable. As for Asamir, she just likes a good fight."

"Thank you," Sotha said. "With all my heart, I thank you."

Anna and Asamir slipped out of their room just after the lanterns were put out. They had arranged their beds to look as if they were asleep, and they knew their roommates would not tell on them. Anna climbed into a tree and sat so that she could easily swing down; Asamir sat on a stump.

Sotha joined them a few minutes later.

"Did you have any trouble getting away?"

"No, though my roommates called me names as I went through the window. What do we do now?"

"We wait," Anna said.

The bell tower chimed the hour. As the peals died out, they heard footsteps come toward them from the boys' barracks. Sotha walked to the edge of the wooded area, making himself visible. Asamir stood up and Anna swung down in time to hear the bully in chief—it was, indeed, Valen—say, "There you are. We heard that you like to hide near the girls' barracks."

"I am not hiding," Sotha said. "I came out so that our discussion would not be constrained by the small size of my sleeping room." He held his wooden sword loosely in one hand.

"You alone against the six of us. I expect this discussion will end quickly."

"He is—" Anna said, coming up to stand on Sotha's right.

"—Not alone," Asamir said. Both held their wooden swords at the ready, Anna's in her right hand and Asamir's in her left, for she could fight with either hand.

"What are you girls doing here? This is a matter between Sotha and ourselves."

"But there are six of you and only one of him. We are here to even the odds somewhat."

"You are still outnumbered."

"We know." Asamir gave him a nasty grin.

"Numbers are less important than skill," Anna said. "I have trained with every one of you at some point, and I have won the matches. The same is true of Asamir. And while Sotha may be younger and smaller than any of you, his knowledge of strategy is far superior."

Sotha said, "If you attack us, the swords will make a certain amount of noise. And if you attack, all of us are prepared to make even more noise by yelling and screaming. We are only twenty feet from the nearest windows, and the dorm mother sleeps quite close by."

"You would not dare," the wiry boy said. "You would get in as much trouble as we would."

"We do not mind a certain amount of trouble," Asamir said.

"And perhaps the dorm mother will listen to us when we explain that we are out here screaming to protect a fellow student from a gang of bullies," Anna said.

The boys mumbled among themselves. Anna could not hear what they said, but in the moonlight she could tell from their gestures that at least two of them were arguing for an attack, while another was already edging back toward the boys' barracks. From behind her, she heard the sound of a window being raised, followed by the voices of several girls.

Valen froze, glanced in the direction of the window, and made his decision. "This is not over," he said to Sotha as he and the others ran back for their barracks.

"Thank you," said Sotha. "I better go back now myself. I hope those girls have not alerted the dorm mother."

"They have not," said Asamir.

"Oh. Of course, they are friends of yours."

Asamir smiled.

Anna said, "Those boys will continue to pick on you unless you challenge Valen and beat him."

"I will try," Sotha said. "I do not want to spend all my time avoiding bullies. But I am not a very good fighter yet."

"Neither is he," said Asamir.

"We will teach you what you need to know," said Anna.

A week later, during the late afternoon break, Anna sat on the low stone wall. Asamir, who for once had not gone off to clean up immediately after class, sat beside her. They watched as Sotha, padded sword in hand, walked over to Valen.

"I challenge you," he said formally. "Name a time and place."

The older boy laughed. "Here and now." He walked over and picked up his own padded weapon.

They bowed to each other and began.

They struck and parried, stabbed and blocked, going through the formal moves that both had learned. And then the older boy broke through one of Sotha's blocks and ended with his sword tip about six inches from the boy's throat.

Sotha lowered his sword, as if he were about to concede the fight, and then, using the smooth movement Anna and Asamir had been teaching him in private, slapped the other boy's weapon aside with the palm of his hand, and hit him over the head with his own.

"Ow," said Valen.

"Thank you for an enlightening match," Sotha said, and bowed without taking his eyes off the other boy.

Sotha was beaming as he walked over to Anna and Asamir, who both clapped him on the back and exclaimed over how well he had learned his lessons.

After that, the three of them went everywhere together—except at bedtime, when Anna and Sotha went virtuously and separately to bed and Asamir dallied with one of her many boyfriends.

"Let us hope that Sotha remembers our friendship from school and not the ongoing battles in the last war," Asamir said, as Anna sat over her list of supplies needed for their expedition. "I would prefer to spend the rest of my life without being arrested or worse in Foraoise."

"So would I," Anna said. She made another note on her list.

Chapter 8

AND SO IT was that, in less than a week, Anna was en route to Foraoise with Asamir, Cecile, and Nicole, a younger member of the Guard who was as thrilled as Cecile by the opportunity for adventure. Asamir, to her delight, was attired as a wealthy abbess, and they rode in a carriage suitable for one of such rank. Nicole served as driver, and Anna as bodyguard, with Cecile in her usual role as page. Cecile was somewhat less content in her position, since she was dressed as a novice and required to respond to Asamir's whims when there were others around. But the robes of the religious are copious, allowing both Asamir and Cecile to have weapons at hand; further, to address both the warm summer days and make it easy to reach for a knife or sword, the robes were much lighter than those commonly worn by those in holy orders. Nicole, dressed in keeping with a coach driver for a noble, kept a sword hidden under the driver's seat. Only Anna was able to travel openly armed and very much as herself. Her story, should she need it for purposes of getting to Sotha, was that she had been expelled from the Queen's Guard and had taken up employment with the abbess. Sotha would likely recognize Asamir as well and see through the story, but she could hold to her disguise until they were able to meet with him.

Their realm's ambassador to Foraoise had been expelled in a tit-for-tat response. The foreign minister had arranged for Anna to meet with him before their expedition left. But he had little to tell her.

"The Queen of Foraoise did not even meet with me, but sent a messenger accompanied by a troop of soldiers to order me to leave as soon as she received the news of their ambassador's expulsion. Since I had no warning of this action and no instruction from Their Majesties, there was nothing I could do, not even file a protest, except leave. Until this occurred, our relationship with Foraoise had been improving, despite some raids on their mines at Airgead, which they blamed on the governor of our Andalucie province, an assumption that, alas, I knew to be true for all I tried to put it down to outlaws when asked for a response. I had felt certain that we were not at risk of war. But now..."

On their first three nights on the road, the four women traveled through a well-settled part of the Realm, allowing them to stay at comfortable inns each night. Asamir had played her role to the hilt, sending both Cecile and Nicole running to and fro. However, when she tried to do the same to Anna, she was met with a frosty response. "Your nonsense will not harm the young ones, but I will not be party to these games."

By the end of the fourth day, however, they were in a lightly inhabited forest region. There would be no more fancy inns until after they crossed the border into Foraoise, and on that night there was no possibility of any kind of lodging, even a farmstead. A clearing in the trees not far from the main road would be their refuge. They were well-prepared for this situation; they had brought along a large tent that would provide them with cover should it rain. Anna would have preferred to camp out of sight of the road, but with the carriage, such a choice was impossible. She was beginning to regret that she had chosen to put together such an elaborate disguise. None of them were actors or trained spies. It might have been a better plan if Anna and Asamir had simply slipped into Foraoise at a lightly guarded station on the border, or at some easy-to-ford section of river between border stations, and managed to find Sotha by stealth.

"Child, hand down my cases," Asamir said to Cecile in the voice of the haughty abbess.

Cecile glared, and Nicole looked at Anna, who said, "There is no audience here. Handle your own cases. Cecile, Nicole, set up the tent. Asamir, you can gather some wood."

Asamir said, "We should stay in character, just for the practice."

"You do not need any more practice. We are in the middle of nowhere, and we will camp like soldiers on the road, not like nobles who are too important to do their own work."

Although Anna had been charged by the Queen with putting together this expedition, she did not outrank Asamir within the Queen's Guard and had no right to give her orders. Asamir threw back her robes, and put a hand on her sword.

"Do not be absurd," Anna said. "You are not going to fight me just because I reminded you that you are a guard, not the abbess of your dreams. We are all tired, and we will all do the work necessary to make ourselves as comfortable as we can be tonight." She turned her back to Asamir and began to unload their food supplies.

Asamir stood there a moment longer, then sighed audibly before she started beyond the small grove to find some good logs and kindling in the denser forest.

Before long, their tent was set up and a small cookfire was burning. Anna had water boiling for soup and was chopping vegetables and dried meat to flavor it. It was still summer, but it was cooler under the cover of the trees than it had been in the Capital, and the warmth of hot food and drink was welcome.

Asamir sat on a nearby rock, feeding twigs into the fire. She said nothing, but Anna could tell she no longer felt anger over their words earlier. Nicole poured wine into everyone's cups— good wine, since an advantage of traveling by carriage was the ability to carry comestibles—and Cecile cut slices from a cheese. Soon they were in merry conversation, with Anna and Asamir telling war stories and the younger women sighing with envy. Nicole was not much older than Cecile and had not yet been in battle. Likely she would be pleased if a war did break out with Foraoise.

But even if they prevented this one—and Anna was by no means sure they could—there would be another war. The world was not a peaceful place, and the various realms jostled with each other for power. Silly, really, she thought, though the tales had reminded her that she, too, loved a campaign. So had her mother, but after some ten years in the Andrean Guard before reunification, she had returned home, married a man from another family of farmers, and settled down to raise children and pigs. Perhaps she would make her mother's choice, soon enough.

As it grew time for bed, Anna said, "Put out the fire."

Cecile objected. "We should just leave it low, so that we can rekindle it easily for breakfast."

"No," said Asamir. "It shows where we are. We may not have seen anything untoward in these woods, but it is possible that we are not the only ones here. No fire tonight, and we shall take turns on watch. Cecile, you will take first watch. I will take second, Anna third, and Nicole will do the early morning."

That was a schedule that put the two experienced women at the times when it was most difficult to stay awake. Cecile picked up her sword and chose a rock to sit on as Anna and Nicole smothered the fire.

"I suspect she is thrilled to be on guard," Anna whispered to Asamir.

"I will make noise when I relieve her, in case she falls asleep. It would not do to hurt her pride this early."

The night passed without intruders, and Anna, though worried about any delays in their travel, consented to wait in the morning until they could rebuild a fire for a satisfying breakfast.

The road through the forest was quite well kept for an area so devoid of people. The horses trotted happily along, and they made good time. They might make the market town of Ruisseau by nightfall, if nothing untoward happened.

But, of course, the untoward was a common feature of their lives. They were less than ten miles from Ruisseau when they were attacked. As they traveled through an area where the trees formed a canopy over the road, two people dropped down. One landed astride one of the horses pulling the carriage, facing toward Nicole and Anna on the box. From the expression on his face, he had hit the horse's backbone with a sensitive part of his anatomy, but he managed to wave a sword at them even though he was too far away to do anything with it. "Halt," he squeaked.

The other thudded onto the roof of the carriage. Anna took up a staff with greater reach than a blade and knocked the man on the horse to the ground, where he barely managed to avoid cutting himself with his sword. As the one on the roof staggered to his feet, Nicole encouraged the horses to pick up their pace while Anna struck backwards with the end of the staff toward his midsection, collapsing him to his knees. As the carriage gained speed, he was swept off the roof by an overhanging branch.

It would have made a funny story, but for the two people on horseback who blocked their path, and the two archers on the ground, who were pointing arrows at Anna and Nicole. Nicole pulled up on the reins. Anna laid down her staff and kept her hands easy.

"Well met, mesdames," said one of the riders. Both wore swords, though neither had unsheathed them. She opened her mouth to say more, but was distracted when both archers were hit by knives that flew out from the carriage. The one on the left side was hit on the hand that held his bow, so that he dropped it, sending his arrow wobbling into the ground. The other was struck in the shoulder; her arrow shot into the air. Nicole whipped the horses forward, the two on horseback veered to the side to keep from being run down, and Anna again wielded the staff, knocking the one who had spoken to the ground.

"Stop the carriage," Anna said. She pulled out Nicole's sword and handed it to the other woman, then jumped to the ground, drew her own sword and pointed it at the throat of the rider she had dehorsed. Cecile and Asamir descended from the carriage, robes thrown aside and swords in their hands. "I got her," Cecile yelled. She was almost dancing with glee. The remaining rider decided retreat was in order and spurred his horse down the road.

The archers both lay in the road, moaning. The two bandits who had first jumped them were slowly getting to their feet fifty yards to the rear. They stared toward the scene at the carriage and began to limp into the forest. Nicole jumped to the ground, ran around to catch the horse of the leader, mounted quickly, and rode toward the two on foot. Within a minute she had them rounded up.

Asamir walked over to the archer she had hit with her knife and pulled it carelessly out of his hand. The archer howled.

"Get your knife," Anna told Cecile. She wondered where the girl had learned to throw a knife with such accuracy, given that knife fighting had not been part of her training so far. Perhaps knife throwing had been one of her childhood hobbies, along with sneaking out at night.

Cecile copied Asamir's moves in retrieving her knife. "What are we going to do with them?" she asked, standing over the archer with her sword at the bandit's throat in imitation of Anna.

"We could let the young ones practice their sword cuts on them," Asamir said. "It is said that the best way to learn the art of the sword is to use it to cut human flesh."

Cecile smiled at her archer and raised her sword.

"Mercy," croaked the leader around the sword Anna held at her throat. "You have come to no harm. Let us go, and we will trouble you no more."

"But you will trouble the next person who travels this road," Anna said.

"We are grievously injured," the leader said. "We can do no harm to anyone."

"You will heal," Anna said. "More's the pity."

Nicole joined them with the other two. "We should take them into Ruisseau. Likely they are wanted by the authorities there."

"No, no, please no," said one of the two she herded. "We will be hanged."

"And well you should be," said Anna.

"It would be a lot of trouble to take them to Ruisseau," Asamir said. "Why not do justice here?"

"Oh, please mesdames," one of them cried, while Asamir's prisoner said, "We should never have chosen you leader, Clotilde. First those two men get away from us and now we find we cannot even succeed against women of the cloth."

"I doubt it is your leader," Asamir said. "It appears that you are all incompetent at your trade. If we do not kill you, someone else will soon enough."

Anna said, sharply, "What two men?" She pressed the point of her sword in the leader's throat.

"Gentlemen, they looked like. Riding good horses, laughing and joking. Easy prey, they looked like, and just the two."

"Except they threw Albion into the trees and cut Aram so deep that he may not recover. And then rode on as if they had not exerted themselves at all. Clotilde said we should not go after them, that better pickings would come along."

"How long ago was this?" Anna said.

"Two days."

"Describe these men."

Their descriptions overlapped and were confused. Dark. No, one was fair. Dark, I say. A bay horse and a sorrel. No, it was black.

"The swords were by Ormont," said one of the two Nicole held, a person who had not spoken before.

"How do you know of such swords?" Anna asked.

"My father was a swordsmith. He taught me the trade."

"You should have kept at it. Even if you were a poor sword-smith, 'tis a better occupation than outlaw."

"I would have, but for the fact that my father was murdered and our smithy taken from us by Greybonne after he became our governor."

"None of us chose this life out of desire to rob," said the woman under Anna's sword. "The people here have been badly wronged by Greybonne, and we have few choices in making our way in the world."

"Outlaws are a pox on society," said Asamir.

Anna shook her head. "Some are, but if this one speaks truly, and I believe she does, we may share a common enemy. I have heard of this Greybonne."

"Who is he then?" asked Asamir.

"Not now. Fine swords, you say." She indicated Nicole's prisoner. "You have the best eye. What else did you notice?"

This time the description was precise. Anna exchanged a look with Asamir. Roland and Jean-Paul, no doubt in their minds, though neither said so.

Anna took her sword from Clotilde's throat. "Let them go." She watched Clotilde climb to her feet, saw the injured manage to get onto theirs. One of the others collected their horse.

"Go quickly, before we change our minds," Anna said.

The outlaws, too damaged to go very fast, moved slowly but with great purpose back down the road.

"And find another profession," Asamir shouted. "You are not cut out to be outlaws."

Once they were out of hearing range, Asamir said, "We are not the only persons being sent to Foraoise to find out what is going on. I suppose the King's captain has concerns as well."

"King's men?" asked Nicole. "Are you certain?"

"Very certain," said Anna, picturing the two men in her mind. "They must have left before us, since we have not seen them on the road. Likely they know nothing of us."

"And they are traveling by horse and will arrive in Foraoise ahead of us," Asamir said. "Perhaps they are already there."

"True, but do they know anyone in Foraoise?"

"Not to my knowledge, but I do not know all of their personal histories. I do not think they are aware that we know someone in Foraoise."

"Well, our missions are likely to be the same. We must hope that their presence does not complicate ours, but I see nothing we can do but continue."

"Why did you say we might have a common enemy with those outlaws?" Nicole asked.

"Governor Greybonne is known to be a partisan of the Hierofante," Anna said. "And our ambassador mentioned raids from this region into the Airgead mines. There are many in Andalucie who believe the mines should belong to our Realm. The governor may well be stirring up trouble with Foraoise."

The inn in the market town did not boast the luxuries of their earlier stops, but they were able to obtain a private, though small, sleeping chamber. For their evening meal, they had no choice but the common room. It was week's end, the night before the holy day, and in the way of hard-working people everywhere, the local people were celebrating or drowning their sorrows in the inn's execrable beer and worse wine. Asamir set up court in a corner, playing the grand abbess to a steady stream of locals who sought her blessing and her assistance in getting them a new priest for their church. The old priest had died six months back, but their requests for a replacement had gone unanswered.

Asamir promised them she would speak to the Hierofante as soon as she returned to the capital. Yes, she knew her personally, she told them. She patted hands, even blessed children, and listened to whispered confessions. In between, she sent Cecile and Nicole on various errands to refill her glass or fetch a scarf or book.

Anna, freed from such attendance by her role as a bodyguard, stood at the bar, drinking as little as possible of her wine and picking up bits of gossip about the two fine gentlemen who had passed through two days back. They were traveling to Foraoise, the innkeeper said, refilling Anna's glass though she had not asked for more wine.

"Aye, to Foraoise," agreed the old woman leaning on the end of the bar. The innkeeper's mother, Anna thought. Or maybe grandmother. "The young one, he said they were looking forward to seeing a different place. The older one seemed a bit put out that he was so open about their travels. And you, Madame, are you also traveling to Foraoise?"

"My lady abbess is traveling there, and it is my duty to guard her. We are given to understand that those of the church are welcome there, even though most of their people follow a different faith. My lady hopes to help those of the church in Foraoise." Better to give out their cover story than seem too quiet, though she sympathized with Roland's frustration with Jean-Paul's loose tongue. The two men were much of an age, but she could understand why the old woman thought Jean-Paul young. Odds were, he would still be a fool at eighty, should he live so long.

"If they are not so welcoming, please ask my lady if she would consider settling here. We have much need of ministry in this place."

Anna managed not to laugh at the idea that Asamir, even were she a real abbess, would set up shop in this town forsaken by all, including, in all likelihood, God. She gravely promised to convey the message.

"Of course, we need more than priests and nuns here. Times have been hard, with many put out of work, since Greybonne became governor over these lands."

That name again. "Oh?" said Anna, treading carefully. "Are there difficulties then?"

Perhaps the old woman realized she should be more discreet, because her voice got quieter. "Several long-time guild people have been turned out, and their shops turned over to strangers."

That fit all too well with what they had heard from the out-laws. Anna shook her head in response.

"That older gent, of the ones through here before, he seemed upset when he heard who had become our governor."

What did Roland know of the man, Anna wondered. The old woman motioned her closer, and Anna leaned in.

"Do you think my lady abbess might have a word with some-one in the Capital about our plight? Churches are all very well and good, but we need other relief."

"I will convey your message," Anna said, resolving to speak of this to the Queen.

When the four of them had retired to their quarters, Anna told Asamir about the old woman's request for her to establish a convent here. She was surprised that her friend did not laugh.

"I would not want to come here myself, but I must think of some way to help these people get the priest and other churchly services they need," she said.

"Surely it is a sin for you to allow these people to think you are a woman of the cloth and that you know the Hierofante," Anna said.

"'Twould be a worse sin to ignore those in need," Asamir said, a tone of piety in her voice.

Her concern for the locals sounded almost genuine. Perhaps Asamir's religious feeling was more sincere than Anna had ever believed.

"And I have met the Hierofante," Asamir added. "She bless-ed me."

"She did not know who you were, or she would likely not have done so," Anna said. "But the old woman had more to say than that." She explained about the governor, though she did not mention Roland's reaction.

"By God, we will do something for these people," Asamir said.

"I think we might do more if we consult Her Majesty than if we rely on the current emissaries of God," Anna said.

Chapter 9

GIVEN THE RECENT departure of the Foraoise ambassador, the travelers were not surprised to find an increase in the number of guards on the border. Fortunately, a combination of Asamir's haughty manner—really, she was far too good at playing the abbess—and liberal spending of the Queen's gold allowed them to enter Foraoise with a minimum of trouble. Whatever the difficulties between their two nations, things had not deteriorated so much that those with funds would be turned away.

"Perhaps things are not as bad as they seemed when we left," Nicole said to Anna as they continued on their way.

"At least we are not yet at war. But had the diplomatic breaches been patched, I think we would have been admitted without paying quite so much in gold."

When they stopped to rest several miles in from the border, Asamir said, "It would be lovely to always have such liberal funds at our disposal. So many things in life are easier with wealth."

"Fine sentiments for a lady of the church," Anna said.

"The church is not impoverished."

"Indeed, some appear to have built great wealth for their families while serving God. But is that good, given those in need whom it ignores?"

"Wrongdoing by some does not make accumulation of gold a bad thing in itself," Asamir said. "Should I have more gold, I would do good with it."

"I am sure you would offer it liberally to the vintners and clothesmakers."

"I give alms to the poor. Or would, if I were not usually among the poor."

Anna shook her head. "I wonder if Roland and Jean-Paul crossed at the border in an official manner."

"I would guess that they did not. We would not have, if our disguise did not require us to travel by the road. On horseback one can cross in many places, especially this time of year when the rivers are not so full."

"My thought as well. We should do our best to avoid them, then."

"Do you not think we should join forces with them, should we find them?"

Anna shook her head. "I am worried that the King's interests in this matter may not align well with the Queen's, or why else would they each have sent people to explore the situation when they could have sent a combined expedition? It pains me to think we might be at odds, but the possibility is there. Besides, you know well that Jean-Paul lacks all discretion. Should he see you in those robes, he will blurt out something unfortunate."

Asamir grinned. "That is certainly true. But the capital of Foraoise is not as large a city as our own. We may cross paths with them."

"We can but hope that we do so in a place where such meeting does not draw additional attention to us."

The capital city of Foraoise differed markedly from its counterpart in the Realm. The buildings were plainer; they lacked the ornate stonework and statuary common in their own Capital and rarely rose more than two stories. Even their houses of worship were simple affairs in contrast to the towering cathedral where the Hierofante resided and held services.

However, it smelled much the same as their city, an aroma that managed to combine the odors of baking bread and roast-

ing meat with that of stale wine and beer, all striving to cover
the omnipresent odor of human waste. The capital of Foraoise
was no cleaner than their own cherished city. After days spent
traveling through forest and countryside, where the fresh aroma
of flowers and even dirt provided a treat to the senses, the city
smells were a pungent reminder that humanity in large groups
had its unpleasant side.

They passed a small church of their own religion, confirm-
ing that, indeed, the Foraoisians allowed worshippers of other
faiths alongside that of the national church. Unlike the native
religious houses, it had statues of saints set before it, including
one of the Holy Fool. "Should we look for lodgings near that
church?" Nicole asked.

"God forbid," Anna said. "We should keep as far away from
them as possible, lest they figure out that we are not whom we
seem—and lest they be spies for the Hierofante. It may be necessary or even useful for "our lady abbess" to meet with them, but
we do not want them to be in a position to watch our daily com-
ings and goings. I am given to understand that the river district
will be the best place for us to find an inn."

The Inn of the Swans, a quiet place on a inlet from the tributary river that flowed from the capital city down to the border, was located at the edge of the government district. Anna put
her foot down when Asamir argued for a livelier inn. "My lady
abbess, in such a place you would be disturbed by parties at all
hours, even when you were deep in prayer and meditation," she
said, pointedly ignoring Asamir's desire to participate in such
parties. After they had settled in, Asamir sent Cecile to the ministry for religious affairs, seeking an audience, as well as to the local bishop of their religion, with the same purpose. Those actions
seemed an appropriate way to establish their reason for being in
Foraoise, though Anna felt it would be best if neither audience
were granted.

Anna thought of going to the neighborhood of the defense ministry to see if she might find Sotha on his way to or from his offices. Observing those in the government offices might also give her a feeling for how Foraoise was responding to the ambassador's return. She also considered visiting the barracks of the Foraoisian Guard—their soldiers all answered to one authority—since she had made friends of a sort with several guards who had been at the embassy in the Realm. But in the end, she decided that the first expedition was unlikely to result in any useful information and the second posed too many risks. Her friendly relationships with the guards might not be enough to keep them from arresting her, if relations were as sour as they had seemed, particularly given that she had entered Foraoise under false pretenses. Instead, she dressed herself as an ordinary woman of Foraoise—tunic and leggings, covered by a shawl even though it was warm—and went out to tour a noble neighborhood during the afternoon, returning just before the evening meal.

After a fine dinner of capon and fresh greens, the abbess and her women retired to their rooms, where Anna and Asamir quickly changed into nondescript clothing. The two younger women were quite put out at being left behind, but Anna assured them that their presence was necessary to keep up the illusion that the abbess remained in residence. Their rooms being at the back— "the abbess must be away from the noise of the road"—the two of them were able to jump down into the back garden and then to easily scale the outer wall into the alley, which smelled of rotting fish and worse, as alleys are wont to do.

"I hope this odor does not attach to us," Asamir whispered as they moved carefully toward the street, making certain they were not seen. "Or they will smell us coming."

Soon after the three of them had graduated from Saint Demetrius, Sotha's family had been allowed to return to Foraoise from exile. The relationship of the two realms at that time had been peaceful; that Sotha's family had been allowed by both sides of the divided Realm to live there during their exile had provided a measure of peace despite the usual tensions. Anna was invited to visit him once the family had reestablished itself. It had been an uncomfortable visit, since his father, knowing of Anna's loyalty to Sotha when the two were at school during his years of exile, thought she would make a good wife for his son. Anna's friendship with Sotha had never been romantic on either of their parts, though they liked each other well enough that a marriage of convenience would have been acceptable had she been willing to marry. But Anna had applied for membership in the Andrean Guard—this being a time a few years prior to the reunification of the Realm, a time in fact where the end of the Great Divide did not appear possible—and she had hopes of being accepted and becoming part of the elite forces who guarded the Queen, the Princess, and others in the royal family. Some guards did marry, but their spouses were not highly placed persons in a foreign realm and, in any case, anyone who married Sotha would have significant duties in Foraoise, given his family's position. Fortunately, Sotha's mother felt that Anna was not of sufficient rank for him to marry, particularly when she learned that Anna's mother had never risen past lieutenant of the guard and had retired to raise pigs. Sotha was embarrassed by this, but Anna was glad that things had been resolved in a way that kept her from officially declining the unwelcome honor. Sotha had married a woman more to his mother's liking soon thereafter, and there had been no more trips to Foraoise.

But because of that expedition, Anna knew the city well and, more to the point, knew where Sotha lived. On return from exile, his family had moved back into their compound, which was in the neighborhood Anna had visited in the afternoon. On her previous visit, Sotha had shown her the rooms that would be his when he married, as well as showing her his bachelor dwellings. At school they had disregarded the rules about male and female socializing even though they were not lovers doing so for romantic reasons, and their casual attitude about these matters extended into adulthood.

The compound was a one-story building that extended from one street to the next. A solid fence of well-laid stone shielded it from the street, and it was, of course, well guarded, given that Sotha served as minister of defense and his father as an advisor to their Queen. But Anna and Asamir had developed the skill of avoiding guards at an early age. In her afternoon excursion, Anna had found a way to enter, though it—like their egress from the inn—was odorous.

"Surely we could have found a way in that did not involve latrines," Asamir muttered. But they managed to move quickly from the outhouses to the pig sty, past the chickens, and onto the porch off the kitchen without being noticed. There, they heard voices. Some of the kitchen staff were still at work, cleaning up from the evening meal. The two guardswomen blended into the darkness as a young man came out through the porch to throw dishwater onto the herb garden. Fortune shone on them, for he seemed to be the kind of person who did not notice what he did not expect to see.

A few minutes passed, and the voices disappeared. A door slammed. They decided they could risk moving through the kitchen into the main part of the building. Sotha's rooms were at the front, about halfway around from the kitchen. Anna and Asamir crept through silent halls, hiding once behind a large pottery urn when they heard voices. Servants carrying laundry walked by them, noticing nothing.

"He lives well," Asamir breathed in Anna's ear after the servants had passed, and Anna nodded.

At Sotha's rooms, they stopped to listen. A murmur of voices came from within. Hiding behind a large plant near the door, they waited and listened. The door opened. "Are you certain you will need nothing more, my lord?" a man said.

"I will be quite comfortable, Ivan," said a familiar voice. "Go along to bed. I must read more of these dispatches before I retire, but there is no need for the rest of others to be disturbed."

The servant closed the door and headed toward the kitchen area with a tray. Anna, deciding that in all likelihood Sotha was alone, and also tired of stealth, walked over and opened the door. Asamir followed her.

"Is there...oh, god in heaven," Sotha said before Asamir was behind him with one hand on his mouth and the other on his arm. Her pale white hands made a sharp contrast with his dark brown skin. Anna stood between him and the bell on his side table.

"We are not here to harm you," Anna said. "Or to cause you or your realm any grief. Matters between our nations have gone awry for no reason that we can understand, and we seek your help in determining the cause. You know us to be women of our word. Will you hear us out without summoning help?"

Sotha nodded, and Asamir took her hands away. They were taking a risk. Sotha was not so foolish as to try to fight them, for he was aware that either of them alone could defeat him with her eyes closed and one hand tied behind her back. He was a great strategist, but barely adequate as a fighter, a fact well known to them, who had taught him most of what he knew of swordwork. However, if Foraoise were bent on war, he might well hear them out, let them leave, and then take steps to have them arrested or even executed as spies. But if the march toward war were the result of meddling, not state policy—as Anna suspected—Sotha might keep their visit secret, since both realms would benefit from frank talk.

"How in the name of the Seven Wonders did you enter the country? I admit our border guards are not our most brilliant citizens, but even they know better than to admit guards for the Queen of Grande Terre."

"As long as you have known us, and you doubt our ability to cross a mere border?" Asamir said. "We are women of many talents."

"Then you, who work for the rulers of your realm, should be smart enough to know that the awkwardness between our countries began on your side. Our ambassador was forced to leave and escorted to the border by armed troops. It is my understanding that such things rarely happen without a royal order."

He made it a statement, but Anna thought he also intended it as a question. She did not yet want to acknowledge that the Queen—and apparently the King—had known naught of the exiling of the ambassador until after the fact. Instead of responding directly, she asked, "Would there be someone powerful here in Foraoise who might desire chaotic relations between our countries? Someone who might be willing to risk charges of treason against your queen and conspire with someone in our Realm?"

He had not expected that response. He looked at both of them and took a deep breath. "There might be such a person. Might you be saying that someone—a powerful someone—in your realm has reached out to a counterpart in ours without royal approval?"

"Royalty can always reward success after the fact, just as it can disavow failure," Asamir said. "Our…person might be using yours to gain something Their Majesties could be persuaded to find useful."

"Or it could be that those who conspire have the interest of neither realm at heart," Anna added. "Perhaps they conspire for reasons of their own advancement."

"To the potential detriment of both realms," Sotha said. "Know you of someone within your realm who might be willing to take such a risk?"

It was phrased as a question, but Anna knew Sotha was well aware of the Hierofante. He had learned much of how their Realm functioned in his years of exile. "We might," she said.

"Such a conspiracy would require that these someones meet," Sotha said. "People who would betray their realms for their own reasons are not likely to trust intermediaries. And if they do not trust each other, that is even more true."

"Might they have been able to meet in some manner using other than normal means?" Anna asked.

Asamir made the religious gesture.

Sotha smiled. "Magic, you mean?"

Asamir repeated the movement. Anna thought Sotha had used the word "magic" just to get that response from her.

"More likely that they met in the normal way, but used some powers to cloud the minds of any who might have noticed," Sotha said.

Asamir repeated the gesture a third time.

Sotha shook his head. "After all these years, you remain superstitious about the world of magic." He caught her hand to prevent the move. "Your Church misunderstands it, and, as is not uncommon, fears and condemns that which it cannot understand. What you call magic is simply the practice of a powerful form of natural philosophy. Prohibiting it, as your realm has done, simply pushes it undercover, to back streets and forest huts."

"But even here, where it is permitted, it seems to inhabit such back streets as well," Anna said. "If our supposition about conspiracies between two persons of our realms is correct."

He sighed. "It can hold too much sway here, a different problem from that in your realm, but with a similar result. But would someone in your realm who desired to cause such disruption truly use magic, given how the church opposes it?"

"It seems unlikely," Anna said. "And yet, we have reason to believe that someone may have dabbled in such areas before."

Sotha rubbed his eyes. "There is someone—not the someone I might suspect, were I the suspicious sort—who might be of help in finding out if your suppositions are true. Give me two days to see what I can discover, then meet me at the market grounds. I think you should be prepared to leave shortly afterwards. I will be discreet, but the asking of questions often leads others to ask their own."

"Reasonable," said Anna. She had begun to think they might abandon their carriage and travel home on horseback as themselves.

They left the way they had come and made their way back to their inn. Nicole and Cecile awaited them, having laid out a late-night feast of wine and cheese and the olives that were the specialty of the countryside.

"The child is quite gifted at finding the best foodstuffs available," Nicole said. "A few words with the innkeeper, and suddenly we are gifted with a fine vintage and the best of this year's olives."

Cecile gave a modest smile, no doubt the result of her lady-in-waiting training. Anna and Asamir sat at the table and recounted their adventure.

"I think we should abandon our carriage and leave here on horseback, avoiding borders," Anna said. "'Twill be safer, should any pursue us."

"Do you think Sotha will betray us, then?" Asamir asked.

"I do not. He could, but I will be surprised if it happens. No, it is that I think our disguise will have worn thin ere we leave. And I do not want to spend time with the border guards from our Realm, some of whom we might know. We will leave the inn early in the day before we again meet Sotha and pretend we are leaving the country, then take the carriage to the woods beyond the city and abandon it. We can cross at some unguarded spot and ride the horses home."

"And how do we get back for the meeting with Sotha?"

"I will remain behind to meet him, and meet you afterwards, on the road."

"And what happens if Sotha has you arrested? Or if someone betrays him and captures you both?"

"Then it will only be one of us caught in their net."

"You will need someone to watch and see what happens," Cecile said. "Otherwise, your sacrifice will be of no use, should your meeting go wrong. I could come with you and hide nearby to see what may happen."

The child was right, Anna thought. While she hesitated to put Cecile in a place of such risk, it made more sense. She nodded. "Asamir, you and Nicole will take the carriage out, pretending that you the abbess and Cecile are within. We will remain behind, and Cecile will go to find you should I be arrested."

Both Asamir and Nicole wanted to play the hero's part, but in the end they agreed to the plan.

The young ones went off early the next morning to seek more easily portable foodstuffs for the journey home, and to explore the town. They were entitled to a bit of fun, Anna thought, though she did worry about their discretion. After they had left, a messenger arrived from the local bishop of the Church of the Realm—here called the Church of Grand Terre—inviting Asamir to meet with him.

"Damn him to the lowest rung of hell," Anna said. "I had hoped to avoid this."

But Asamir was delighted. "I shall play the grand lady, and we will see what the people here would like to receive from the Hierofante."

Anna drove the carriage and escorted Asamir to her meeting. In her capacity as guard, she waited outside the door while the two met privately. However, despite the presence of the bishop's attendant, she managed to make sure the door was slightly open, so that she might hear what transpired. For her part, Asamir told the bishop she had poor hearing. "Please speak more loudly," she said in what was almost a shout, "so that I may follow your words."

The state of the church in Foraoise was not good, they learned. They were obligated to follow the direction of the Hierofante, having no equivalent ruler of the church in their own realm, and the Hierofante had given them little. They would be very grateful if the abbess would endow a convent in their realm, and if she could perhaps speak to the Hierofante on their behalf. That woman had visited Foraoise not long ago, but though she had stayed in their best rooms and been attended by their people, she had not deigned to speak officially with any of the church leaders.

Sotha had said the conspirators had met in person, and this provided additional proof of that. Asamir kept her wits about her, apologized for the Hierofante's failure even as she attributed it to matters of state, and asked when this might have taken place. "For as you likely know, the relationship between our realms is now on shaky ground."

The Hierofante had visited two weeks before the ambassador returned home.

Anna lost herself in thought as they returned to the inn, and neglected to pay attention to those around her. Two horsemen passed her, and then turned abruptly in the street and raced back toward her.

"What in the name of all that may be holy are you doing in Foraoise?" said Roland de Barthes.

Chapter 10

IT WOULD NOT do to have a discussion in the street. Anna indicated a tavern nearby. "I will meet you there in an hour. My word on it."

Roland nodded. "Let us go," he said to Jean-Paul, who was trying to peer inside the carriage. The men rode off, though Jean-Paul kept twisting around to look at them.

Asamir was banging on the communicating panel at her back. "Are we discovered then?"

"I am, at least. I will see what truce I can negotiate."

"We can negotiate," Asamir said. "I will not miss this. Is Jean-Paul with him?"

"He is," Anna said. She wondered yet again whether bringing so many people along on this expedition had been a good choice. Perhaps she should have simply come alone. But it was good to know that the Hierofante had visited Foraoise and that her lack of attention to church matters here had offended people. They would not have discovered that without Asamir's disguise.

The two men had arrived ahead of them and secured a quiet table in the back of the tavern. It was mid-afternoon, too early for those who sought dinner or other end-of-the-day refreshment. Over passable wine—though not as fine as that Cecile had procured for them the day before—the four toasted each other and tried to find a way to broach the obvious questions.

Asamir had changed her garb, and they had once again used the inn's rear exit. They did not want to share her impersonation with Roland and Jean-Paul. Anna hoped neither would ask what she was doing driving a closed carriage.

"I think we can assume," said Roland, "that we are on similar missions. Relationships between the Realm and Foraoise have gone awry, but the cause of—and therefore the solution to—this failure of diplomacy is murky. Our captain thought we might be able to discern some of the problem if we traveled here. I gather your captain thought the same."

"Seeing that you are not wearing the uniform of the King's Guard, I assume that you are using indirect means," Anna said. She pointedly did not mention the Queen. Had the men been sent by their captain without the King's knowledge?

"And we assume the same of you," Roland replied.

"Is that why you were driving a carriage?" Jean-Paul asked.

"Of course it was," Roland said, in a tone that let Anna know that he had larger suspicions but was refraining from asking blunt questions.

"Have you had any success in your inquiries?" Anna asked.

Roland hesitated just long enough to let her know that he had. Almost too long, because Jean-Paul leapt in. "We have…"

"Heard some rumors," Roland finished.

From the look on Jean-Paul's face, Roland had stepped on his toe.

"We do not think the Foraoisian ambassador left the realm of her own accord, or on the orders of her ruler. Both the officials here and the ordinary people are angry, which does not bode well for the relationship of our countries," he said.

Anna did not want to mention Sotha. But sharing some information could be of use in loosening Roland's tongue and in creating a stronger alliance between them. "We have heard that"—she paused to make certain no one was nearby who might hear what she said—"Her Eminence recently visited Foraoise."

"How did you hear that?" Roland asked.

"You know that Asamir is very devout," Anna said, hoping that her friend would follow her lead. "She felt the need for spiritual reflection and happened to hear about the visit while in church. It appears," she went on before Roland could ask more about the church visit, "that the gentlewoman has been neglecting her duties among the church's followers in Foraoise. We gather that her visit here did not allow for time with the local members of her congregation and did not address the significant needs of the church here, though apparently she did have other meetings."

"Did she meet with someone not of her religious persuasion on this visit?" Roland asked.

"We do not know with whom she met nor what was said, though we have hopes of learning more. But our time here grows short. Best we do not overstay our welcome or our disguises."

Roland nodded. "We are planning to leave soon as well."

Asamir and Jean-Paul had reverted to form. Anna gave them an exasperated look. "Can you two not stay focused on the matters at hand for even a few minutes?"

"We have not seen each other in forever," Jean-Paul said.

"Allow us some fun," Asamir added.

"Go off and play," Roland said.

"And do not get yourselves arrested," Anna added. "Or even noticed."

Their departure left things more awkward than Anna had expected. Roland started to speak, and then seemed to think the better of it. She almost said something, but did not.

Finally Roland said, "I am certain that both of us know more than we are sharing. But perhaps that is wise. We should meet again when we return home; it may be of more use to compare our knowledge then, once we have finished our missions and reported to our captains."

"Yes. For we must be careful to make sure that we do not betray the interests of our royal patrons."

"Though we are all sworn to defend the Realm," Roland said. "We must think of that above all."

It pleased her, to hear him say it. She smiled, remembering their fight on the road some months back. "We have heard some other disturbing news. It may or may not have any bearing on the matter at hand, but it appears that the man appointed governor over the Andalucie region has forced out or even killed artisans and caused general disruption in the social order."

Roland stiffened. "I heard that as we traveled here. I have reason to know that he is a man whose only loyalty is to lining his pocket and increasing his power, and that he would sell out anyone, even his most eminent patron, to that end. Though so far he has no reason to turn on his patron."

Eminent patron likely referred to the Hierofante. "Have you had dealings with him before?"

"My father did. We once had a small estate in Alejara, on the southern border. Greybonne was appointed governor there before Andalucie. He confiscated our family's holdings and took over our barony. My father died soon after, of a broken heart."

Anna could feel the anger arising from him. "I am surprised that you are willing to serve the King, given that history."

"This happened before reunification, before the King ascended the throne. A failure of the King's father, not the King. Nor was Her Majesty involved; it was a Meloran decision entirely. I doubt either of Their Majesties understands what kind of man Greybonne is, or they would never have given him the governorship."

"Yet another situation where the influence of someone besides the true rulers is causing difficulties for our Realm," Anna said. "I think we should consider ways of having this man removed from his governorship."

Roland smiled for the first time since the name of Greybonne had been mentioned. It was not a friendly smile. "Indeed. A better lord for Andalucie could certainly be found. And if we cannot bring the power of their majesties to bear, there might be other ways."

Anna must have looked startled at his words, because he added, "For the good of the Realm."

"So long as our actions for the good of the Realm do not end with our heads on a block or our necks in a noose," she said.

Roland smiled again, more gently this time. They left the tavern together. Anna was thinking of ways to take her leave before she headed to the Swan when Roland said, "We seem to have attracted the interest of someone. We are being followed. I will turn at the next alley; you continue on. Let us see which of us they follow."

Roland was dressed in the attire of ordinary Foraoisians—tunics, leggings, and light cloak—but he wore his sword under his cloak. Anna had remained garbed as a bodyguard, allowing her to carry her sword openly.

She nodded in response to Roland's words and continued on when he turned, keeping her attention behind her. Two people followed Roland; otherwise, the street was quiet. She retraced her steps to the alley where Roland had turned. Overhanging trees and buildings whose upper stories extended over the road made the route dim, but the clang of swords told her all she needed to know. She drew her own sword as she ran toward the sounds.

Roland had a good position and was keeping his two attackers at bay, but there was no reason to allow him to have all the fun. Anna smacked the backside of the closest one with the side of her blade. He—no, it was she—turned to deal with this new threat, only to see Anna's blade arcing to slice her neck. She ducked under it, losing feathers from her cap as she did, and tried to recover with a lunging strike of her own. Anna blocked her sword with such force that she dropped it. As she dove to grab the hilt, Anna stepped on her arm at the elbow.

Meanwhile, Roland had made short work of the other, who now knelt on the ground, bleeding from his shoulder. "Why did you attack me? Speak," Roland demanded.

The man on the ground shook his head. "I do not know," he said, sounding like someone coming out of a daze.

"Nonsense," said Roland, brandishing his sword.

"Please," the man said. "I know it sounds absurd, but hear me. My companion and I were walking down the street, when we were suddenly overcome by the need to follow and attack you. I do not know why."

"He speaks the truth," the woman said. She had ceased to struggle against Anna's foot on her arm. "If it did not sound like the ravings of the mad, I would say that someone took over our minds."

"A likely story," said Roland. "In a place where magic is common, to blame magic for misdeeds must be the miscreant's first refuge."

But Anna felt that vague awareness of something other that she was beginning to associate with the world of the uncanny. Looking at the two attackers more closely in the dim light, she shook her head. "I think they speak the truth. You," she said to the woman. "Take your friend to a medico and get him seen to. And tell no one of what you saw and heard here." She moved away from the woman, who scrambled to her feet and went to help the other.

Roland stepped back and let her take him. He and Anna watched them walk out of the alley.

"But why?" Roland said.

"I think someone else might be watching. Someone who might want to know if we are friends and whether we are better than ordinary fighters."

"And now they know it. We would have done better to simply elude them. I was moved by anger."

"It only occurred to me after the fight, when I saw how confused they were." She did not want to tell him that she could sense that something was off, particularly since she was barely willing to admit that ability to herself. "You and I are not accustomed to living in a place where other than natural means may be deployed. I suggest that both our parties should leave Foraoise as quickly as possible."

"I will go collect Jean-Paul...." Roland stopped. "Do you suppose someone followed him and Asamir as well?"

"We'd best find them. Where do you suppose they might have gone? Another tavern?"

"I suspect some place where they could be alone."

"The place where you are staying?"

"Perhaps. Though our room is small and stuffy. More likely some place outside. Is there not a large park in this city?"

There was, and Anna knew it well from her long ago visit to Sotha's family, though she had not visited it on this expedition. But the city had not changed overly in those years, and she remembered where it was. "It is not so large as the Governor's Gardens, but it includes small glades and other private places." She led the way.

"You know this city well," Roland commented as they walked quickly toward the park, which was in the heart of the government district.

"I have made good use of my time here." She did not specify which time there.

Although the Royal Park was small by comparison with its counterpoint in the Realm's capital, it still covered quite a bit of ground, much of it wooded. Given that it was a fine day, much of the populace was out enjoying it as well. "A lot of territory to cover here," Roland said.

"There is a grove back through those trees," Anna said. Sotha had brought her to that place on a picnic to escape the unending parade of social affairs at his home. They had even practiced some sword fighting as a respite from polite conversation. "I do not know if our friends would have discovered it, but I suspect they are skilled in finding private places to meet."

As they approached the grove, they heard sounds of a scuffle. Both drew their swords when they heard the fighting. Entering the grove, they found Asamir and Jean-Paul fighting off four ruffians. Their friends had been caught unaware, for they were only partly clothed and their swords were not in their hands. One ruffian had a knife, but the others appeared to be unarmed. As Anna and Roland approached, the knife-bearer rushed Jean-Paul. Their friend easily sidestepped the attack, grabbed the man's wrist, and twisted the knife back toward him, forcing him to drop the blade.

Asamir had thrown one of the others down an incline, and the other two were circling her warily, looking for an opening. Despite having been interrupted at what was clearly a delicate moment, she was grinning widely and encouraging them to attack.

"What ho," shouted Roland.

The ruffians attacking Asamir swung around at his very official sounding voice, giving her the opening to kick one of them in the side, which sent him tumbling into the other.

"Halt," yelled Anna in an equally official voice.

All the ruffians picked themselves up and ran in different directions. The one who had lost his knife to Jean-Paul ran too close to Roland, who grabbed him by his injured wrist.

"You have spoiled our fun," said Asamir.

Anna often wondered which Asamir liked more: intimate relations or a good fight. Keeping in the voice—if not the appearance—of an official guard, Anna said, "We cannot allow these ruffians to prey on people enjoying the park, even if their victims might be able to protect themselves."

"Who sent you?" Roland said to the person he had caught, who turned out on closer inspection to be more of a boy than a man.

The boy was scared enough to tell something like the truth. "Some swell pointed them out to us, said they was carrying gold for all they looked ordinary. Don't know about the gold, but they wasn't ordinary."

No magic here, Anna thought. Just the time-honored method of finding a criminal looking for a likely victim and giving them one.

Roland hustled the ruffian on his way with a kick in the rear. Anna said, "Someone has noticed us and is trying to cause us trouble. We must back to our quarters immediately, for they may be trying something there as well."

"And we should leave now," Roland said, "before more trouble occurs. Will you two not join us?"

"No," said Anna. "We have more duty here and must continue as we have begun. But we will follow you in short order."

He nodded, saluted her, and grabbed Jean-Paul. "Now," he said firmly.

As they watched the two men hurry off, Asamir said, "Do you really think that was more than just the low-lifes of this city seeking some fun?"

"I do." As they returned to their inn, Anna told her of the attack on Roland. When she mentioned the apparent magic, Asamir made the religious gesture.

"It might be best if we left before morning," she said.

"I still must meet with Sotha, or our trip here is incomplete. And it would cause commentary if you were to leave suddenly after having told the inn you were leaving on the morrow."

"We could sneak out," Asamir said.

"No. Let us stay with our original plan. While those who are watching now know you and I are connected with our friends of the King's Guard, they may not be aware that we are also the abbess and her bodyguard. Let us return to the inn and make a major appearance in that guise in the common room."

Chapter 11

THE WOMEN LEFT the Swan early the next morning, ostentatious in their departure, with Asamir sending Cecile running for this and that at the last minute. Anna rode inside the carriage, leaving Nicole on the box alone. "No need for a bodyguard in the city," Asamir said loudly as the carriage was loaded, providing an excuse for Anna to travel out of sight. Due to the early hour, the streets were lightly traveled. When they reached a deserted area near the market grounds set as the meeting place with Sotha, Nicole slowed just enough to let Anna and Cecile jump out. Both moved to the shadows as Nicole urged the horses along. They saw no one else.

Anna and Cecile walked over to the grounds. Farmers who lived near the city brought their wares in each week, but this was not a market day, and the place was deserted. Cecile, freed at last from novice's robes and for once dressed in simple clothes rather than the formal attire required of her as a page, ran around the space, stopping occasionally to investigate an interesting stall or a small animal hiding in the grass. Anna looked about for a likely place for them to await Sotha, one that would allow Cecile to hear everything that was said but would provide her a safe hiding place, assuming no uncanny means were employed. She found one near the livestock pens: a rundown building that had once been a barn, complete with a hayloft, standing next to a tall chestnut tree whose full branches obscured the building. Anna could sit under the tree to wait, and Cecile could hide in the hayloft. "If I am betrayed," Anna said, "you must stay hidden in the loft until the people leave. Only then should you seek out Asamir and Nicole."

Cecile looked as if she wanted to argue the point. Anna said, "The purpose of having you here is to make certain that everything that happens is still reported to the captain and the Queen should anything happen to me." She did not remind the girl that she was not skilled enough for daring rescues, because that would have encouraged her to do something foolish. Emphasizing the importance of her job was the best way to gain her cooperation. She let Cecile explore some more to calm her down, then sent her into the loft as midday—the time appointed for their meeting—drew near.

Their location not only allowed Cecile to hide herself, but also gave Anna an unobstructed view of the market entrance. At just past the hour, Sotha rode in astride a bay horse. He entered through the gates and slowly picked his way among the empty structures. If anyone had accompanied him, they had waited outside, for no one else came into the marketplace.

Anna stood in plain sight. He was methodically scanning the stalls and other structures, looking for where she might be. Once he saw her, he dismounted and led his horse toward the chestnut tree. He stopped at a small patch of weeds, dropped the reins, and patted the horse's neck. It began to graze.

"I do not think I was followed," he said by way of greeting. "It is known that I often go for a ride at midday—it is a soothing practice—so I do not imagine anyone thought my actions unusual. But…"

"Discretion is always advisable," said Anna, reciting the oft-repeated admonition of one of their teachers at school.

Sotha smiled.

"Have you news?" Anna asked.

"Barun Meara, the man whose ascent to prominence during my childhood brought about our family's exile, has regained some of his former power. He has the ear of the justice minister, which gives him entrée to the Queen, although it is known by all that she does not trust him. And he has been seen dealing with those who sell their sorcery skills to the highest bidder, with little concern about what that person might be hiring them to do."

"Has he perchance met with our Hierofante?"

"No one has seen such a meeting. But he did, in fact, travel to the region of Andalucie in your realm about a fortnight before your authorities sent home our ambassador. I am given to understand that he was well-received by the governor of that region, and it is within the bounds of possibilities that he met with your Hierofante on that occasion."

"The governor is known to be of the Hierofante's party," Anna said.

"Ah," said Sotha. "That would explain a great deal. The ambassador has always opposed Meara's influence, even going back to the time when he had my father exiled, so having her ejected from your realm in such a provocative manner would have pleased him personally in addition to furthering any untoward ends of his own and others. I gather you think your Hierofante might have acted against the ambassador without the knowledge of the royals?"

"It appears to be the case, though the manner in which it was handled makes it impossible for anyone to make a direct accusation against her. Did our Hierofante also meet with this man on her recent visit to Foraoise?"

"I did not know of the Hierofante's visit."

"That meeting also occurred before the ambassador was sent home. Perhaps your Barun Meara's travel to Andalucie was for the purpose of bringing the Hierofante into Foraoise. The bishop of our church here in your capital was quite offended that the Hierofante did not address church affairs—outside of requesting a well-appointed room and meals—while she was here."

"If they are conspiring with each other, they must have met. It is possible that Meara brought her here to meet with others among his allies. However, one suspects that the mind of anyone who knew of that meeting will have been clouded. We are unlikely to have any true evidence."

"Well, this is more information than either of us had before, regardless of whether it provides the kind of proof necessary to hold anyone officially accountable. I hope it will be sufficient to encourage those in our Realm who want to avoid war to take action to repair this breach of diplomacy. And I hope there are those among your leadership who can make some use of this knowledge, assuming they will not believe that I am playing some deeper game to cause them to distrust their own."

"I was not planning to tell anyone that I heard of these matters from you," Sotha said. He smiled again. "I will have to come up with an explanation of how I was able to learn of the Hierofante's visit here. It is known that I visit all houses of worship, so perhaps I could have made a friend among your clergy."

"I assume you also find houses of worship soothing."

"Working for the defense ministry leads one to consider ways of finding comfort," he said. "I know what will happen should my strategies be followed."

"You are too gentle a soul for such work," Anna said.

"Indeed. I would prefer to retire to a life of philosophic studies, but the way of the world conspires against me. But in answer to your question, yes, your information is most valuable, and I believe I can mention it in the quarters where it will do some good." He started to walk toward his horse. "I do not think anyone of importance knows that you are here as yet—that is, they know of the abbess and her retinue, but not who you really are."

They had not told Sotha of their disguise, but the abbess must have provoked some comment among the Foraoisians, and he was certainly aware of Asamir's fondness for matters of religion. Anna smiled like a child caught out.

"But you should not remain much longer. The wheels of war have not yet been put in motion, but the seeds of distrust are being well tended. I hear much about a threat from your realm to retake the Airgead Mines."

That was a piece of information worthy of further study. The Hierofante had always criticized the failure of the last war to retake Airgead. "I will take your advice about leaving. But I hope our time here has been fruitful, and that we will soon see the restoration of diplomatic relations. As for the mines: we have fought enough wars over them. I would hate to see us undertake another."

"Wars are always bad. But the return of Meara to power would cause much greater harm than simple war. And here in Foraoise, at least, we have great qualms about the influence of your Hierofante."

"Those qualms are shared by many on our side of the border."

They touched hands formally. Sotha mounted his horse and started to leave, then stopped suddenly. "You should leave now, and quickly. Take special care to protect the child you have with you; there are those who would find her a valuable hostage. Do not go back for Asamir and the other one; I will see what I can do for them."

"Asamir should be out of the city by now." Anna was startled enough by his behavior to speak truthfully.

"Then I will check at the gates and make certain she has been allowed to leave." He took off the blue silk scarf he wore and tossed it to her. "Tie that under your tunic until you are outside of our realm." He cantered off without waiting for her reply.

Anna stared after him. Had what he just done been a demonstration of something uncanny? Sotha had never admitted to having sorcerous powers, but had never denied it either. And she, of course, had never asked the blunt question. He could have known of Cecile through the rumors, but why had he suddenly changed his advice from leave soon to leave now? And what use was the scarf? It felt warm in her hand and she again felt the vague sensation of something just beyond her ken.

Whatever might be going on, Anna trusted Sotha enough to do as he said. She whistled Cecile down, and the two of them hurried off to meet Asamir and Nicole in the forest just beyond the city walls. The streets outside the market bustled with afternoon traffic, making it impossible for them to run, but as they were wearing the tunics and leggings common to ordinary inhabitants of Foraoise, they attracted no attention. They exited the city gates with a group of other citizens headed for farms or nearby villages.

The meeting place in the forest was an hour's walk from the city gates, yet when they arrived Asamir and Nicole were not present. The scarf, tied around her waist under her tunic, continued to feel oddly warm—not the warmth of clothes on a summer day, but something that felt as if it were inherent in the object. Anna was glad she had brought her sword with her, clumsy as it had been to hide under a cloak while posing as someone who did not go armed. She attached it to its proper place on the sash that closed her tunic. If she were forced to defend Cecile, she was as prepared as she could be.

The sound of hoof beats made her shove Cecile into the foliage and draw the sword. But the riders were Asamir and Nicole, bringing with them the other two horses from the carriage along with the things they needed for travel.

"We were delayed at the city gate," Asamir said by way of greeting.

"Asamir played the haughty abbess to the hilt," Nicole added, "but we still feared they would not let us go. And then someone rode up on a bay horse and spoke to a guard, and after that they waved us on."

"Sotha," said Anna.

Asamir nodded. "It was indeed him. He did not look at me, but I am sure he was aware who I was. We hurried from there to leave the carriage in a place where it should soon be ransacked by those in need rather than mentioned to the authorities. I am glad we sorted the belongings last night, because we were able to transfer them quickly and rode as fast as we dared. I was worried that you might also have been detained, or that you would come back and search for us."

"Sotha aided us as well, I believe. Though his methods un-nerved me."

Asamir read her meaning and made the religious gesture. For once, Anna did not feel the urge to laugh at her. It was one thing to be complacent about the sorcerous realm so long as you did not experience it directly, but quite another to think that your longtime friend might not only be intimate with it, but have just saved you by use of it.

"We should keep moving," Anna said. "I will not feel safe until we are across the border."

"Yes. Though you will not like the horses. I said when we left that these horses were not meant to be ridden. And now that I have ridden one for some little distance, my opinion has been upheld. We will be unable to outrun even a mule on these nags."

"We will nonetheless move faster than we could have in the carriage. And if anyone is searching for us, we can hope they will be searching for it rather than riders. These horses will be sufficient."

The four of them rode off through the forest. Traveling by horse allowed them to avoid the main road, and they did not see any other persons on their route. By the end of the second day, they were back in their own Realm, having forded the river that divided the countries at a shallow point some distance from the of-ficial border entry. The nuts and berries of late summer abounded, giving them more than enough to eat, especially with the added delicacies that Nicole and Cecile had found in the city and packed in the saddlebags. Even the weather had cooperated. Anna won-dered if that was Sotha's doing as well. Regardless, she felt safer. And she had noticed that the scarf was now cool to the touch.

"The inn we stayed at before is not far beyond this place," Asamir observed as they stopped to set up camp that night.

"We stayed there as the abbess and her retinue. They will remember us too well and note our change of costume."

"There must be other inns."

"Not along our route. We will be home in a few days, and you will be able to indulge yourself to your heart's delight. For now, we travel like practical guardswomen who do not wish to be noticed."

Asamir muttered something that sounded like "Just because the Queen likes you does not put you in charge," but she said it quietly enough that Anna could pretend that she had not heard it. Managing people was difficult enough when one had official authority. Anna had noticed the pressures on their captain. It took even more skill when you lacked a title, particularly when the person you needed to manage was your old and volatile friend. She allowed Asamir to set the watches for the night, so that she asserted herself in an appropriate place. Asamir might complain about the lack of luxury, but she knew as well as Anna that they must move with care.

Chapter 12

ON THE FOLLOWING day, they were again traveling in the region where they had been attacked by the incompetent outlaws. While they were not concerned about those particular miscreants, it had occurred to them that the governor's abuses might have caused others to turn to robbery and worse to feed their families. The forest was thick enough here that they were riding close to the main road even though they were using the small trails made by the local people when they foraged. The region was sparsely populated, and this year's good weather had brought on lush vegetation; no one needed to travel far into the forest to gather wood, herbs, berries, or fungi, so the only people who traversed the deepest parts were those who did not care to be found, and such people did not create much in the way of trails. The four women rode quietly—their horses made the occasional sound, but the women did not. In the quiet, they heard a man cry out, followed by other voices and the clang of a weapon. They halted.

"Someone is in trouble," Nicole whispered.

"'Tis probably those fool outlaws again, trying to get themselves killed," Asamir said in an equally quiet voice. "We should leave them to their fate."

"We are in our own country and are sworn officers of the Realm," Anna said. "Our duty requires us to investigate." Before Asamir could protest that their mission gave them a more important duty, she added, "And to see if there is something we can or should do without endangering our mission." They dismounted. Anna and Asamir walked soundlessly toward the road,

118

leaving the horses with the two younger women. The voices became clearer as they drew closer to the road. Anna climbed up one nearby tree while Asamir moved toward another.

Anna slid forward carefully along a thick branch about ten feet above the road. Below she saw Roland and Jean-Paul, afoot, being held at bay by two men with matchlock pistols. A third man held their horses. Those who had trapped them were not the outlaws of their earlier adventure—all three wore identical tunics indicating they were members of a guard unit of some sort. The governor's men, most likely, unless some local lord also maintained a guard.

"I tell you, we are members of the King's Guard, traveling through this area on the orders of our captain. You have no reason to hold us," Roland said.

"We have not been told that guardsmen would be traveling through here," one of the others replied.

"Perhaps no one thought you important enough to be so told," Jean-Paul said.

Roland did not make a sound, but Anna could feel his internal sigh. As usual, Jean-Paul was making the situation worse.

"And perhaps you are lying," the man with the musket, who appeared to be in charge, said. "These woods teem with outlaws. Disposing of such is a boon to society."

"You must take us before a magistrate and give us an opportunity to prove our story," Roland said.

"Must we? I see no need to waste time and effort on such a course of action."

Anna heard rustling in the bushes just beyond her tree. One of the men with the pistols turned toward it. Knowing that Asamir would not have made noise without a purpose, Anna leapt down behind the other armed man, knife in hand, and had the blade at his throat before he could respond. The man who had moved at the noise wheeled back and fired toward Jean-Paul, who was closest to him.

But while Jean-Paul was often a fool with words, he was never at a loss when it came to action. He had moved when the man turned, diving for his knees. The bullet went into the empty air where Jean-Paul had been, and the tackle caused the man to fall hard to the ground, hitting his head on a rock. Asamir leaped over him, sword in hand, heading for the man holding the horses. He dropped the reins, drew his own blade, and rushed toward her with his sword extended. Just as he reached her, she stepped easily to the side, slicing his wrist from underneath. He dropped his sword and grabbed his bleeding wrist, howling in pain.

Roland, who had not moved, said, "I believe you are right. There is no reason to trouble any magistrates on anyone's behalf."

Anna whistled loudly—a signal for Nicole and Cecile. Asamir said, "What shall we do with them?"

"What they planned to do with us," Jean-Paul said. The man he had tackled was moaning and holding his head.

"You are in the province of Andalucie. We are the Governor's Guard. You harm us at your peril," said the one Anna held at knife point.

"You appear to us to be highwaymen," said Asamir. She flicked blood off her sword.

Nicole and Cecile joined them, bringing their horses. "Could you not have saved one of them for us to fight?" Cecile said.

Roland laughed. "You can make yourself useful by finding the horses belonging to these gentlemen, which I suspect are not far from the road." He turned to Asamir. "I do not believe they are highwaymen; they are too well-outfitted to be outlaws. But they appear to prey on travelers as if they were. Few would miss them, should they disappear in the forest."

"You will make powerful enemies should you harm us."

"You are assuming that someone will discover what happened to you," Anna said. "We are not so foolish as to leave evidence behind us."

The man Asamir had cut was beginning to tremble. "Please," he said. "Please."

"One of you has manners, at least," Anna said. She looked at Roland. "Monsieur, would you have some rope?"

"Aye, enough for hanging," he replied.

The third man cried out "please," his voice almost a wail.

"That should suffice for tying them up. And here are their horses," Anna added as Cecile and Nicole walked up with three well-formed geldings in tow. "Even should they manage to get loose—and I am known for my knots—it will take them some time to walk rather than ride."

Roland came forward with his rope and took the man's matchlock, sword, and knife as Anna bound his hands. Soon all three were disarmed and bound. They led the three men into the forest, and tied them each to a separate tree.

"Are you certain this was the right action?" Roland asked Anna as they walked back to the road. "They will likely find a way to get loose and might either come after us or report what they have seen to other authorities."

"We will be long gone ere they do so, and they know little of us. And they will not be armed, unless they pick up sticks in the forest. Given the circumstances, they are unlikely to make an honest report. And I would be reluctant to kill a man just to prevent his report."

"I, too, but I hope we do not endanger our mission unduly by leaving them alive."

Anna nodded. "It is a concern, but I am willing to chance it."

"I notice that you have other companions. You did not mention that when we were in Foraoise," Roland said.

"We all have our secrets. Nicole and Cecile have proved their value on this adventure."

The captured horses were much more to Asamir's liking. She, Anna, and Nicole each took one, to Cecile's annoyance. Their goods were distributed among their other mounts, leaving all the horses traveling lighter. They used more of their rope to link them together, something that seemed to please the coach horses, who were used to moving in tandem.

"You are better provisioned than we. Shall we travel together, then?" Roland asked.

"Not if you are keeping to the road. We prefer more discretion."

"We are willing to follow your route. Traveling by the road has proved less than wise."

"Then please to join us. It seems numbers are useful when dealing with the dangers that beset this forest."

But they met with neither guards nor outlaws on the remainder of their travels. Asamir and Jean-Paul bickered, as was their wont. Anna and Roland spoke of nothing in particular as they rode. Anna felt certain that Roland knew more than he had told her, and she knew she had not shared everything with him, but for now it seemed wiser to wait until they had talked with their captains—and she with the Queen—before saying more.

They did, however, speak more of the governor. "I think we must do something to make sure that man is removed from office," Anna said. "First the incompetent outlaws, who have only taken up thieving because they have been driven from lawful occupation. Then the reports about him from the citizenry that indicate he is taking what he pleases and ignoring his responsibilities. And finally the fact that the guards who are supposed to maintain order in his realm are attacking travelers, likely for their own benefit and perhaps for his as well."

"It is possible," said Roland, "that those men knew exactly who we were and set on us for that reason. In which case..."

"In which case our decision to leave them alive was perhaps a bad one. Why did you not mention this before?"

"Because it has only now occurred to me. I was thinking back on the initial attack, and I remember someone saying 'I thought there were three of them.' Mayhap the reports on our skirmish in the city led someone to believe you and I were of the same party."

"Even more reason to be rid of the governor, if he is aligned with the powers trying to force us to war with Foraoise." Anna thought of mentioning what she knew of the governor and Barun Meara, but decided it was not necessary to this discussion. "That may provide more of an argument than his abuse of the citizenry, which those of noble rank often consider unimportant, though I hope Their Majesties will consider it."

"I cannot directly oppose the man," Roland said. "My history with him is well known."

"I have no such history. May I speak of the attack on you and Jean-Paul to my superiors? It is possible that I can get this information to someone with much authority."

"You would go to Her Majesty with this?"

"You honor me, sir, to suggest that I am welcome in such august circles."

Roland smiled. "You are an honorable woman, and I am given to understand that your renown is spoken of at the very highest levels of the Realm."

Anna did not bother to protest further. "The only other who could do what is necessary is His Majesty, and I do not have his ear. And, as you say, it would be more difficult for you to request the man's removal."

"Even had I the King's ear, which I do not. Madame, my family and I would be greatly in your debt if you succeed in this matter. It may be true that we have but little left of our resources for paying such debts, but you would have the lifelong gratitude of the entire Famile de Barthes if you can bring about this man's downfall."

"I will do my best. That he may be part of the conspiracy to cause war makes it my duty, and the harm he has caused to so many makes it my pleasure."

When they were within a day's ride of the capital, they decided to risk travel by road.

As they reached the edge of the Capital, Anna said, "I will report to my captain and you to yours." She did not mention the

Queen. "Perhaps they will decide they should meet and share information, which will be my recommendation. But even if they do not speak to each other, we must encourage them to tell those in higher places what we have discovered. For now we best leave things at that."

"And what shall we do if those in higher places are not willing to listen?"

"Then we will reconsider," Anna said. "For we must consider the Realm above all."

Chapter 13

THEY ARRIVED IN the capital late in the evening. Anna dispatched Cecile back to the palace, requesting an audience with Her Majesty at the earliest opportunity, with very specific instructions on what to say. She herself went to the captain to report before retiring to her own abode.

"What you describe smells of treason," the captain said. "Treason to both our Realm and to that of Foraoise."

"Indeed. Though I do not believe that the Hier...the person from our Realm intends to betray us into the hands of a foreign country, but rather is playing a dangerous game to force us into the policies that she wants in place, policies that will also strengthen her power here. She is loyal to the Realm in her own way, but I do fear her way is not the path Their Majesties would choose, unless they were given no choice. I know little about the man in Foraoise, though from what I am told he is likely looking to develop his own power; it is possible that he would betray his queen to do so, but at the very least he wants to be the power behind her throne."

"I care little about that man, except that anyone from our Realm dealing with him is clearly risking far too much, whatever the motive. And the actions so far have opened the Realm to the possibility of war with Foraoise, something that is not in our interest no matter what resources could be so attained," the Captain said.

"And her motives might be much worse than I believe. Regardless, our discoveries require assumptions. We do not have enough evidence to condemn an important figure for these activities."

"Even if we did, it might be of little use. Seeking to bring a formal action for treason against someone powerful could well harm us more than them, even could we prove it. We need another kind of response."

"Yes, but what should it be?" Anna asked.

The captain shook her head. "I have no ideas. Perhaps you will learn more meeting with Her Majesty. For my part, I will endeavor to meet with my counterpart at the King's Guard. We have had our differences, the Great Mother knows, but I do believe him to be an honorable man with the Realm's interests at heart. Perhaps we can form an alliance."

"It is my fervent hope that we can," Anna said. "If we can prevent dissension between Their Majesties, we will have greater success."

The captain shook her head again. "Even with cooperation between their guards, it will be difficult. Our enemy is powerful, and your report leads me to fear that she is willing to engage in treachery to gain her own ends. And she has always had His Majesty's ear. She nurtured a relationship with him when he was but a babe in arms."

Anna had expected to find Cecile in her rooms when she returned, but instead found only enough dust to indicate that her landlady had been neglectful in her absence. The lack of cleaning had one blessing: no one had found the wine she had secreted under her bed. She poured herself a cup. Despite all her exertions of late, she was not tired enough to sleep. Her discoveries troubled her on a deep and abiding level. While she had known that the Hierofante constantly schemed to increase her power and influence over the policies of the realm, it was disturbing to discover that she would engage in both treason and the magical powers she had always condemned as heretical to do so. Anna had set aside her suspicions about the rain that had frustrated her travels from Beaufort's castle, but now she felt certain that the Hierofante, despite all religious preachments, was regularly engaging in such practices. Her concerns were not religious; she felt no worries about whether the Hierofante was endangering her immortal soul. But the use of such powers on the sly by someone who proclaimed a moral opposition to them in a place where they were prohibited both angered and frightened her. And to conspire with a discredited official in Foraoise, even to the point of encouraging war!

The sins of the governor of Andalucie and his guards might be easier to resolve. His meetings with Barun Meara would likely be enough to dismay Their Majesties, and the behavior of his guards would displease them, regardless of whether they cared about his treatment of artisans in his province. That, at least, she could bring to the attention of Her Majesty.

She found herself hoping that by bringing all of the matters to the attention of the Queen, she would be freed from any duty to determine a strategy for saving the Realm. She was glad to go and fight, even to go and gather information. But she was only a guardswoman, not even a captain, much less someone of true authority. Surely there must be someone more important and more knowledgeable than she who could solve all of the problems. Though if magic were involved—and she believed that it was—how could she hint at that to Her Majesty, when she dared not mention it even to the captain? If no one but she knew that the Hierofante was dealing in the uncanny, who but she could take action to counter it?

And it seemed that she not only knew someone of power in Foraoise, but that he, too, trafficked in what the country people called the old ways. She trusted Sotha, but it was a trust based on youthful fellowship. He did not seem to have changed in character, but he had a weighty job and a family and realm to whom he owed allegiance. Anna did not expect him to harm her without cause, but perhaps he might have cause. Further, his use of magic on her behalf had made her acknowledge that the uncanny scared her quite as much as it scared Asamir, for all that she pretended to others that a country-raised woman such as herself did not find such things troublesome.

"Perhaps the magic influence is petty. Perhaps the captain will meet with her counterpart of the King's Guard, and all will be well," she told herself as she poured another glass of wine. "And surely Her Majesty and her advisors will know what to do." It took a third cup of wine before she was able to believe herself enough to sleep.

From which rest she was awakened an hour later by Cecile climbing in through her window. "Her Majesty's respects, Guardswoman, and she would like to see you forthwith."

"Does the woman never do business during daylight hours?" Anna said, crawling out from under her covers. She noticed Cecile staring longingly at the bottle standing on her table. "Pour yourself a glass of wine while I attire myself."

The Queen was duly apologetic when they arrived. "We regret the necessity of calling you out so late, Guardswoman, but I wanted the minister to hear your report as well, and she was involved in some delicate negotiations until now."

"I am ever at your service, Your Majesty, no matter the time of day." She gave her report, leaving out any suggestion that the Hierofante might have trafficked in magic, but mentioning the prelate's meetings with Barun Meara, Sotha's enemy in Foraoise.

"These are treacherous waters," said the Queen. "But I find it hard to believe that the Hierofante's intent is to betray our realm. Is she perhaps persuading this Meara to betray Foraoise? Though to what end, I cannot imagine. Our relations with Foraoise were in good repair before she intervened. And I see no reason to expand our borders to include another realm. Any value we might gain would not be worth the cost in lives and destruction."

"Her Eminence has always believed that the Airgead Mines belonged to our Realm," the defense minister said. "Perhaps her goal is a war that brings those mines under our control. She might believe it would be worth the cost."

"But one of the terms by which we last settled things with Foraoise included an acknowledgment that they controlled the mines. While they would be of benefit to our Realm, starting a war over them that would likely extend into winter would be perilous, especially given that their country lies to our north and that our last encounter with Foraoise was so unsuccessful. Why would she think we would have success on this occasion?"

"Perhaps," said Anna, "she believes Meara will betray Foraoise. I am given to understand that he is the sort of man who might betray his country for his own purposes."

The Queen said, "Oh," as if the very idea were horrible.

The defense minister gave a grim smile.

"And I think he might well be a sorcerer," Anna added. She had decided that she could mention magic by someone in Foraoise, even though Meara had met with the Hierofante.

Both women made the religious gesture. "Would Her Eminence..." the defense minister began.

"It is possible that Her Eminence does not know this," Anna said, though she very much doubted that was true.

"I certainly hope she does not," said Her Majesty. "But regardless of her own knowledge, if he is a sorcerer, her dealings with him, even should she believe them to the benefit of the Realm, portend great danger and should certainly be halted. But we still lack enough information to address this in an open manner. She is far too powerful, and, of course, His Majesty respects her, as well he should. She is his aunt as well as head of the church. So what action can we take?"

"We can undercut her by opening negotiations to re-establish diplomatic relations with Foraoise," the minister said. "I would suggest that we attempt that, if you think His Majesty can be convinced to support such actions."

The Queen looked hesitant. Anna said, "I should inform you that members of the King's Guard were also investigating matters in Foraoise. It is possible that His Majesty has his own suspicions. And it is likely that he is even now receiving a similar report."

The Queen brightened. "We did hear something of your meeting with the King's men as you traveled home."

"It would perhaps not be politic to mention to His Majesty that we found it necessary to rescue them."

That brought a laugh. "We shall be most politic. But the fact that he, too, sent someone to investigate bodes well for the minister's proposal."

Her Majesty looked as if she were ready to make a formal dismissal, so Anna said, "Your Majesty, there is one more matter that I think may be of use to you. The governor of Andalucie province appears to be working with Her Eminence in this matter. The men who attacked His Majesty's guardsmen appeared to have knowledge of their mission in Foraoise. And they presented themselves as the Governor's soldiers."

"It is well known," said the minister, "that the governor is Her Eminence's creature. His removal would certainly make things more difficult for her. And that his guards dared to attack King's men will not please His Majesty. Do you have more such evidence?"

"I am told that Her Eminence met with Barun Meara in Andalucie not a fortnight before the ambassador left."

"Hmm," said the minister. "That seems to confirm the governor's connivance, but it does not give us a way to be rid of him without mentioning Her Eminence, something I am loathe to do. Anger at excesses by his guards will not suffice."

"If I might suggest, my lady," Anna said. "The governor is not well-liked within the province. It appears that he might be abusing his office for his own profit and that of his friends. Perhaps a royal audit of his reign?"

The minister smiled. It was the first time that Anna had ever seen her do so, and the effect was terrifying. "Guardswoman, should you tire of the life of the sword, you might have a second career in my office."

"With the greatest of respect, my lady, I find the life of the sword less perilous."

Cecile came for training two days later. She had run all the way from the palace to give herself more time to train. Pleased by this show of commitment, after the girl went through her basic exercises Anna rewarded the child by sparring with her using blunt-point blades that lacked a cutting edge. Determined to score on Anna, Cecile kept diving in with a stab or cut at the smallest hint of an opening, regardless of the risk to herself. Since the openings were ones Anna had manufactured for the purpose of drawing in her opponent, she blocked or sidestepped each attack with ease, occasionally ending with her point at the child's throat. Within five minutes Cecile was breathing hard and had failed in all her attempts to even touch Anna.

"The art of the sword is not all in the attack," Anna said. "You need more strategy. Let us sit and watch Asamir spar before we do more training."

Asamir was dueling with three opponents, all junior members of the guard. Each time one attacked, she managed to move so that the attacker missed her entirely and attacked one of her comrades instead. Periodically, Asamir hit one or the other of them on the head or touched another on the throat. Her evasions frustrated her opponents and caused them to attack more wildly. The wilder they got, the calmer Asamir became, and all three continued to be unsuccessful.

After a few minutes, Cecile said, "No, no," when one of the junior guardswomen attacked. "There's no opening."

Anna smiled. "It is easier to see when someone else is fighting."

"Yes. Rushing in does not work," Cecile said. As they spoke, Asamir used a spiral move of her sword to knock aside the blade of the one opponent who had not been attacking, then continued to press forward until the tip touched the other's heart. "But neither does holding back."

"No. It is always a balance between patience and action, between attacking and defending. There is no one simple strategy."

Cecile nodded, keeping her eyes focused on the match.

"So tell me, what news from Her Majesty?"

"I was privileged to attend Her Majesty when she met with His Majesty yester even. The minister was also there, and I am to inform you that the two of them agreed that they should make overtures to Foraoise in the hopes of reopening diplomatic relations."

"Ah. One hopes that will happen."

"The King was most unhappy about the attack on his guardsmen. I gather the report given to him was not completely accurate as to what transpired, for it appears he believes that his men escaped without undue assistance. Her Majesty did not disabuse him of this notion, though she did have a most unseemly attack of giggles once His Majesty had departed. However, that was after they had agreed to send a team of auditors—well-guarded auditors—to inspect the governor's accounts. His Majesty shared Her Majesty's concern that the man was lining his pockets and abusing his office."

"Most excellent," Anna said. "Come. Let us spar again, and you can show me what you have learned by observation."

And, indeed, Cecile was more cautious in her attacks and more deliberate in her defense this second time. Anna found she had to pay more attention to keep the girl from scoring on her.

"You are making good progress," she told the child as she sent her back to the palace.

The captain summoned Anna for a conference the next day. "It seems that the ministry is sending an assistant minister to Foraoise to investigate the possibility of re-establishing diplomatic relations. Since I fear your face might be too familiar from your last expedition, I thought to send Sylvie to accompany her," she said, naming an older guardswoman who commanded much respect within the troop.

"A good choice," Anna said.

"I must also send some guardswomen to accompany a team of royal auditors to examine the work of the Governor of Andalucie. Given your recent adventures with members of his guard, I cannot, of course, send you or Asamir, but I would like your suggestions on which of our women would be best suited for such a task. They will have to work closely with members of the King's Guard, so that is a further consideration."

Anna provided some names. "I am encouraged by this joint action," she told the captain.

"As am I. So long as Their Majesties work together, the Realm is in good hands. It is only when bad influences try to prevent such cooperation that we end up with difficult times. I have hope that the mission to Foraoise will be successful in repairing the breach between our countries."

Anna agreed. "We do not need to fight another war with that country."

"No," said the captain, herself a veteran of far too many campaigns. "The younger ones think they would like a war for proving their mettle, but you and I have been guards long enough to know that the best wars are the ones avoided."

Chapter 14

SEVERAL DAYS AFTER both delegations had left the Capital, Anna and Asamir repaired to the Maudite for refreshment after a long day of training. Although the captain hoped that the efforts to re-establish diplomatic relations with Foraoise would bear fruit, she was schooling her troops hard in case diplomacy proved unsuccessful. Indeed, all of those who led soldiers within the realm had increased their training regimens, and all of the soldiers' schools had added extra classes in tactics and strategy. To encourage hard work, a tournament that would pit forces from different guard companies against each other had been scheduled in the Capital. No captain wanted to see their charges fail in public, especially since Their Majesties were likely to attend. Anna and Asamir were too senior to compete in such affairs, but they were charged with supervising much of the training, making their days long.

They arrived somewhat late at the tavern, Asamir having found it necessary to spend time repairing her appearance after their hard work. She drew many eyes as they made their way through the crowded tavern, though not one of the men who gave her admiring looks was foolish enough to speak out of turn. Her skill with the sword was too well known, and everyone remembered her first bout with Jean-Paul.

They spied Roland and Jean-Paul sitting at a small table in the corner. The men beckoned them over. Roland gave a shout to another guardsman, who brought over his own stool and another for the two guardswomen. Anna caught the sleeve of the serving woman as she scurried past and bespoke a bottle of wine and some bread and meat for the table.

Asamir and Jean-Paul had barely greeted one another before they resumed their usual bickering. "It is as if they recall the very words they uttered upon last meeting and begin again at that point," said Roland, leaning over to speak into Anna's ear.

"Indeed. One would think they had engaged in no other conversations in between," Anna said. "It is our good fortune that this place is far too noisy for us to hear the actual words they are uttering."

"Though one can easily guess what they are."

"I shall pretend I cannot. I am given to understand that royal auditors are on their way to examine the books of the governor of Andalucie. Perhaps we will have good news on that front before too many weeks pass."

"Even if nothing should come of it, I remain grateful for your actions in that regard. And perhaps they will find sufficient irregularity to remove the man from his position. It also appears that delicate negotiations are afoot in the diplomatic vein with Foraoise."

"One hopes they also bear fruit. The drumbeats for war are pounding far too loud in both our Realm and theirs."

Roland gave a sober nod. They drank in silence.

Asamir and Jean-Paul rose to leave together, still carping at one another. "I wonder if they continue such conversations even as they engage in more—intimate—relations," Roland said, catching Anna's eye.

"'Tis likely. I shall do all I can to not find out if that is true," Anna answered.

He laughed. "Madame, since my companion has robbed you of your escort, might I see you home?"

She acquiesced with pleasure.

Due to the lateness of the hour, the streets were all but deserted and blessedly quiet after the noise of the tavern. They strolled toward Anna's rooms without speaking. When their hands accidentally brushed each other, Anna felt a frisson. But she did not take Roland's hand. Both wore the uniforms of their guard, and it would both be unseemly. Besides, it would block his sword hand.

At the mouth of an alley, they saw a man look out at them, and then slink back into the darkness. When they reached Anna's door, she found it natural to invite Roland in. She had recently replenished her wine supply and, as Cecile had not visited of late, was able to offer him a decent vintage. They sat across from each other at her small table.

"I feel I should have taken action against the governor before now." Roland drank some wine. "But my mother has always cautioned me that attacking the man might damage my prospects within the Guard and with His Majesty, and thus bring more harm to my family."

"Your mother might well be right."

"She is rarely wrong. The loss of our estates and my father left my family in poor circumstances, and Greybonne compounded the evil by taking our title upon himself. My mother is dependent upon my brother-in-law for her sustenance. I can contribute but little, given the meagre pay of the Guard. We are fortunate that my sister's husband is a good man, and of decent means and rank, but it still pains me that I cannot assure my mother a good life. If I rise through the Guard, it is possible that I will someday receive a livelihood that will enable me to care for her in a proper manner and restore our family's honor. However, hearing of the many evils done by that man, I begin to think that I should have acted before now. One must consider the greater good, not just one's personal prospects, when dealing with corruption and dishonesty."

"We can hope that the audit leads at the very least to his removal from office. Though given the other matters at hand, removing him may not be a priority with Their Majesties. Should they not find it reasonable to act, I stand ready to help you. That man is a danger to the Realm, whether they know it or not."

"I thank you for that, though I share your hope that he will be deposed by means other than my hand."

She nodded in agreement.

Roland placed his left hand on hers. "We have spent too little time together in recent months."

"We are too much at the mercy of the politics of our betters," Anna said. She did not remove her hand.

"So many duties," Roland said. "Mine to the King, yours to the Queen. And both of ours to the Realm, to our families, and to the good of the people of the Realm, who should not be forced to suffer under the ill deeds of the powerful. But we should not let all those responsibilities cause us to neglect the very important duty of spending time with our friends."

Neither of them moved quickly to the next step. When Anna finally rose to pour them another glass, Roland moved his chair to her side of the table. When that glass was finished, they repaired to her bed and engaged in deeper explorations.

An hour later, Roland, dozing in her arms, said, "I suppose it is much too late for me to take my leave. Should anyone have been watching, they will have counted the hours and leapt to conclusions."

"Then stay," she said. And he did.

As he departed at sun rise, he eschewed the large chestnut behind her window so beloved by Cecile and left by the front door, like the honest man he was.

Later, at the headquarters of the Queen's Guard, Anna was called away from her teaching duties to meet with the captain. "I have arranged to meet with my counterpart of the King's Guard at a country inn on the River Road. We have hopes that we will not be observed by too many talebearers at such a place."

"The landlady there is discreet," Anna said, "though I fear the spies of the city might venture that far."

"I share your concern. But he and I must meet. There is no place within the Capital where we would have any possibility of remaining undiscovered, and neither of us can spare the time to travel a farther distance. I would like your company on this venture."

"I am honored," Anna said.

They saddled their horses. The Guard had grooms who were quite competent to do so, but both women felt that it behooved a horsewoman to tighten her own cinch and to be aware of the mood of her horse as it was done. At a sign from the stable manager that no other was about, they left through the back gate and took less-traveled roads toward the inn.

Two hours later, they were ushered into a private chamber. Roland had accompanied his captain, which pleased Anna for reasons both personal and professional: she was glad to see him, and she suspected his presence meant that the King's captain shared their concern for the health of the Realm.

The two captains knew each other well, for they were frequently together on formal occasions. But they had never before ventured to hold a private meeting on matters of importance to the Realm. It soon became clear to Anna that neither of them knew how to approach the delicate topic of how they might work together, given the ever-present possibility of differing interests between Their Majesties and the fact that they had spent many years on opposite sides during the Great Divide. The four of them took their time ordering wine and food and spoke of inconsequential matters.

It was Roland who opened the path to a more robust conversation. "When my captain and I took our oaths as members of the King's Guard, we of course swore allegiance to His Majesty. In the same way, Madame Captain, you and Madame d'Gart swore your oath to Her Majesty. None of us are fools; we all know that those oaths might bring us into conflict with each other's forces, much as we might prefer to be always on the same side. The reunification of our Realm is recent history, and many of our colleagues still hold to the Andrean or Meloran positions. But all of us also swore oaths to defend the Realm. It is our duty to keep our Realm safe from dangers inside and out. That is, I believe, why we meet here today. Pardon me, captains, if I speak out of turn."

"No, no," his captain said. "That is indeed a fair statement of our situation. I am sure that all of us take our oaths to defend the Realm most seriously."

"Indeed," said the Queen's captain. "We must walk a careful line so that we each protect the interests of our principals, but it seems to me that their interests are, in general, aligned in the matter of avoiding unnecessary wars. That both your men and my women were sent to Foraoise to find the truth of the withdrawal of diplomatic relations indicates such agreement."

"The information gathered on those expeditions does indicate that some of those trying to influence our policy may have… misjudged the best interests of the Realm."

Anna could tell that neither captain wanted to name the Hierofante or speak directly of what she had done and might do. Roland having started the difficult discussion, she felt it her duty to take the risks inherent in continuing it.

"Madame. Monsieur. If I might speak plainly. Our expedition determined that Her Eminence has traveled to Foraoise, and that such travel took place not long before the expulsion of the Foraoisian ambassador. We are all aware that Her Eminence acted on her own in expelling the ambassador, only seeking approval of Their Majesties after the fact. While we must take care what we say of Her Eminence to Their Majesties or to anyone else, for she is the leader of the Church, and I am certain that she is acting in what she believes are the Realm's best interests" —or at least those of the Meloran side of the Great Divide, Anna thought, but did not say—"it falls to us, in our duties to the Realm, to ensure that her travel to another country and possible communications with others there do not produce an unwanted outcome."

Both captains nodded thoughtfully. The Queen's Captain spoke. "I think, perhaps, we should compare our information. Anna, please tell the gentlemen what you discovered in Foraoise."

"Messieurs. You may not be aware that I am personally acquainted with Sotha of the Foraoisian defense ministry. We were at school together, and while our duties to our own realms caused us to be in conflict during the recent war, our friendship has survived. From him, we discovered that a Foraoisian man who in the past caused major unrest in that realm may be involved in this affair. He was removed from power when the current Queen of Foraoise attained her majority, but he is once again acquiring influence at the highest levels and appears to be using...," she hesitated, "magic to do so."

The King's Captain raised a hand as if to make the religious gesture, but stopped short of actually doing so.

"Sotha has no proof that this man has met with Her Eminence, but in making inquiries among the church leaders in Foraoise, our expedition discovered that Her Eminence has, in fact, visited that realm. This man, Barun Meara, has a grudge against their former ambassador to our Realm. It is not unreasonable to conclude that he is stirring up trouble to consolidate his own power. However, the conversations we held with Sotha lead me to believe that those in Foraoise who oppose Meara may act to stop him even as we are trying to rebuild the relationship between our countries."

"If I might be so bold, Mesdames and Monsieur," said Roland, "the information we were able to obtain in Foraoise suggests that Her Eminence might similarly be causing problems with Foraoise for her own purposes." Both captains looked nervous. "I do not suggest that she is doing such things for the benefit of Meara or Foraoise itself. I am certain that she does not intend to give them an entrée to take power over our Realm, even if they might believe she is doing so. But I am willing to believe that she is creating problems so that she might provide a solution and thus increase her own power, perhaps at the expense of Their Majesties."

"She may also," Anna said, "think that a war would allow us to regain the Airgead mines. While a war over that would be difficult, if it succeeded it would be popular among both nobles and commoners from that part of the Realm. That, too, could increase her power."

Both had spoken with care, but their words were still dangerous, and all of them knew it. No one spoke for several minutes.

The King's Captain broke the silence. "She has long held that the Airgead mines should belong to our Realm. Though I am not certain how she plans to win a war against Foraoise to obtain them, particularly since the stirrings would lead to a winter war, putting us at greater disadvantage. I do not wish to disparage our soldiers, but our previous endeavors to defeat Foraoise have been unsuccessful, and I do not see that anything has changed. Unless, of course, she might be courting this Meara to betray them."

Or, Anna thought, unless she might be using magical means to force such betrayal or cause the Realm's forces to succeed. But she dared not say that aloud, even to those here who shared her concerns.

Anna's captain said, "We must continue to share our information, so that we can defend the interests of our principals. It is difficult for you and me to meet openly," she said to the King's Captain. "Perhaps Monsieur de Barthes and Madame d'Gart can meet more easily, disguising their meetings as mere flirtation."

Anna willed herself not to blush, though she was not certain she succeeded. Roland looked uncomfortable. The King's Captain might have been suppressing a laugh. The captains might or might not know where Roland spent the previous night, but they appeared to be well aware that the flirtation would be no disguise.

The King's Captain cleared his throat loudly. "An excellent suggestion, Madame. If the two of you have no objections...?"

Both Anna and Roland nodded their agreement, Anna not trusting herself to speak.

The landlady came into the room and whispered in the ear of the King's Captain. When she had withdrawn, he said, "It appears that some members of the Hierofante's Guard have stopped in the common room. It would not do for them to know of our presence here. Roland, if you and Madame d'Gart were to leave openly, perhaps they might make an erroneous assumption."

Anna gave up any effort to hide her blush. "If they follow us, or even just jest with us, it would give you captains the opportunity to slip out unobserved."

"It might be particularly effective if you act as if you are trying to slip away and let them discover you. You might use that color to your advantage, Anna," the Queen's Captain said.

Anna left first. She had no faith in her acting ability, but her face still felt warm enough to indicate that the reddish color remained and was likely visible to all, even on her brown skin. She went down the main stairs and tried to put on a mask of surprise when she saw three Hierofante's guards in the common room, including that same Lefevre who had led the troops that had tried to stop her return to the Capital with the Queen's necklace.

"Well met, Madame," said Lefevre. "What brings you to this out of the way place?"

"The food and drink is most good in this establishment," she said, but she thought of Roland, which brought back her blush.

"And perhaps you found good company with which to share those bounties."

Roland came down the stairs at that point. When he entered the common room, his eyes widened, as if he had not expected to see the guards.

"Ah. And now we have our answer. 'Tis a long way to come from town for luncheon, but perhaps you found other amusements." The other guards laughed at Lefevre's words and at Roland's obvious discomfort.

Anna's face remained red. Roland said, "Perhaps we hoped that by going some distance our private affairs would remain private." His voice had a tone of bluster.

"Given where you slept last night, monsieur, I would suggest that your private affairs are well known," Lefevre said.

Anna drew herself up. "And how would such matters be known to you?"

"The friendship between the two of you is no secret, for all that you appear to skulk around."

"Indeed," said Roland, letting anger show in his voice. "There is no shame in our friendship. We have not taken religious oaths. I would suggest that those who skulk about looking into the affairs of others have more reason to feel ashamed."

"Are you accusing me of spying, sir?" Lefevre said, putting a hand on his sword hilt.

"Someone is spying," Anna said. "Perhaps it is not you, but it is not unreasonable to assume, given your statements, that you have been the recipient of information." She hoped the captains were slipping out the back way as they spoke, since the possibility of a duel of honor in the courtyard appeared to be imminent.

"I do not skulk in the streets or spy upon others."

"Then what brings you out so far from town in the middle of the day?" Roland asked.

"We were doing a training ride and stopped to refresh ourselves before we returned. We are not spies." His hand remained on his hilt.

"Then how…," Roland began, but Anna interrupted. "Then we are found out by pure happenstance. Ah, well. 'Tis no use to try to keep matters of the heart quiet in this Realm. We would ask you, monsieur, you and your companions, if you would forebear to gossip about our dalliance."

Lefevre leered in a way that suggested he was already planning to spread this news both far and wide. "Of course, Madame," he said.

Roland looked as if he wanted to challenge the man further, but Anna said, "Come, sir. We both have duties back in the Capital."

Lefevre stayed in the inn, but one of the others followed them out. Neither Anna nor Roland had stabled their horses at the inn, instead secreting them in a nearby glade along with those of their captains. Anna sent up prayers to her patron saint that the captains had already made their departure. Those prayers were answered. Only her horse and Roland's still grazed there.

The member of the Hierofante's guard was amused that they had taken such precautions. "You should have availed yourself of the stables, for all the good it has done you."

Roland put his hand on the hilt of his sword. "I am grown weary of taunts, sir. I suggest you return to your fellows and leave us be."

A look passed over the man's face that suggested he would like to challenge Roland, but he did not. Either he had orders only to taunt, or he knew too much of Roland's skill. He returned to the inn.

Anna and Roland managed to hold their laughter until they were some distance from the inn. "I think we succeeded, sir," Anna said, when she had caught her breath. They had stopped under a tree.

"Indeed. Though I would have liked to run that nosy bastard Lefevre through when he pretended to take offense at accusations of spying. It is clear that they are paying far too much attention to our affairs."

"But if they are convinced that our affairs are merely personal, it will be useful," Anna said. "I do not enjoy the mocking, but I feel no shame."

"Nor I," Roland said. He reached for her hand and kissed it, and they started back to the capital.

Chapter 15

THERE WERE MANY advantages to Anna and Roland serving as intermediaries for their captains. It gave them an opportunity to meet on a regular basis, and while that opened them to ribald commentary from members of all three guards, those meetings were pleasant nonetheless. The amount of amusement at their expense indicated that their secondary purpose had not been discovered, which allowed them to privately mock those who mocked them publicly. The serious information they passed on to each other let both of them keep abreast of the ongoing matters of the Realm. Between what she and Roland shared and her regular reports from Cecile, Anna felt herself at the center of all important activity within the Realm—an unusual position for a simple soldier of the Queen's Guard.

From these sources, she gleaned that Her Eminence's star had dimmed with both Their Majesties, even the King, who, as her nephew, had duties to her beyond the religious. Ongoing careful negotiations seemed to be leading toward a resumption of diplomatic relations with Foraoise, and further reports (overheard by Cecile when the defense minister met with Their Majesties) suggested that Barun Meara was losing his influence with the Foraoisian Queen and her ministers as well. It seemed likely that Sotha and his family had undertaken their own political actions. Anna wondered if they had ventured into sorcery, but preferred not to know.

The relationship of the royal couple was once again blossoming, with a return to slow walks about the palace grounds—ones appropriate to a woman approaching her fifth month—and elaborate teas in the courtyard. There were no more reports of His Majesty making decisions without consulting first with Her Majesty and their wisest advisors.

Cecile also reported that Their Majesties were most displeased by the auditors' reports about the Governor of Andalucie. Indications were that he would soon be removed from his position. Anna began to believe that she might never have to mention the Hierofante's excursions into magic to anyone, nor take any action on her own, and she and Roland both began to hope that Greybonne would be driven out without any further action on their part. It was still a time of uncertainty, but Anna was enjoying the relative peace and quiet.

On a sunny afternoon, a man from out in the provinces arrived at the Guard barracks with a letter for Anna. Her father had fallen while repairing the house roof and broken his leg. While the letter, from her sister who had married into the farm family next door, included words intended to keep her from worry— "we expect him to recover soon"—it also suggested that she might want to visit now rather than later.

It had been far too long since she had seen her family, Anna realized. She often went for the winter solstice, but the previous year a blizzard had forced her to cancel her visit, and since then duty had called on a regular basis. She begged leave from her captain and went to her lodgings to pack. The man who had carried the message would not be returning for some time, so she would arrive ahead of any reply letter. Not for the first time she thought that the Realm could use a regular service for letters among its people.

She set out early the next morning, taking the road north and not making any effort to conceal her route. It was satisfying to travel with an ordinary and straightforward purpose for a change. The weather caused no trouble, though the sun was warm. She crossed the Adabarean in the afternoon and rode into the night, for the moon was almost full and she had paced her travel so that her horse was not over-exerted. It was usually a three-day trip to her family's home, but she hoped to shave off some time.

Traveling north of the Adabarean made her realize that she had passed within a short distance of her childhood home on the wild trip to retrieve the Queen's necklace, which further made her aware that the old witch in the forest did not live that far from her family. The woman had seemed familiar in some way; perhaps she had seen her at a market or fair when she was a child. She had not spared a thought for her family on that trip, and had not even questioned the witch, despite the woman's obvious recognition of her. That led her thoughts into uncomfortable regions, and she brought her attention back to finding a campsite.

She reached the family homestead on the morning of the third day. Her youngest sister Susanne—now almost grown and due to finish soon at Saint Demetrius, where Anna had also studied—met her at the gate. "I said you would come right away, just as I did," the young woman said as they hugged in greeting. "I told Jeanine her letter made things sound much worse than they are, but she still refuses to listen to me even though I have a real sword now." Susanne indicated it at her side, schooled enough not to brandish it, but not yet so accustomed to it that she would set it aside even when home with family. "Father is healing well, though he will not be climbing anything in the near future."

Anna's mother and her middle sister Berthe, now a midwife but also noted for general healing skills, met her at the door of the house. "I hope Jeanine's letter did not drag you away from important duties," her mother said. "Your father is not at death's door, though he will be laid up through harvest."

"His leg was broken in three places, but the breaks were clean enough to set them properly," her sister added. "He should get back full use of the leg by spring."

"Three places!" Anna was shocked.

"We are lucky he did not break his head as well," her mother said. "The pitch of the roof is so steep. I told him to let the young ones do it, but he was unwilling to wait until Robert or Jeanine had time to help. Summer is busy for everyone, and of course the roof needed repair ahead of any serious rain, but it could have waited. That man is just impatient." The complaint was an old one, delivered with her mother's usual mix of exasperation and fondness. "He's in the old bedroom," her mother said, referring to the tiny room in back where her grandmother and great aunt had lived when Anna was small.

The house had been expanded many times since Anna's childhood. At first it had been one large room, with sleeping lofts above. The old bedroom had been added when her grandmother had come to live with them, since she was by then too old to climb ladders for sleep. Other rooms had been added as well, and the loft space turned into a full second story. Most of the windows in the house were still mere holes in the wall, covered by shutters at night and in the winter, but Anna noticed that two windows on the south side now boasted leaded glass. Last year's harvest must have produced a nice return.

She walked in to find her father stretched out on the bed, his leg encased in a contraption of long shafts of wood tied in place with strips of leather. A young boy sat on a stool beside the bed, getting his instructions.

"Jeanine's eldest," Berthe whispered in her ear. "He is helping out over here. And do not let Father move that leg."

"Anna," her father said. "Just what an old bag of broken bones needed." He nodded to the boy. "Run along and take care of that right now while I talk to your aunt." As soon as the boy left, the old man sighed and said, "It is too much work for a child. But everyone is very busy this time of year. It is good to see you, daughter."

She leaned over to kiss his cheek. "Fortunately, things are slow in the Capital."

"I hear there is risk of war with Foraoise," her father said.

"I am one of those trying to prevent it. I have been traveling quite a bit on those duties, but now we are waiting to see if we have been successful."

"Ah, that would be good. We do not need soldiers tramping across our fields, and I am in no position to stop them now." He waved at his leg.

"I am told you are to keep still," Anna scolded.

"Ah, these healers worry too much. Berthe even considered fetching the old witch to look at me, but in the end she decided that she had my care under control. Not her usual work, fixing legs, but she did well by me."

"The old witch?" Anna asked, her memory darting back to the old woman who had stopped the rain.

"Yes. You remember her. It was you who fetched her for your mother when she had so much trouble with Susanne. Never been sure exactly what she did, but your mother made it through and Susanne was born the next day. A little cranky, that woman, keeps to herself when she can, but she has been good to us. Berthe studied with her for a while."

Anna started to say that she did not remember going for the witch, and then, suddenly, she did. Her mind harked back to the feeling of déjà vu she had experienced when she had sought out the woman to stop the rain. She had indeed once before walked up to that cottage, as a child of twelve years, frightened and yet resolved. She could think of nothing to say.

But her father, deep in his own memories, had not noticed her reaction. "That midwife we had then was horrified when you came back with the witch, threatened to walk right out and go get the priest. She was new here. The one we had for the rest of you had passed, and the priest brought her in. But Madame calmed her down, even put her to work. After all was said and done, your mother and Susanne both doing fine, the old witch found a midwife for the community who was not afraid of using the old ways when it was necessary. I think she pushed the bad one off on a religious noble somewhere — sent her off to a place where they would rather die than get close to something uncanny."

"Of course," said Anna. "I recall it. That was quite a night. I am glad your injury did not require such action."

"And so am I. That woman always terrified me, though not as much as watching your mother in childbirth. I have always been glad I defied the midwife and sent you along. But tell me, what have you been doing?"

Anna managed to come up with a heavily edited version of her adventures, leaving out all mention of her suspicions about the Hierofante's involvement and even waxing humorous in her description of the "abbess's" trip to Foraoise. But her own mind was on her trip to get the witch so many years back. Her father had told her to take a horse and to ride toward the west. If the witch were willing to be found, Anna would find her. Anna had ridden as fast as she could, but the ride back with the witch had gone even more quickly, and it seemed that little time had passed when they returned.

The witch had shut down the midwife's protests with a word and collared Berthe, who was not yet nine, to help her. She had chased Anna from the room and only allowed her father to stay if he promised to sit in a corner and keep still. Anna and the other children had huddled around the table in the main room, waiting for they knew not what. As the oldest, she kept reassuring Robert and Jeanine, though she herself was terrified, her fears stoked by an awareness that something she could not fathom was going on just beyond her ken.

They had fallen asleep there, she remembered, and woken to delight in their new sister cradled at their mother's breast. Anna had gone out afterwards to help the witch with her horse, and had asked her if the midwife would cause either her family or Madame any trouble with the church.

"She has already forgotten what happened," the witch said. "Most of the others have as well, for all that your father is thanking me so graciously. He knows that I did something, though he is no longer sure what. But you, though you lack all talent for the old ways, you remain aware that they are present. There will come a time when that ability will be of use to you, but for now it is better that you forget it."

And so Anna had, until her father had brought it up. Now she remembered it all, and knew the witch in the forest for the same woman. It left her in some discomfort, though she hoped she had hidden it well enough from her father while she told her stories of adventures and listened to his reports on the farm.

After the visit with her father and a dinner that included both Jeanine and Robert and their families, come to see their big sister, Anna found time to sit down in a corner with Berthe, who was staying with her parents though she usually lived on the edge of the village with her wife, also a healer.

"The old witch in the forest," Anna said. "What do you know of her?"

"Madame Herboriste," Berthe corrected her. "The local priest is horrified at the idea of witches, though even he consulted her for the care of his mother. We are careful to always use her name."

"Father isn't."

Berthe waved her hand. "You know how he is."

"You studied with her to become a midwife."

"Extra studies. She encouraged me to become a midwife after that night with Mother, and told me to come to her for additional training. You remember."

"I did not know that part."

"Of course. You would have been off at school and likely only got vague reports of what your siblings were doing. Madame is a help to every healer and midwife in these parts. My wife trained with her longer than I did. It is how we met. We do not ask too many questions."

"And now people do not ask too many questions of you or your wife. I am not an inquisitor for the Hierofante. I met the woman while on an errand for the Realm, and wondered about her."

"Anyone who practices healing arts must fear witch hunts, whether we have such power or no," her sister said. "But if you or those you serve have need of her, she will do well by you, regardless of their silly beliefs. Though she charges great fees to those who can pay, so that she can treat the ones who cannot."

"I have noticed that. But she is trustworthy?"

"I would stake my life on it," Berthe said.

They were quiet for a few minutes. Then Berthe said, "Those you serve may well have need of her. I fear there is much disquiet in the Realm these days."

"It is true that there are rumblings of war," Anna said.

"This disquiet is not only about war. More than that troubles our Realm."

She said nothing else and Anna did not ask. It was disconcerting to realize that her sister had knowledge of the uncanny; she did not want to know more. She had meant to ask what the witch had meant when she had told Anna about her own ability to sense the old ways, but found that she feared admitting that skill to her own sister. Still, it was useful to have such good report of the witch from a source as reliable as Berthe. Should Anna find she needed her, she would seek her out, much as she hoped to avoid any more excursions into the ways of magic.

Fortunately, her time with Susanne was free of such concerns. She barely knew her youngest sister, having left for school when she was but a year old. But they shared a passion for the sword and the way of warriors. They did sword drills together and even some light sparring. "I must keep up my practice while I am away from school," Susanne told her with that level of seriousness that only the young can demonstrate without irony.

"She worships you," her mother told Anna. "I am certain her schoolmates are tired of her constant stories about my sister in the Queen's Guard."

"Obviously you trained her as well as you did me—or maybe better. I do not think I was so skilled at her age."

"Unlike the others, she sought it out. I think she will be very good indeed. And despite her youthful enthusiasm, she has a great deal of common sense, something I know I came to value back in my day. The person who can avoid trouble is of more value than the best fighter."

Anna stayed only a couple of days, having ascertained from her mother that, in fact, the duties of their farmstead were being well-handled with the assistance of Jeanine and Robert and their children and in-laws. The family was delighted to see her, but they did not need her help. Farmers pulled together in this part of the Realm, and there was talk of combining all three estates in the next generation. "Though of course there will always be a place for you here, should you decide to retire from the soldier's life," her mother said. "And Susanne as well, though she will do all she can to follow in your footsteps."

"And yours," Anna reminded her mother.

"Ah, yes. I enjoyed those years, but I have enjoyed the others as well. I am not sure you would be as happy here as I, and I suspect Susanne of being cut of similar cloth. She does well at school and is hoping for an appointment to your guard, though she does not say it."

"I will see what can be done. If we avoid war, and I hope that we do, we may not take many new juniors this year, but there are some other troops that would provide good training for her."

"If I must have two daughters pursuing the warrior's path, I confess to hoping that no wars of any kind come about. Though that was not my feeling back in my day. Take care of yourself, my dear, and remember that there are other ways of life besides that of the sword."

Susanne was returning to school as Anna left, so they rode together for the first half day. They discussed her training, her other schoolwork—she enjoyed history and military strategy—and her desires for the future.

"I hope to serve the Realm," Susanne said. And then, quietly, "I would most like to serve in Her Majesty's Guard along with you."

"You have the makings of a guardswoman," Anna told her, because it was true. "I will not make you any promises, but if you continue working as you have done, your prospects will be bright in the future."

They parted at the road to the school, Anna having decided that she must hurry back to the Capital in case some new disaster had occurred in her absence. "You will visit again soon," Susanne shouted as she rode off. It was more a command than a request.

Anna waved in response. She hoped it was true that she would visit again soon, but it was clear to her that she no longer had a place in the family homestead. They would help her should she need it, and without complaint, for those of her family cared about each other, but there was no role there for her. And while she did not desire such a role, while in truth she was most happy to think that she might never again need to slaughter pigs or rush to get a crop in ahead of rain, she still felt a wash of sadness to think that she had turned a final corner on that life. What would be the next stage of her life? She was not yet thirty and could be an effective soldier for easily another ten or fifteen years, possibly more. But the time would come when superior skill would not compensate for a slowing body. She wondered if Susanne, too, would come to that point if she continued on the warrior path.

Thinking of Susanne made her wonder if she should have promised her sister more, should have said she would do everything to make it possible for her to be in the Queen's Guard. In truth, she did think her sister was highly qualified, but was it honorable to advocate for family? And on the other side, was it a violation of her duty to family if she did not take such a stand? It occurred to her—because she was, at heart, a self-reflective woman—that she wanted Susanne to join the Guard in part because then she would have family nearby, not just friends and colleagues. Anna knew her desires affected her judgment. When she was Susanne's age, and even during her years in the Andrean Guard, before reunification of the Realm, the honorable choices and duty had seemed to be obvious and not in conflict. Now, though, she found complexities at every turn.

Contemplating all that left her in a melancholy turn of mind as she made her way back to the Capital, to home.

Chapter 16

ANNA RETURNED TO find the diplomatic efforts proceeding slowly, while rigorous training continued apace. Cecile had won permission from both Her Majesty and the Queen's Captain to engage in the upcoming tournament, though the Queen had insisted she compete under a false name and wear a mask to keep her true identity unknown—at least officially.

Cecile arrived at the Queen's Guard barracks early on the morning of the tournament. Anna supervised her outfitting in a tunic—slightly too big—and gave her a live blade to carry, though all the tournament matches would be conducted with padded wooden weapons to avoid serious injury. It would not do to lose valuable fighters to mistakes and the heat of a fight, especially since the purpose of the tournament was to encourage everyone to train hard in case war broke out. The Queen's Guard marched en masse to the arena, Cecile in their midst. The other juniors had adopted her as a kind of mascot, appreciating the hard work she put in, especially since she was, as Nicole put it, "one of those nobles." Most soldiers came from modest backgrounds, unless they were second cousins once removed or otherwise very far down the line of succession or had suffered losses such as those of Roland's family.

The arena had been built in the days when Andrea and Melora ruled the Realm. It stood at the edge of the city, an imposing edifice of hand-hewn rock, decorated over the entrance arch and around the top of the outside wall with carved grotesques. The inner area held thousands, with the nobles seated on velvet-covered chairs in comfortable boxes, while everyone else sat on wooden benches or even stood near the top. The fighting area itself was quite large, since it was used for all types of spectacle. The showplace venue was set in front of the Royal Box, so that the most important people could view the best fighters. The sizes of the other spaces were set up to be adjusted quickly; the large demonstrations that opened the tournament would be held in a sufficient space that could be divided up afterwards so that multiple challenges could go on at the same time.

As with most such events, the participants were divided into different groups based on choice of weapons and years of experience. In addition to duels with blunted swords, there were jousting matches, archery competitions, and bouts of staff fighting. The whole tournament began with demonstrations: several group performances of training forms and then individual bouts by those among the most renowned in that field. In swordfighting, Asamir was dueling Jean-Paul.

It seemed likely to be a rousing event, not least because both of them enjoyed being the center of attention and were determined to put on a spectacular show. They had choreographed most of their performance, incorporating flying leaps, gymnastic rolls, and last-minute blocks that prevented certain injury. The only part of the show that had not been agreed upon in advance was which of them was to be the ultimate victor—a debate that had fast degenerated into the usual bickering. A suggestion by Anna that they end it with a tie had been rejected with scorn by both parties.

Anna left Cecile with Nicole and the other juniors who were competing, and then took her place in the stands with the rest of the Queen's Guard, who were seated behind the Royal Box and next to the King's Guard. She and Roland contrived to sit next to each other. They endured a certain amount of teasing, but under cover of the event they were able to share their captains' opinions on reports that troops were to be sent to remove the governor of

Andalucie forthwith. A marquessa renowned for handling delicate matters involving artisans and craft workers had been selected to replace him, a choice that found approval with both Anna and Roland. They both hoped they might be included among the soldiers sent to take the man into custody.

Their Majesties arrived with members of their court, and after a formal parade by the participants, who made bows and other courtesies to the royals, the tournament began with the formal demonstrations. The archery show was marked by a broken bowstring that shot an arrow into the crowd, sending spectators diving to safety, but fortunately causing no injuries. The musket shooting event did not include live ammunition, possibly to avoid any similar errors; even in expert hands, muskets were notoriously difficult to aim. Then came the demonstration all had waited for: the sword fight.

Asamir and Jean-Paul's performance was as flashy as promised, involving cartwheels and back flips and so many occasions in which a deadly attack was stopped only by a quick turn or block that Anna lost count. Having watched their rehearsals, she knew when the ending was due and watched with interest as Asamir began a charge and suddenly switched her sword to her left hand—a move Jean-Paul had not anticipated—and stabbed toward his chest. He twisted at the last minute, so that the sword slid harmlessly across his torso. His triumph at this defense was short-lived, though, because Asamir hooked his foot as he twisted, sending him sprawling to the ground. She waited a moment to savor her triumph before putting her sword point at his throat, and that gave him time to put his at her stomach. While neither cut the other, the end result was clear: mutual destruction.

The crowd roared with approval, though neither combatant appeared satisfied. Anna laughed so hard that Roland had to pat her on the back.

The tournament began in earnest, with a dozen different divisions running at the same time. At this point, most of the audience decided that it was time for a glass of wine or other snack, or even a stroll outside to gossip with others. Their Majesties joined this exodus, repairing to a suite set up for their use. However, the members of the guard forces who were not competing stayed in their places, eager to track the performance of their junior members, on whom many had bet not inconsiderable amounts of money. Anna made regular use of her spyglass, for otherwise it was impossible to determine who was fighting whom. She noticed that the captains of the various guards, including her own, moved to a point where they could easily see the fighters from the less celebrated troops, leaving their seconds and seniors to watch the fights featuring those of Queen's, King's, and Hierofante's Guards. Recruitment of new soldiers was ever on their mind, particularly since the drums of war had not yet been silenced.

Cecile, fighting in the juniormost guard division (there were three of these in an effort to award as many victories as possible), began with a quick decision over a recent graduate of one of the soldiers' schools who had joined a border guard, and then dispatched a young member of the Hierofante's Guard in a hard-fought match that left the opponents with a grudging respect for each other.

The events continued throughout the afternoon. Even members of the various Guards who were watching took a break now and again, for it was hard to sit still for too long. Some, disgusted with the performance of those they had trained or bet on, left to drown their sorrows. But as the time grew near for the final matches, all returned to their seats, even Their Majesties and the other nobles.

In the junior guard finals, Cecile met a young man new to the King's Guard who showed himself to be much more skilled than she. He scored one point, then another, before she managed— borrowing a move from Asamir—to take him off his feet and land what was ruled a killing blow. Since the tournament was built on training for possible war, a killing blow gave her an automatic win even though the other fighter was ahead on points. Anna, looking up at the Royal Box, noted Her Majesty applauding with enthusiasm, while His Majesty appeared to be frowning at the defeat of his soldier by an anonymous young woman.

In the end, Cecile's victory provided the points that made the Queen's Guard the overall victors—by a hair—over the other guard units. Given her mask, there were many grumbles that she was a ringer, but if those disputes led to any physical altercations, they took place in the taverns after the tournament ended.

Cecile's success obligated Anna to take her out with the other Guardswomen for a celebration. With regret, Anna took leave of Roland, promising to see him on the morrow, and joined the happy throng. Mindful of her duty to Her Majesty and of Cecile's youth and high position, she drew the girl away from the party before too many bottles had been opened.

Cecile protested, but Anna was firm. "Her Majesty was very good to let you compete, but now you must return to your true duties. She will be expecting you. Besides, she will want to hear your account of the fight."

The summer days were starting to wane. Dusk overtook the Capital as the woman and girl strolled along the streets from the tournament grounds toward the palace. The streets were crowded—the tournament had made for a festive day among the Capital's populace—and many of the less savory inhabitants were eyeing those coming from the taverns, evaluating which ones might be sufficiently intoxicated to be susceptible to a pickpocket or cutpurse. These ruffians steered clear of Anna and Cecile, who looked far too formidable.

They took a short cut down deserted streets—ones that less well-armed and skilled women might have avoided. As they walked, they heard a commotion ahead and turned a corner to find several men holding a young woman, around whose neck they had placed a noose. A boy was shinnying up the lamp pole with the other end of the rope. One of the men clutched a rag to his face, which was bleeding copiously. He was screaming, "No young bitch will get away with cutting me."

The girl spat at him, which increased the fury of his commentary.

"We must stop this," Cecile said.

Anna nodded. She let Cecile take the lead. The girl drew her sword and waded into the crowd, knocking one man off balance with her hilt and sweeping another off his feet before he realized she was behind him.

"Let her go," Cecile said.

"This is none of your affair, guardswomen," the bleeding man said. "We handle our own down here."

"Not this time."

"Your skill with that blade will not stop us all."

"I suspect it will stop enough of you to end this farce, or would you care to try me?"

The bleeding man was angry enough to charge a woman with a sword, but his friends were not so foolish. One of them pulled him away, and another, having noticed Anna watching, shooed off the remainder. The two were left there with the girl.

"My thanks, me ladies. I thought sure I was done for this time."

"Will you be safe from them now?" Cecile asked.

"If I can avoid them. That scoundrel is convinced he should have his way with every female out here, and he will surely try again. But I have me knife."

"Come with us," Cecile said.

Anna raised her eyebrows. "I am not sure..." she began, thinking of what the Queen would say if she saw this girl, with her dirty hair and ragged clothes.

Cecile ignored her. "I cannot offer you luxury, but I can find you work in the palace stables or perhaps in the laundry, which-ever might be your preference."

The girl looked startled, and a bit of hope rose in her face. "I used to look after some horses, before me mother lost her position in Andalucie and we had to come to the Capital to see if we could make our way."

Andalucie. Another family ruined by the governor, no doubt.

"The stables it is. They are always looking for grooms. Most likely you will be cleaning stalls."

"'Tis better than avoiding whoremongers, me lady. It seems I have more reason to thank you. But...." The girl hesitated. "But I must get back to me mother, or she will worry."

"And 'tis late," Anna said. "The head groom will be abed."

"Then I will meet you on the morrow and take you to him," Cecile said. She named a place and time.

"I will come, me lady. Me mother is scarce feeding me and my brothers on what sewing she can take in. Work will be of help to us all."

They saw the girl to her home—hardly more than a hovel. The child was embarrassed by it, but given the cutthroats in the street, Anna agreed with Cecile that she should not be left to her own resources.

"On the morrow," Cecile said, and the girl promised anew.

As they continued toward the palace, Cecile said. "I hope she will come."

"I suspect she will. She seems a likely lass, one who will take advantage of an opportunity."

"She has pluck. She might have the making of a squire, should my father allow me to become a soldier."

"More likely that than servant to a lady in waiting," Anna said.

When they reached the palace grounds, Cecile regretfully removed her mask and sword. "It seems I am always changing one disguise for another."

"You fought well today, but you have many good skills. Do not be in too much hurry to pick one path over another." Anna knew Cecile would enjoy the soldier's life for a time, but she felt certain the girl was ultimately destined for some high position.

For the Good of the Realm

Both her brains and her compassion marked her for more than a simple role in the future of the Realm.

Chapter 17

Two days later, the captain sent for Anna and Asamir. As they walked up the stairs to her office, Asamir said, "Did you not say they were sending an armed delegation to remove the governor of Andalucie? Perhaps we are to be included."

"That would be most satisfying," Anna said.

But the captain had a different assignment for them. "The negotiations with Foraoise are progressing, but Their Majesties are becoming impatient. They want to take advantage of your relationship with the defense ministry, but they also want to make the delegation official. To that end, they are sending the Count of Rabelais to meet with him, with the two of you escorting him and his party. You leave on the morrow. Anna, you will command this expedition. I am sending Lily and Blanche with you; I believe four guardswomen will be enough. The Count will bring some men of his own."

"Bah," said Asamir when they left the captain's office. "Another damned diplomatic mission. It would be much more fun to throw out the governor."

"Possibly, but anything we can do to avoid war is worthwhile. And we do know Sotha. Though it may take some finesse to get the Count to let us make the negotiations smooth. He is a blunt man."

"He is a rude man," Asamir said. "And why are you so eager to avoid war? We have not had a good war in two years. I fear my skills are rusting from disuse."

"You have fought five duels in the last two months, successfully, I might add. I do not think you are at risk of losing your skills. May I remind you that the end of summer is almost upon us? Should war break out, we will be fighting in the winter. And they will employ sorcerers." She said the last bit just to make Asamir nervous, and, indeed, the abbess-manqué made the religious gesture.

But despite her automatic reaction to the mere mention of magic, she said, "Perhaps the negotiations will continue over the winter, but fall apart as spring comes upon us, so that we can fight in reasonable weather."

"And the sorcerers?"

"We have defeated Foraoise before, even in the presence of magic. Surely we can do so again."

"True. My mother fought in that war," Anna said. "But the conflict was the result of their raids into Andalucie province and there was much speculation that Foraoise did not put all of its resources behind that endeavor. I do not think we should rely on that victory."

In the evening, Anna proceeded to the Maudite to wait for Roland. "I am very sorry to report that I must away in the morning," she told him when he arrived close on her heels.

"Are you part of the expedition to remove the governor, then? Jean-Paul and I also leave on the morrow to assist in that venture."

"Alas, no. I have a different assignment, but one that I believe may be profitable in the prevention of war with Foraoise. 'Tis likely to involve tedious diplomacy, though, rather than forthright effort against a wrongdoer. Important, but I am sure your expedition will be more satisfying."

They parted with regret after sharing a bottle of wine, since both needed to make their preparations.

Anna and Asamir were surprised to learn that the Dowager Countess of Rabelais—the Count's mother—was traveling with them. True, the Countess had been a guardswoman in her youth before marrying well and pursuing a diplomatic career in tandem with her husband. It was not unreasonable to assume that she would be of value to the expedition. But she was not young, and the travel, even with coaches and a staff, would not be comfortable.

Both Anna and Asamir's evaluations of the Count of Rabelais were revealed as understatement. By the end of the first day on the trail, Anna concluded that the best word to describe him was insufferable. He berated his servants in front of everyone for their every failing—real or imagined. After he screamed at his coachman for the third time for both driving too slow and hitting too many holes on the poorly maintained road, Anna was moved to inquire of one of his personal guards how the man retained staff.

"Her ladyship takes care of us," the man said quietly.

"I begin to understand why the Countess was included in this expedition," Anna said.

They stopped for the night at a small inn, where the landlady found herself flustered by such a large party, particularly one that included nobility. When the Count tried to bully the poor woman, Anna stepped between them. "Your lordship, please calm down and let her do her work." That, at least, caused him to vent his ire on Anna, which was annoying but allowed the landlady to set up their rooms and meals.

Later, the Countess sought her out. "Madame, I apologize for my son. His manners are frightful; alas, his father had charge of his raising and taught him arrogance. Our people are used to it, and I am sure you can protect yourself where necessary, but it is difficult when he abuses outsiders. If you would please give the landlady this purse for her additional trouble, I would be most appreciative."

A variation on that routine was repeated on each day of the trip. By the time they reached the last village before the Realm of Foraoise, Anna had concluded that the Countess was the actual diplomat, even though she had officially retired from such work. "Her

Majesty should have explained that to the captain so that she could inform us," she told Asamir. "We will need to let Sotha know."

"Yes. Although given his brilliance, he will likely deduce it."

"We will let him reserve his skill for the task of keeping the Count content while negotiating a true agreement with the Countess."

"And hope he will not be angered by this absurd arrangement," Asamir said.

"Sotha is not prone to anger," Anna reminded her. "His challenge will be convincing others in his government to recommence diplomatic relations when our supposed envoy is so undiplomatic. But I suppose using the Count is the only way for Their Majesties to continue to avail themselves of the Countess. I wonder if her marriage to his father in the first place was for the purpose of placing a talented diplomat in partnership with a well-placed man who lacked all such skills."

"Sometimes I am moved to question the value of noble classes," Asamir said.

Anna smiled. As the daughter of a guardswoman turned pig farmer, she had few illusions about nobles. In her experience, far too many among the highborn behaved as the Count. Those who did not, such as Roland and Sotha, had often suffered adversity despite their families' ranks. Asamir, though, was prone to confuse rank with ability. If dealing with the Count had caused her to think anew, it made the experience slightly more bearable.

They ensconced the Count and the Countess, together with their entourage, in the one inn in the village large enough to accommodate their party. Accompanied as it was by the Count's usual boorish behavior, this process took an hour longer than it should have, though the Countess's largesse smoothed things somewhat. Then Anna undertook the difficult task of explaining to the Count that as it was her task to meet with Sotha so as to prepare the for negotiations, she and Asamir would be traveling ahead to Foraoise to arrange matters.

Although the Count had been told by Their Majesties that Anna and Asamir were accompanying the party not just as soldiers but also as persons with connections to the Foraoise defense ministry, he was, of course, inclined to argue.

Once again, the Countess managed the situation. After allowing him to rant about the disrespect to his authority and the need for him to be present to ensure that these girl guards would not betray their mission—Anna had to stomp on Asamir's toes to forestall her from drawing her sword when he uttered those words—the Countess soothed him by reminding him that the mission was supposed to be discreet. Unless Anna and Asamir traveled ahead to arrange matters in advance, he would be forced to sneak across the border, an uncomfortable adventure at best.

They wasted the better part of another hour in resolving the matter, so that it was approaching sunset before Anna and Asamir were able to take their leave. Under normal circumstances, they would have waited until the following day to depart. But both were so relieved to be shut of the Count that they managed to insist it was best to cross the border in the dark of night.

"And what we will say to him if it is necessary to sneak him across the border to facilitate the meeting, I do not know," Anna said as they saddled their horses. "I bid you pray that Sotha will convince his superiors to agree to an official meeting with a formal gate crossing so that we are not forced to devise another explanation."

"Praying for such is blasphemy," Asamir said. "You should have let me kill the Count for his insults to us, and then we would not have had to put up with his nonsense."

"And I would have, but for the fact that you would have been hanged for murder forthwith."

"A duel is not murder."

"A duel between you and the Count would be."

They did not, in fact, cross the border in the night, as the day had been long and they decided that a meal and sleep would improve their chances of doing so unseen. Though Asamir grumbled as they built a fire and toasted bread and cheese for their dinner. "We could have had soft beds and roast chicken at the inn."

"But here we will have peace," Anna said.

The river that divided the two realms had swollen with late summer rains since the last time they crossed it. When they had left Foraoise after their expedition as the abbess and her retinue, they had found a location shallow enough that the horses could wade it, but now it was too deep. "The horses can swim if we remove their saddles," Asamir said.

"But that does not get us and the saddles across," Anna said. "Let us walk along the bank and see if we can find something we can use."

They had traveled through the forest north of the main road to reach this crossing. "I do not think there are any other bridges or other means of crossing except at the official crossing point," Asamir said.

"No? Then how do the people of our realm and the people of theirs handle informal trade matters? I doubt we are the only people who seek to cross without bringing ourselves to official attention."

And, indeed, they did not go far before spotting a tall tree that sported a rope swing. Across the river they saw a raft pulled up under some bushes—more visible from their side of the river than the other. "The horses will still have to swim," Anna said, "but we can make it across dry shod."

She climbed up the tree to give herself some loft, then swung across the river on the rope, landing on a soft pile of dirt. Before rafting back, she scouted around to make sure no guards were hiding nearby to catch illegal crossers. The place appeared deserted.

"Odd that no one has put guards in this place, given the tensions between our realms," Asamir said as they poled across. A handy ring on the raft had provided a place to tie the horses' leads so that they could swim along behind.

"I suspect local officials at both of the close-by villages do not want to interfere with informal trade."

"You mean that they have been bribed to look the other way so that smuggling can go on."

"I mean that people who live at the boundaries between countries are not inclined to take borders very seriously."

They reached the Foraoisian capital just before nightfall. A sheepherder's hut a few miles outside the city had provided a place to hide their belongings and leave their horses. "I hope no one brings sheep here before we return," Asamir said.

"No one will," Anna replied. "Look at the grass. The sheep left here a week or so ago and will not return until the grass has time to grow back."

"More of your country knowledge?"

"It is useful to know how the world outside of the city works."

By late afternoon they reached the capital city, where they endeavored to blend in with others, having left their guard tunics (though not all their weapons) at the hut. "Understanding city ways can also be useful," Asamir observed as they stared down a man who offered an indecent suggestion.

Anna grinned. "I suggest we once again go the back way to Sotha's home."

"Must we skulk through latrines and garbage?"

Anna gave her a look. "Of course we must. Onward."

As before, their trip was odorous, but not difficult. "Really," Asamir breathed in Anna's ear. "You would think a high official in the defense ministry would have better security."

"Perhaps he is hoping for a visit from such as us."

And, indeed, Sotha was not surprised when they entered his room. "Ah. The ambassadors return," he said. He rose to greet them.

"Only their emissaries," Anna said. "The official party waits just across the river. We were not certain whether you might be ready for more open negotiations."

"Things have changed in Foraoise since your last visit," Sotha said. "Meara has been de-fanged, and our gracious ruler has once again proclaimed her faith in my family and myself. Your realm's quiet work with our ministry of foreign affairs has made true negotiations easier. We are ready to meet your ambassadors and re-establish relations."

"I had not expected such an open welcome," Anna said.

"In truth, had we not been able to discredit Meara, it would not have been possible. But the fact that he, supposedly a devotee of our native religion, had met with your Hierofante, who is well-known for interests beyond the holy, was useful in destroying his influence. I am very grateful to you for that information, for it carried the day.

"I assume the two of you crossed into our realm informally. If you can return the same way, I will give you a safe conduct for yourselves and your ambassadors, and make this matter above-board."

"It is almost as if you had been expecting us," Asamir observed.

"We did hear some rumors," Sotha said. "But where are my manners? May I offer you some wine? Have you eaten?"

"We would be most grateful for some wine," Anna said. "And in truth, our dinner was a hurried affair at a tavern best forgotten." Conversation over wine and food would also allow her to tease out a few more answers.

"I can also offer you a bed for the night, if you have not made other arrangements." He rang for a servant.

Asamir could not hide the delight on her face. "A bed would be most welcome."

The servant showed no surprise at his orders. He quickly returned with plates piled high with meats and cheese along with an assortment of late summer fruit and said that their chamber was just next door, when they were ready. Sotha poured them all some wine.

Anna sipped hers slowly. An excellent vintage. She nibbled a bite of cheese and thought about what she wanted to know. On the principle that sharing information often leads to more open conversation, she said, "You should be aware that the Count of Rabelais, our ambassador, is—how shall I say this—a man of limited intellectual gifts who covers this shortcoming with a rude manner. Fortunately, he is accompanied by his mother, who once served the realm as a diplomat in her own right. He is the official envoy, but..."

Sotha smiled. "I will let the ministers know. We will endeavor to work around him while seeming to work with him."

"The Dowager Countess will be of great assistance to you there, as she is often called on to do this. From watching her, I believe that letting him bluster and then ignoring much of what he says and moving to the essential matters is the best strategy. Also, he responds well to flattery, although he deserves it not. But of course you will be able to find a way to work with him. Your understanding of such tactics has always been better than mine."

"The key is knowing your opponent's weaknesses and using those against them. I learned that from training in the sword with the two of you."

"I have always found it easier to discern and use weaknesses in a swordfight than in a diplomatic exchange," Anna said. "But I am told that rudeness is at times a ruse in negotiations. In this case, should the Dowager be rude, you should take her seriously."

"But tell us," said Asamir, who was finishing her second glass of wine and impatient at the pace of conversation, "how were you able to bring about the downfall of Meara? Was he not the man who forced your family out of Foraoise when we were children?"

Sotha nodded. "Yes. Fortunately, when the Queen attained her majority and was able to rid herself of her uncle, who had been a poor regent, Meara lost his influence. Her Majesty knew of the great service my family had been to the realm for generations and brought us back.

"Our position here has always been somewhat precarious. My great-great grandfather came here from the country of Alhambra at the request of the then-king, who met him while traveling on youthful adventures. His service to the realm brought him a title and our family lands, but three generations is not long enough in Foraoise to be considered true nobility or even a true Foraoisian to some, so there were many who believed Meara's lies. He was weakened when the Queen took power, but not exiled or imprisoned as a sop to his family heritage. So it was no surprise to find that he was once again meddling in foreign affairs."

Sotha took a sip of wine. "We had noticed, of course, but we had no lever with which to uproot him until you told me that he had been meeting with your Hierofante. That gave my father and myself the opening we needed. He will not trouble us or you again."

The words were ordinary, but Anna picked up darkness in what he said. She wondered what had truly become of Meara, but could tell from Sotha's voice that she was not supposed to ask. And, indeed, she was more than a little afraid to know too much. However, there was something that she needed to know—an equally tricky issue and one that would frighten Asamir by its mere mention—but a vital one. She chose her words with care. "We have reason to believe that our Hierofante has used...uncanny measures within our realm."

Asamir's eyes widened, and she lifted her hand as if to make the religious gesture, though she did not do so.

"Magic? Your Hierofante? Does she not condemn it at every turn?"

"The highest religious officials in every faith have been known to say one thing and do another," Anna said. "I do not accuse her of this lightly, but unnatural things have happened, and there are sufficient indications to permit the assumption that she is behind them. Given that the meetings between her and Meara were apparently conducted with the help of some magical influence, I have wondered whether Her Eminence might be getting assistance from, or through, your enemy."

"She could have been." Sotha hesitated. "I will trust you with this information. Barun Meara is a sorcerer of some power. He could have provided assistance to your Hierofante. It would depend on whether the assistance the Hierofante sought was related to something Meara would also find useful. I do not think mere gold would influence him."

"Would causing friction between our realms or within our Realm be of interest to him?"

"Yes, if he thought he could use it to gain power here at home. I am sure that is why he was dealing with the Hierofante. But if that is the case, do not let it trouble you further. Meara is no longer able to cause difficulties either here or in your Realm, and if the Hierofante was relying on him, she will be unable to do so in the future."

Anna heard the unspoken command to let the subject go, and turned the conversation to inconsequential matters. Not long after, they retired for the night.

"Do you suppose he used magic to spy upon us?" Asamir asked as they prepared for bed.

"Possibly. I wonder how he dealt with Meara. There was always talk that Sotha's father was a sorcerer. But I do not think we will ever know the story. He does seem grateful for our earlier assistance. That bodes well for the negotiations."

Chapter 18

THE COUNT GLANCED at the safe-conduct from Sotha and said, "We cannot trust these people. This is likely a ruse to have us arrested or murdered at the border."

"You are wise to always question the motives of others," the Dowager said. "But I am certain that our guards will be able to handle any treachery."

"These girl guards? Hmph."

"And it appears that our passage will be quite difficult if we do not cross at the border," the Dowager continued, ignoring his comment and pleading with her eyes to Anna and Asamir that they do the same. "Did you not say, Madame, that you found it necessary to swing across the river on a rope?"

"Indeed," said Anna, who did not mention that she had left the raft on the Realm's side of the border. "Our horses had to swim the river and, of course, there would be no way to transport your carriage across. We would have to proceed on foot or on horseback from there to the city. I fear, my lady, that it might be very difficult for you." She knew full well that the Dowager was respected for her riding ability, despite her years, but she also knew the Count was not a horseman of note.

The Dowager smiled with understanding. "It would be very easy for you to ride hell-for-leather as these guards do, my dear, but it would be a sore trial for me, at my advanced age. If the Foraoisians will not come to us, I fear we must take their invitation at face value and go to them in an open manner." Neither she nor the guardswomen pointed out that their expedition would not be successful if it were not officially recognized and sanctioned in Foraoise.

The Count continued to bluster and complain, but the Dowager's careful strategy of flattery and accommodation was eventually productive, and they obtained his consent. Once the Guardswomen were finally alone, with nothing more to do than plan all the logistics of the morrow's expedition, Asamir said to Anna, "The world would not suffer if that man should fall victim to a stray round of shot—or a misdirected bit of steel."

Their fellow guardswomen laughed. "You missed even more of the man's abuse while you were in Foraoise," Blanche said. "Asamir is not the only one among us to harbor such feelings."

"Nonetheless, you—any of you—would suffer if you were on the other end of either of those items," Anna said. "Though I confess to exhaustion. How does the Dowager manage to stay so cheerful when she expends so much of her energy working around that man? I know she was trained as a diplomat, but even so, it must be dreadful to do this for every tiny matter of daily life."

"I have no idea. I cannot imagine tolerating a man such as the Count for any purpose," Asamir said.

"Nor can I. I have heard that his father was equally ill-behaved, so I suppose the Dowager has years of practice. Be more grateful. So long as she manages him well, we may end up with fruitful negotiations, and no war."

"War would be preferable," Asamir said.

As they drew close to the official border crossing with Foraoise, Anna and Asamir rode ahead. Anna had the safe-conduct from Sotha tucked in her inside pocket. She wanted to be certain all matters were in order before she brought the Count's party across.

It was past midday. Even if all went well, they would arrive in the Foraoisian capital at a late hour with the need to find an inn that would take a large party. They had got off to a late start despite all of Anna's careful planning. The Count had renewed his objections to crossing officially at the border over breakfast, and it had taken the Dowager an hour to persuade him to follow the plan.

"I am certain that even the Dowager would be pleased if someone throttled him," Asamir said when they stopped at a pond to give their horses a drink.

"I cannot deny that the world would be much improved," Anna said. "But it cannot happen until after he returns home with a successful pact. If anything happened here, the Foraoisians would be blamed and war would certainly result."

"Perhaps when we return home, then. Surely there must be a way to dispose of him without bringing harm on the one responsible."

"Perhaps if he fell off a cliff in the presence of someone of unimpeachable integrity who was willing to swear by all that is holy it was an accident," Anna said.

"I shall see what I can do in the way of finding such a person."

Anna rode up to the bridge, with Asamir waiting in case someone needed to ride back quickly to warn the official party. The other two guardswomen rode alongside the carriage. Two sentinels on their side of the border greeted Anna. "You are later than expected. The official party over there is getting impatient."

Sotha had not only issued the safe-conduct, but had come to the border himself, accompanied by several ministers. He was waiting for her just across the bridge.

"Go tell his lordship to get a move on," Anna yelled to Asamir as she led her horse across the bridge to meet the officials.

When the Count and the Dowager alit from their carriage some forty-five minutes later, Sotha, along with the three nobles in his company, greeted them effusively.

"We have opened and cleaned your embassy so that you may stay in comfortable surroundings. Her Majesty's favorite chef is there now, preparing a welcome dinner and overseeing food preparations for your stay. We have heard so much about you, your lordship. I am certain our negotiations will be most fruitful. Tomorrow morning we will present you to Her Majesty, so that you will be well-assured that she supports our endeavors here."

The Count kept trying to respond but the Foraoisian party kept up their relentless praise and greetings. The Dowager murmured, "So kind," at regular intervals. In a matter of minutes they were on the road to the capital.

"I begin to fear," said Anna, "that the Count will be flattered into giving away everything."

"The Dowager will keep him in check. Did you notice her speaking quietly to Sotha before they left? Both of them know who the important players are in this drama," Asamir replied.

Indeed, the plans put in place by the Foraoisians kept the Count mollified for the rest of the day. He had regained his usual irascible form by the next morning, and snarled and yelled throughout his people's efforts to get him breakfasted and properly dressed before his audience with the Queen of Foraoise. That event went off without a hitch despite the Count's threats to give Her Majesty a piece of his mind. The Dowager, who had met the Queen when that royal was a child chafing under the authority of her uncle the regent, managed to take charge of the conversation and keep her son from making a fool of himself.

The negotiations began in earnest in the afternoon. To their horror, Anna and Asamir found that their continued presence was expected, apparently due to their friendship with Sotha. The other guardswomen and the Count's personal guards took turns serving as security personnel, but the two of them were seated behind the Count as part of his entourage.

"How do ladies in waiting and ambassador's aides stand their work?" Asamir complained at the mid-afternoon break.

"They must grow used to extreme boredom and allowing outrages to pass without comment," Anna said. "It was wise of the officials here to insist that all weapons be left outside the room."

"Yes. I would have stabbed the Count half a dozen times by now. Not that the people from Foraoise are much better."

"The Dowager has things well in hand, though," Anna said. "The substantive work is taking place between her and Sotha. And for all that he is a great strategist, I fancy she has taken a few pawns this round."

"How do you even notice such things?"

"It may be boring—it is boring—but things do happen, and it would be wise to be aware of them in case aught should go amiss."

"Better you than me, Madame," Asamir said. "I shall continue to amuse myself by thinking of ways to dispose of these useless people."

"That is not seemly behavior for one who aspires to a religious vocation."

"I cannot imagine that God will disapprove of my contribution to the peopling of Hell."

The negotiations dragged on for a week, but over that time an agreement was forged. The Foraoisians requested that the Count—with the assistance of the Dowager Countess—remain as ambassador, which was an unexpected success. Such a decision required that messengers be sent back to obtain permission for such an appointment, along with a message recommending that Their Majesties issue an invitation to the Foraoisians to send a new ambassador.

Anna and Asamir took advantage of their rank in the guard to appoint themselves to the duty. They forewent a celebratory dinner with the excuse of getting on the road and instead had dinner with the guards of their Realm after crossing the border. And while they were careful not to gossip about their mission, they did assure the guards that peace looked to be in the offing.

Chapter 19

THEY SET OFF early, with the goal of making it to a town with an inn by nightfall. Since there would be little opportunity to change horses en route, they planned to pace their travel so that they could rest their mounts at well-managed stables when possible while still making good time, though they were also prepared to camp if necessary. As they had discovered on their previous expeditions, the villages and towns of Andalucie province were not close to one another. The region was more densely populated near the provincial capital, which was north and west of their route.

"I wonder if the effort to remove the governor has met with as much success as our mission," Asamir said when they stopped to rest their horses after a few hours.

"I would hope so. It should be a straightforward matter, and one assumes that Their Majesties sent sufficient troops to convince the governor that resistance would be futile. But, of course, the man is under the patronage of Her Eminence, which might make the mission something less than straightforward." Anna did not mention magic, but it had occurred to her.

Given the expression on Asamir's face, it had occurred to her as well.

"Perhaps we will hear something at the inn when we stop for the night," Anna added.

The inn was bustling with business when they arrived. That it was market day contributed to this bounty of patronage, but the two guardswomen soon learned that rumors of the governor's downfall had led even locals to spend their hard-earned money on celebratory ale.

"Success, then," Asamir said as they claimed two spaces at the end of a common table.

"So the rumors have it," Anna said.

As they quietly broke bread and sipped ale, they picked up more of the story from the conversations flowing around them. Their Majesties' troops had indeed ridden into the provincial capital and taken charge of the government. A new governor had been put in place, and word—official word, as near as they could tell—had gone out to those displaced of their livelihoods by the deposed governor: your lands and businesses will be restored. In this very town, the son of the late swordsmith had already taken up his forge.

"Apparently those failed outlaws are able to return to honest work," Asamir said under her breath.

"'Twould be good. They would not have lived long in outlawry.'"

But as the two women continued to listen, they began to realize that although the provincial government was now in the hands of a more honorable person, the former governor remained at large. It seemed he had left before the troops arrived at his palace.

"One suspects he received a warning," Anna said. She did not have to specify from whom.

Troops were hunting him across the province. At least one woman claimed to have seen them in pursuit. The crowd's speculations about where he might be found were all over the map. In Foraoise, more than one said, but others said he was making for the Capital, or possibly an abbey, where his eminent patron would protect him.

"I do not think the people of Foraoise would take kindly to him at this point," Anna said. "Though perhaps one of us should return and let them know of this possibility."

"By one of us, you mean me, since you have the ear of Her Majesty. And I shall not return to Foraoise and the Count without much more detailed information than tavern rumors."

And so, after an uncomfortable night in a shared bed in the common room, they left early the next morning, getting on the road ahead of those returning from market. By midday they rode alone in the forest, its silence broken only by the footsteps of their horses and by birds chirping to warn their fellows of riders on the road.

A large flock of birds took suddenly to the air in front of them, squawking loudly. Farther away they heard rustling in the brush. The guardswomen reined in their horses.

"Maybe some of the outlaws have not given up their sordid ways," Asamir said quietly.

"Or perhaps these are newly minted outlaws." Anna let her horse move forward at a slow walk, while Asamir faded off the road to the south—the opposite direction of the noise.

Twenty yards down the trail, a man leaped into the road, brandishing a musket at Anna. "Your horse, lady. I need your horse."

"And so do I, sir. And since she is mine, I do not think I will part with her."

He waved the musket toward her. "Your horse or your life."

At which point Asamir rode out of the trees and ran her horse into the man. He fell to the ground, and the musket flew out of his hands. It went off by itself, fortunately hitting nothing but the top branches of one of the trees. The birds scolded at full throttle.

"My apologies, Madame," Asamir said to Anna. "I did not think that it was loaded." She jumped from her horse and drew her sword, pointing it at the man's throat and preventing him from rising.

Anna, who had not moved, said, "No harm was done. Who do you suppose we have here?"

"Mercy, my ladies. Mercy."

"We might have considered that, had you started with such a plea. But since you began by waving around a musket, I, for one, do not feel merciful. And you, Madame?" Anna followed Asamir's lead and did not use her name.

"I never feel merciful."

"Please, my ladies. I would not have shot you. I am in great need of help. If you assist me, I can reward you. I have powerful friends." His hand moved, as if he would reach beneath his tunic for something. Asamir pressed the point of her sword harder against his throat, and he froze again.

Anna dismounted and walked over to him. "And have you evidence of these powerful friends?"

"A letter. In my purse."

She squatted beside him and lifted his tunic until the purse was visible. His eyes got wide as she pulled out her knife, which she then used to cut the purse strings. She moved away to open it: a few paltry coins, breadcrumbs, and a document rolled in leather binding. This she opened.

"'To whom it may concern,'" Anna read. "'The bearer has been of service to the Realm and should be assisted if possible.' And a signature that might belong to Her Eminence the Hierofante."

"It is Her Eminence," the man said. "She wished to reward me for my service."

"One wonders what kind of service," Asamir said.

"If this document is even a true one. It might be a forgery. Or, more likely, stolen. I note that it does not refer to you by name. It could refer to anyone."

"Please, my ladies."

"He does not argue. Your suspicion that this document was not honestly come by becomes more likely, Madame," Asamir said. "Shall I run him through?"

"Let us tie him up instead. It is possible that he may have more that he wishes to tell us. We will let him think about it."

Asamir pulled her sword back so that the man could scramble to his feet. Anna tied his hands in front of him and hobbled his legs so that he could walk. "I seem to recall that there is a stream not much farther down the road," Anna said. "Perhaps a mile. We can stop there for luncheon." She strung a rope from the bands around the man's hands to her saddle horn and tied it securely. "Best move quickly," she told him as she remounted and urged her horse into a trot.

The man yelped as he felt the first pull of the rope. He lurched from side to side, not quite getting his balance.

Asamir, riding up behind, observed, "He is most regrettably noisy. Are you certain he is worth all this trouble?"

"He obtained that letter somewhere, either from its rightful owner or a forger."

"It's mine," the man protested, though more feebly than before.

"It is even possible that he is telling the truth, which means that he has done something valuable for Her Eminence. We should endeavor to learn the truth."

"But we do need to travel quickly," Asamir said.

"That is also true. Which means we do not have unlimited patience in this matter." Anna urged her mare into a brisker pace, causing her prisoner to stumble.

"Please, please," the man cried out again as he stumbled along. "All right. I took it from the governor as we ran from the soldiers sent to remove him."

"And?"

"And I know where he may be found."

Anna reined in her horse, hopped down, and untied the man's legs.

"And my hands?"

"They stay tied. You have valuable information for Their Majesties' soldiers."

"I will tell you."

"And should we just trust your word and let you go, given that we know you are a thief and a liar? No, you will travel with us for now."

"Those searching for the governor might be anywhere," Asamir observed. "And we have orders."

"If necessary we will turn him over to local authorities in the next village," Anna said.

But that proved unnecessary. As they drew close to the place she had mentioned, Anna heard a sound beyond the chattering birds and the murmur of the stream. She stopped short, causing the man to stumble and curse.

"Quiet." There it was again, a splashing sound. The sound of a horse wading into water for a drink. And then sudden quiet.

"Someone is at the stream," Asamir whispered.

"And they have heard us."

Again, Asamir moved off the trail, while Anna continued forward with her captive. As they reached the water, they saw a lone man with a horse. He looked up, and then said, "Well met."

It was Roland. He gave a shout, and was joined by Jean-Paul and two other guardsmen.

"We have found friends," Anna said loudly, and Asamir rode up as well. "And," she said to Roland, "We have brought you someone you may find of value. He says he knows where the governor may be found."

"Does he, now?" Roland gave the man a close look.

"He might be lying. He lacks honor. He has already admitted to thievery from his former patron. I recommend that you do not accept his word or believe anything he says that cannot be proven."

"No," Roland said. "But perhaps he might lead us to this location in return for his life. There is now a bounty on the former governor's men, since lives were lost as they fled."

"I have not killed anyone," the man protested.

"We can leave that to the magistrates. Or you can lead us to the runaway governor and we will consider letting you go. It is up to you." Roland turned to the other guardsmen. "Go and question this man further. I must talk with this guardswoman." There was no point in asking Jean-Paul to help with the questioning, since he and Asamir had already walked off together, bickering in a happy manner.

"Well met, Madame," Roland said, offering Anna a seat beside him on a fallen tree. She pulled her provision bag from her horse and left the mare loosely tied. Taking the seat next to Roland, she pulled out the fruit and cheese they had brought for the day's luncheon.

"Even more well-met. We have been hunting the former governor for days and are down to eating what we can forage on the fly. What brings you through the woods?"

"We must report back to Their Majesties about the negotiations in Foraoise."

"Are they going poorly?"

"No. In fact, they appear to be very successful. I do not want to speak out of turn until all is done and new pacts are signed, but I am optimistic that we will avoid war. I hear that you were successful in turning the governor out."

"Yes, but the man eluded us, as you have no doubt also heard. Your capture of this man will be useful, if he be telling the truth. I believe the governor could be in this part of the province. I suspect him of trying to make his way to the Capital in the hopes of obtaining the protection of Her Eminence. This stream runs into the River Adabarean. Following the river would take him to the Capital by way of the Abbey of Holy Angels, where Her Eminence often takes her retreats."

"Those are not unreasonable speculations," Anna said. "I took this from our prisoner, who eventually admitted he stole it from the governor." She showed him the letter.

"'Tis delightfully vague, is it not?" Roland said.

"Her Eminence is skilled at disguising and distancing herself, should she need to. I thought to keep it. It might prove useful."

"A wise step, Madame."

One of the other guards came back to report that the man claimed the governor might be found along with some of his troops several miles to the north and east, camped not far from this very stream. They were traveling by foot, according to their informant. "If, he also says, they have not moved on from there. I cannot tell if he is saying that to protect himself in the event no one is there or if what he says is the truth."

"I dare say that there will be evidence of their encampment if they are not present, which would go some way in establishing the veracity of our informant. We will follow the stream bed in that direction, then."

"Good hunting to you," Anna said. "We must make our way on to the Capital."

"Godspeed to you. It would be good if peace can be restored between the two realms."

Anna collared Asamir and Roland Jean-Paul, and the parties separated.

"I should have ridden with them," Asamir said. "They might have need of my sword."

"Or you of Jean-Paul's," Anna said. "We have our own duties. Come. Let us make time while the horses are refreshed."

They had no other adventures of note on the road to the Capital, though they did collect more rumors of the governor's deposing. "People are happy," Asamir said. "We should feel cheered by our part in these matters."

"One hopes they will remain happy with the new governor. I know nothing of her, but far too many nobles named to high positions by Their Majesties are more interested in lining their own pockets than in taking care of the needs of the people they are appointed to govern."

"Spoken like a country woman," Asamir said. "There are many fine people among the nobility. And their duty is to Their Majesties, not the people."

"It should be to both," Anna said.

"Now you sound like the man hanged for exhorting the peasants during the great bread strike."

"Such men would not find followers if those appointed to handle affairs for the Realm took care of the people."

"Hmph," said Asamir. But she did not argue further.

Her Majesty and the foreign minister were delighted with the news from Foraoise. "We were afraid," the Queen said, "that the Count might offend the Foraoisians, but His Majesty felt he was the best man to send, and we could not dissuade him."

"The Dowager Countess has been a great help to him," Anna said.

The foreign minister smiled. "I am glad we insisted that she accompany him."

"It also appears that Barun Meara, the man with whom Her Eminence met in Foraoise, has lost his influence there."

Said the Queen, "That is good news indeed. What has happened?"

"My friend was unwilling to say, and I felt it prudent not to press him. But if he still lives—and that is questionable—he is in some place where he cannot act."

The Queen and her minister exchanged glances. Matters of magic, their expressions said.

"With that man out of the way, it appears that the Foraoisians are as eager as we are to put this matter down to a misunderstanding and re-establish all ties."

"What a relief," said the Queen. "We did not want a winter war on that border. There are enough problems on our southern one."

After a brief meeting with His Majesty, the Queen provided Anna with a letter inviting the Queen of Foraoise to send a new envoy as soon as possible. She instructed Anna to leave at once.

Asamir was to follow with a party of guards and servants to staff the embassy.

"Please return as soon as the negotiations are concluded," Her Majesty told Anna. "We want to know that all is well."

The captain grumbled that there were other soldiers in the Realm capable of running errands for Her Majesty. "It appears that you are no longer necessary to the negotiations."

Anna privately agreed, but said, "It is a compliment to our company that Her Majesty entrusts us with such delicate matters."

The captain said, "If the dispute between the realms ends peacefully, it will not matter. But I would feel more comfortable if all my senior people were home training and working with the juniors, in the event that diplomacy should fail."

Anna's trip back to Foraoise—really, she was becoming far too familiar with the road—was uneventful. She saw no sign of Roland and Jean-Paul, nor of any of their men, nor of any of those belonging to the former governor. Rumors she heard at various inns along the way suggested the former governor remained a fugitive, but all speculation as to where he might be seemed to be the product of vivid imaginations and not fact.

She had barely arrived in Foraoise before she was hustled off along with the Count and the Dowager for an audience with their Queen. Anna presented Their Majesties' request for an envoy.

"Please convey our regards to our royal kin in your Realm and tell them that our ambassador will be returning forthwith. We are much pleased to have this affair settled amicably. Thank you for your efforts in this matter, guardswoman."

The final negotiations were concluded on the day Asamir arrived with a troop of diplomatic guards and a skeleton crew of embassy staff. The remainder of the staff was expected to follow within the week. The Count expressed great displeasure in the small staff—"Only two secretaries. An outrage!"—but the Dowager calmed him. "The others will be here soon, my dear. You would not have wanted to wait until a complete staff could be put together."

The Count was heard to say he did not comprehend why they could not have all traveled immediately. "It is clear," said Asamir, "that he has never had to assemble a group of people to do anything. I was amazed that the minister's people put together this group as quickly as they did."

"The Count has never managed anything for himself and, if we are all in luck, he will never do so," Anna said. "I must back to the Capital tomorrow. Have you more duties, or will you ride with me?"

"My duties were only to deliver people, and I have done so. I have no desire to spend any more time in the company of diplomats. Tell me again why all this was preferable to a nice, clean war."

After several days in the company of the Count, Anna was hard-pressed to find an answer.

Chapter 20

"I GROW TIRED of this road," Asamir said. "Given your influence with Her Majesty, can you not arrange a mission for us that does not require travel to Foraoise?"

"Her Majesty did mention trouble on our southern border. Perhaps our next assignment will be in the opposite direction."

"Is war brewing there? It would not be so bad to fight in the south in the winter."

"It rains there then," Anna said. "One hopes the diplomats are working to avert such a result."

"For a guardswoman, you are amazingly uninterested in the glories of battle."

"For someone who asserts a religious vocation, you are amazingly interested in killing people."

"God is on our side," Asamir replied.

On the third day, they decided to take their midday break by the stream where they had met Roland and Jean-Paul on their previous return. As they approached it, they heard the sounds of other riders, apparently traveling along the stream. Dismounting, the two guardswomen left their horses by a patch of weeds and concealed themselves among the trees on the bank. And once again, the other travelers proved to be Roland and Jean-Paul. They appeared to be traveling alone.

"Let us surprise them," Asamir breathed in Anna's ear.

"Let us not. They have been hunting fugitives, and mayhap their tempers are short. Well met," she called out as the men drew close. She stepped from the trees.

"'Tis amazing how often we meet on these paths, given how much trouble we are having finding those we seek," Roland replied. "But well met indeed. We are traveling back to the Capital. And you?"

"The same."

"Then we will have pleasant company, if we can convince you to follow our route. We thought to track the stream and the river."

"'Tis a slightly longer route," said Anna, "but while we need to make a report, an extra day will not make a great deal of difference. Why do you take it?"

"We are ordered home, though the deposed governor has eluded us. We thought to take this route to give ourselves one last opportunity to find him."

"And if we do, two more swords will be of value," Jean-Paul added. "He is said to be traveling with companions."

"So the prisoner we delivered to you before lied about the man's whereabouts," Asamir said.

"We found some evidence that the governor had been where the man said, but not as recently as he suggested. A rain washed out any evidence of the route he had taken from there, though we are certain that he did not continue in this direction at that time," Roland said.

"But he has not traveled to Foraoise or to the northwest, which leaves this as his most likely direction," Jean-Paul added.

"Perhaps we will have a battle," Asamir said with enthusiasm.

"Perhaps we will not find him at all," Roland said. "I fear he is safely at the Hierofante's refuge at the Abbey of Holy Angels."

They lunched by the stream and then began their trek along its bank. Asamir and Jean-Paul fell into their usual banter, but Roland was quiet, and Anna let him be. She entertained herself by examining the foliage, trying to commit to memory the shapes of the leaves. Few plants were flowering this late in the summer, and some were starting to lose their green color. Fall was not far off.

They reached the river bank late on the next day, having seen no sign of any other people. "I have not been this way in some time," Anna said, "but I seem to recall a town not too many miles distant."

"Yes," Roland said. "It has a garrison as well. But it is too far to reach before dark."

An isolated cove near where the stream emptied into the river provided a good location for a night's rest. Since the sun had not yet disappeared, they took advantage of the river's depth and went swimming. Asamir and Jean-Paul turned the outing into their usual mock-argument flirtation, but all of them found the relaxation refreshing.

Despite the picnic air that lasted into their dinner hour, which came with a fresh-caught fish, they took turns on watch over the night. "There is always the possibility that the governor will come this way, and even should he not, there are others in these parts who bear watching," Roland said.

And, indeed, in the hour just before dawn, when Anna was on watch, she heard sounds coming from back up the stream.

She woke her companions with whispers, and it was only a few minutes before the four of them had hidden themselves a few hundred feet above the mouth of the stream. They were soon rewarded with the sight of two men, one the former governor.

They were afoot and moved in the footsore manner of those more accustomed to traveling by horseback or in carriages. The man's efforts to avoid Roland and his men might have been successful up to now, but they had come at a cost.

"We are almost to the river, your grace," the man said.

"Good, good. I will rest there. You will walk toward the town and find us a bargeman to ferry us to the Capital."

"No need for that," said Roland, stepping out from his cover. "We will escort you both. Greybonne, you are bound to my custody by order of Their Majesties."

Jean-Paul, Anna, and Asamir also stepped out, and the governor's man threw up his hands in surrender. The governor was not so resigned. He drew his sword at once.

"There are four of us, sir," said Roland.

"Of course, 'tis a trap. Just what one would expect of the whelp of the de Barthes. Instead of confronting me for yourself, you use political means to your ends."

Jean-Paul drew his own sword with a curse, but Roland raised a hand. "The insults of a man who has betrayed every trust ever given him are not worthy of such a response. Sheathe that sword and hand it to me, sir, and we will handle this matter properly."

Instead, the deposed governor jumped forward, swinging his sword toward Roland's neck. But he had some distance to cover, and Roland had not stood still. He drew as he moved directly into the governor, using his sword to cover his head and side in case he had not moved quickly enough.

But he had. Greybonne's sword struck only air, and the effort left him off balance. Roland brought his own sword around his head and laid it on the side of Greybonne's neck, nicking him slightly. "Come, you are taken, sir. Do not force my hand."

Greybonne let out a roar—sounding more like one of the great cats who roamed the northeast woods than a human being—and shouted, "You dare to draw my blood!" He raised his sword.

Roland let Greybonne smack his sword aside and easily evaded a cut aimed at his arm by raising his blade high. Greybonne stumbled as his cut missed. "You are tired, and I am your junior by some twenty years," Roland said. "And even should you succeed in killing me, three of the best sword fighters in the Realm await you. It is no shame to surrender."

"Should I surrender to be murdered on the road?" Greybonne said, though he did not attack. He was breathing hard.

"Give Monsieur de Barthes your blade, and we will protect your life until we deliver you to the Capital," Anna said. "You will be able to petition your patron there for more assistance."

She had thought that might calm him, but instead it appeared to enrage him. Greybonne launched another attack on Roland, stabbing for the center of his body. Roland kept his hands high and dropped the tip of his blade to block the attack. Again he brought his sword around toward Greybonne's neck, but the man had managed to recover enough to manage a clumsy block. He raised his sword above his head and struck down toward Roland.

And this time Roland raised his own sword up so that the tip was at the man's throat. Greybonne tried to stop, but it was too late, and the blade went through his neck. He dropped his own sword and tried to grasp at his neck, then fell to the ground as Roland pulled back his sword. Greybonne's blood made a small river on the ground and he lay still.

Roland sighed. "I did not want to do that."

"He forced your hand," said Anna.

"Mercy, sir," cried the governor's man, dropping to his knees.

"You surrendered, did you not? I am not in the habit of killing those who do as they are told. Find something in which to wrap up this corpse, and we will take it and you to the garrison in Pontmarche. And if you tell the truth about how this happened, how the man attacked rather than surrender, I will put in a good word for you."

The man nodded and began unwrapping the blanket he was using to carry his few belongings. In a short period of time, the body was rolled up in that and tied together. Roland and the man threw it across his horse, who held steady despite the smell of blood. The gelding, like the rest of them, had seen enough battle to be inured to its evils.

Chapter 21

THEY REACHED PONTMARCHE town in the early afternoon, and took the body and their prisoner to the local garrison. The commander there was one Elene Delatour, whom Anna and Asamir knew well because she had served with them in the Andrean Guard before the Realm had been reunited.

"You could not take him alive?" she asked on seeing the governor's body.

"Alas, we could not, though we made every effort to do so," Anna said. "Even though he was outnumbered, he drew his sword and attacked Monsieur de Barthes, who was obliged to defend himself. It was a fair, if foolish, fight."

Their prisoner, perhaps mindful of Roland's promise to speak for him, not to mention conscious of the gallows he had seen as they came into the town, confirmed Anna's statement.

Commander Delatour sighed. "I suppose we had best crate him up and ship him to the Capital. Given the rumors that the royal audit showed the man was stealing royal funds as well as exploiting and mistreating the people in the province, it is important to provide Their Majesties with absolute proof of his death."

Anna nodded. "That is why we did not bury him, but brought him to you, unpleasant a task though it was. The matter of this man's abuse of his authority must be laid to rest."

"And in such a way that no one assumes M. de Barthes acted out of personal malice," the commander said, looking at Roland.

"I would never let my personal feelings interfere with my duty," Roland said stiffly.

"Of course not. We will send the corpse and your prisoner to the Capital on the morrow's barge. Perhaps you will want to accompany them?"

"'Twould be a good plan," Anna said. "We have ridden the road many times over the past month. Another form of transport would be pleasant."

As they began to leave, Elene pulled Anna aside. "Know you that the Hierofante's Guard are found in our streets. I have no authority over them. It will take no time at all for them to discover the death of the governor who, as we all know, was Her Eminence's man. Ware those guards."

"I thank you," Anna said.

"It is possible that some of them will take the barge tomorrow as well."

"Indeed. Perhaps we would be best off to stay with the road and to the north of the river."

"It is terrible but true that we must always consider the politics of a situation, not just the right of it," the commander said.

The four repaired to a tavern for a late luncheon. "It would be best if I traveled with the man's corpse," Roland said. "I would not want anyone to think I meant to hide from the action I was forced to take. And since my connection to him is well-known, despite my own discretion on the matter, I must assume some will make inferences."

"Travel by barge would be much faster as well," Asamir pointed out. "If we take the north road, we must ride past the fork where a tributary turns to the capital, for there is no bridge until we reach the main road. The river is much too wide and full to ford."

"But travel with the Hierofante's guards might prove most uncomfortable," Anna said. "And we would not be able to leave should things become extreme."

"We can chuck them all in the river," Jean-Paul said.

"And be hanged on our return. That is why I say we must consider the problem carefully."

They were still arguing the issue when they stepped out of the tavern and met a handful of Hierofante's guards, under the leadership of a lieutenant named Verlaine, known to them all.

"Well met," he said.

Jean-Paul glared at him and Asamir looked as if she was coming up with the right response, which would not have included words of pleasure. Anna said, "As always. But we have business to attend to, so we cannot stop to chat."

"We also have business, and it is with you, and particularly with M. de Barthes, who has killed a man."

Jean-Paul jumped in, "In the performance of his duty and in self defense, as you well know."

"Do we?"

"God's truth you do," Jean-Paul said.

"I will speak for myself," Roland said. "You know well that I am working on direct orders from Their Majesties. I have fulfilled my orders, which is no crime, and as you are not my commander nor the authority in this place, I have no duty to answer to you."

"But you are outnumbered here," Verlaine said. "And even if that does not deter you, given the reputation of those with whom you travel, I assume you do not want to cause a disturbance in these streets."

Asamir put her hand on her hilt, and Jean-Paul seemed ready to erupt in an exclamation of his willingness to fight anyone anywhere anytime. Anna, wishing to avoid both a fight and a surrender, neither of which would be good so far from the Capital, jumped in. "And we are also under the protection of Her Eminence." She drew the safe-conduct from her pocket and held it where the commander could read it. Roland, following her lead, moved up so that he could block the man if he decided to grab the paper.

"How did you come by this? Did you steal it off the governor's body?"

"Are you questioning my honor, sir?" Anna said. She did not move her hand to her hilt, but her voice carried that threat.

"But why would Her Eminence give you such a document?"

"Perhaps you should ask her. Though I suspect she might be displeased that her words were questioned. You will note that it also covers my companions." Out of the corner of her eye, Anna saw Commander Delatour walking up the street.

Verlaine also saw the commander. "I would, of course, never question an order by Her Eminence. Please, continue on your way. Though it remains highly suspicious that M. de Barthes found it impossible to avoid killing an old enemy."

"Perhaps you should remember that the supposed enemy was also a fugitive from justice." Anna packed away the safe-conduct. "By your leave, sir."

The Hierofante's Guard parted, and the four of them walked along the street.

Once they had distanced themselves from the troops, Anna whispered to Roland, "I think we should give out that we are taking the barge, but instead slip out of town after dark and take the road."

He nodded. "Perhaps we should reserve an inn, and sup there."

They did so, taking an inn that was on the edge of town. A pair of Hierofante's guards came in for a time, but left after seeing the four of them lifting their glasses. Roland and Jean-Paul went out to relieve themselves and found no guards had been posted. The four were among the last to retire. One after another they slipped out to take advantage of the outhouse, but did not return. Retrieving their horses from the stable and taking separate paths out of town, they met up at a prearranged place on the north bank of the river.

"I believe we are safe, but we should ride on as far as we can tonight," Anna said. "They are not fools and will send someone this way if we do not board in the morning."

"You were wise to take that safe-conduct," Asamir said. "It may prove useful to us again."

"I would not want to rely on it too heavily," Anna said. "So we should ride quickly."

They stopped once they were well-past the fork where one part of the river flowed to the Capital while the other continued northwest. It was just past dawn, and they rested for several hours before moving on.

Jean-Paul and Asamir bickered happily as they rode, but Roland was again quiet. Anna left him to his thoughts. That evening, after they stopped to dine—and, indeed, caught a fish in the river on which to make the meal—Roland shared his worries.

"People will believe I killed the man for revenge or my own gain."

"People will always believe what they wish to believe. I was there, and I know you only did what was necessary at the time. And the world is better off without him."

"True enough. I have no regrets, but I dislike being the subject of such speculation."

"If you act in this world, people will mistrust your motives, no matter what they may be. You can only be true to yourself."

"And to my true friends."

"I wonder," said Anna, "why he attacked just after I reminded him of his friend and patron."

"Perhaps he feared that she would disown him, seeing how far he had fallen. That he was stealing from Their Majesties as well as those he governed might well have doomed him even in Her Eminence's eyes."

At mid-morning on the second day, as they drew close to the main road north and the bridge over the river where they had once fought, they came upon an old woman walking in their direction. A large dog—it looked to be part wolf—accompanied her.

They slowed their horses, and Anna called out, "Good morrow."

The woman turned. "Aye, so it is."

Anna tried not to allow shock to show in her face. It was the old witch she and Asamir had consulted during the unnatural rain. Her home had been some miles from here, though near the road north, but Anna knew it to be her. Now that her memories had returned, Anna was well aware that the woman was also the healer who had saved her mother when Susanne was born and who had mentored her sister Berthe. From the corner of her eye she saw Asamir make the religious gesture and heard her murmur a prayer. Her friend had also recognized the old woman.

Anna's effort to control her expression must have been unsuccessful, for the witch gave her a knowing smile. "And what might bring together King's and Queen's guards on the forest road?"

"We met through happenstance," Anna said, forestalling any comments from the others.

"As I have met you," the woman said.

Anna took her meaning to be the opposite. "Have you aught to tell us, Madame?" She remembered that Berthe had used that title for her.

The witch liked her use of the word. She smiled at Anna and met her eyes. Anna nodded back, a slight acknowledgment of the fact that they knew each other. No one else seemed to notice the exchange.

"You will find more troubles when you return home. It is possible that you will need to call on the forces she"—and here the woman pointed at Asamir, who made the religious gesture twice in succession—"if not she alone, fears so much."

"Magic, mean you, Madame?" Roland said.

Asamir made the gesture once more. Jean-Paul looked uncertain.

"It is as good a word as any. And as dangerous. You are dealing in matters far beyond your ken, Guardsman," she added.

"Our duties lead us down difficult paths," Anna said. "But we are sworn to the Realm and must do what we must."

"Indeed. Even those of us who have taken no such oaths must do what we must. Ride on, guards of the Realm. Ride on."

She did not disappear, but they nonetheless found themselves some distance from her in short order, as if time had slowed and then speeded up. Jean-Paul began to ask what had happened and was shushed by Roland. "Best we forget all that," he said.

Anna had no plans to forget, but it was certainly not the time to discuss magic. Asamir appeared to be praying. They all rode on. Anna and Roland were in the lead, while Asamir and Jean-Paul brought up the rear. For once their voices were quiet. The encounter had disturbed them.

As they rode forward out of earshot of the others, Roland said, "I believe you know something of that old woman. No, do not protest," he went on as Anna attempted to interrupt. "I am not asking directly, but only letting you know my thoughts. I do not know all you learned in your travels to Foraoise and what other information you may have, but from all indications, we may have need of a witch. And that one, I am certain, is such, though I do not know her power."

"Do you not fear the uncanny ways, sir? The church condemns them, and it is disagreement on that point that makes our relationship with Foraoise so difficult even in the best of times."

"It is disagreement over who controls the mines of Airgead that makes our relationship with Foraoise so difficult. All else is excuse. As for the uncanny, I respect it as I would any powerful weapon. I do fear the harm it can do in the wrong hands, but I think our country's prohibitions on it also cause great harm. People will engage in the prohibited if it gives them advantage, but all involved will lie for fear of excommunication or even the pyre."

"So you do not believe treating with a witch imperils your immortal soul?"

"It appears to me that there are people in good odor with the church who pose much more danger to me and mine than those who understand the old ways. And you? Are you concerned about the church's position?"

"I do not yearn to be an abbess," Anna said. "But those old ways have other dangers. How are we who lack understanding of those matters to judge what to do?"

"As we always do, Madame. Trust in our instincts and our skills, and remain mindful of our duties to their majesties and the Realm."

Chapter 22

THEY RETURNED TO a Capital that seemed strangely quiet. It was early afternoon on market day, and, since it was close to the peak of harvest season, the farmers' stalls were piled high. But there were few people shopping, and they appeared reluctant to do more than buy the necessities and melt back into their homes.

"I have never before come through the market this time of year without having to dismount and lead my horse," Asamir observed.

The streets where the cobblers and dressmakers did business were empty, and several shops were closed. A lone footman carried a small package. No children tarried in the streets, and even the taverns were quiet, though perhaps they would become more rowdy after dark.

The four parted uneasily, with promises to investigate this unnatural calm and to meet late that evening at the Maudite. Anna and Asamir left the men at the gates to their barracks and went to report to their captain.

The captain seemed distracted, as if she were barely listening to what they were saying. Finally, Anna said, "We have averted war and assisted in the removal of an unworthy from a position of power. While the death of Greybonne was regrettable, it was unavoidable, and while I am aware we may have created more tension with the Hierofante and her guard, we still expected more satisfaction from our report. Instead, we find not just a nervous city, but a nervous Guard. What has happened here?"

"No one is sure," said the captain. "But there are rumors that the Queen is...not well."

Anna thought immediately of the witch. How could she have known? But here were her words made true. "You do not know for certain?"

"There are no reports out of the palace, but people come and go there with worried looks on their faces. I have not been summoned to meet with her for many days, and no one has asked if you have returned. I am, of course, very pleased at your report—despite the unfortunate death of Greybonne—and I am sure Her Majesty will be as well. But I fear you will not get to meet with her to tell her the good news. I will, of course, send a messenger at once."

Cecile, dressed as if she were coming for a lesson, appeared at the barracks within an hour of the messenger's departure. Her manner was subdued. "Madame," she said to Anna when they were alone on the training ground. "Her Majesty wishes to see you this evening. But you may have some difficulty in obtaining that audience."

"Is someone...powerful controlling admittance to her presence? The King? Or perhaps...."

"No, no. It is not like that. The problem is her well-being. The midwife has confined her to bed and keeps telling her to let others manage her affairs. Though I do not think the rest is helping her at all. She seems a shadow of herself. I have never seen her this way."

"Do they fear for the baby?"

"Madame, I worry that they fear for the Queen, though no one says aught to me. Her Majesty told me to summon you after the message sent by your captain was delivered. But the midwife said she should not see anyone, and both the Lady of Honor, who supervises us all, and Her Majesty's personal maid, who scares us all, told me to tell you not to come, that your presence would trouble her even though you have good news."

205

"Indeed, while I do not want to contribute to her ill-health, she needs to hear my report. I will not stay long. Is there a way to her rooms where I will not be seen by the midwife or anyone else who could block me? Surely you know of some such method."

Cecile smiled for the first time. "I think I may be able to assist you, Madame."

Anna set out for the palace in the early evening. Cecile had been told that she would be the page on duty in the Queen's room after dinner. The Queen would not be alone—Her Majesty was never alone—but Cecile thought she would be able to let her know that Anna was coming and to make certain that she was awake for their meeting. She would leave a window open for Anna to use for entry.

When Anna came in through the open window, a large one that required only a slight step over the sill, she saw that the ladies-in-waiting were gathered around the royal bed. Cecile, standing at the foot, was the only one who noticed her entry; all others were too focused on Her Majesty to hear the slight noise that she made.

The Queen's skin looked ashen, but she was sitting up in bed. "Enough of this herbal tea. We have need of something stronger to sustain us."

"But Your Majesty, the midwife…."

"A pox on the midwife. Bring wine."

"Your Majesty," Cecile said loudly, "Anna d'Gart of the Queen's Guard to see you."

The others around the bed turned to look, and her maid—that formidable lady who had been at the Queen's side since she was a babe in arms—moved in Anna's direction.

"Most excellent," said the Queen. "Please approach, Madame, and report. You," she pointed to the formidable one, "go and fetch wine. The rest of you give way for the guardswoman. Go and leave us be."

The formidable one scowled at Anna and gave Cecile a look that did not bode well for the page, but she did not stop Anna from approaching. Despite the order to fetch wine, she did not leave. The ladies-in-waiting backed away from the bed, though they stayed in the room.

Anna came and knelt near the head of the bed so she could be close to the Queen without looming over her. Up close, the Queen's color was even more gray than it had looked from afar. Her hair was damp from sweat, though the room was chilly. And she smelled of something not quite foul, but off—a yeasty odor that did not sit well with Anna.

"Your Majesty, I am sorry to see that you are not well. But I knew you wished news of the latest actions in Foraoise and of the problems in Andalucie province. "

"Yes. Please let me know everything that has happened."

"Your Majesty," the formidable woman said, "this will tire you."

"Mayhap. But it is our duty to know what transpires in our realm," the Queen said. "The guardswoman is mindful; she will take care not to tire me. Step back and allow her to speak with me in private."

The woman bowed and left the room. Anna wondered whether she went to fetch wine or reinforcements.

"Thank you for your trust, Your Majesty. When I left at the end of the last sennight, all was well between our realm and that of Foraoise and seemed likely to remain so. The Dowager Countess has taken charge, as you foresaw, and the embassy is beginning anew. But the death of the former governor of Andalucie province may provoke more difficulties with Her Eminence." Anna dropped her voice as she said these last words.

The Queen closed her eyes as she listened to Anna. The guardswoman noted her pallor, her fatigue. "Your Majesty, I fear I am tiring you. Is there someone to whom I can report that you think trustworthy? The foreign minister, perhaps?"

"No, no. I will want to confer with her, for even though this may not be a matter of foreign affairs at this point, she is my wisest advisor. I do want you to meet with her as well, but I must be involved, especially if there is the possibility of internal strife once again."

"It is possible that Greybonne had become a liability to Her Eminence, and she may not care about his fate. But we did find it necessary to elude her guards."

"All the more reason why we must take great care here, and why I must be involved."

"What is all this?" The woman who walked into the room made no pretense of obeisance. "Your Majesty, did I not tell you to rest and to forego any meetings?"

"You did, but since your order did not also make the rest of the world stop, matters have occurred that need my attention."

"You will be unable to attend to them in any manner if you do not follow my directions."

"I will promise to rest if you will give me something more than herbal tea to drink. And you must allow me to meet with my advisors tomorrow in the post-noon. Guardswoman, please return then."

The midwife—for it was she, fetched, Anna was certain, from her own rest to insure that the Queen was not unduly disturbed—said, "I will allow a sip of brandy in your tea. But this guardswoman must leave now."

Anna got to her feet, bowed to both the Queen and the midwife, and left the room. But she remained outside the chamber, waiting for the midwife to leave as well. The woman came out shortly, told one of her assistants what to take to the Queen, and glared again at Anna.

"Madame, I would speak with you privately as well," said Anna.

"If you are endeavoring to get around my orders for Her Majesty's health, it will do you no good," the woman said.

"It is a different matter."

"Come with me, then."

The midwife had quarters not far from the Queen's chambers. As they entered, she sent a servant for tea for them both. "Madame, if you are asking for my services for yourself, you should be aware that I have agreed to take no other patients at this time."

"That is not my purpose." Anna was not sure how to go on. The midwife had been present at some of her meetings with the Queen, and she felt sure the woman was deeply in the Queen's confidence. But she was reluctant to mention her fears. "Madame, I last saw the Queen a fortnight ago, and at that time she appeared to be in the best of health. I am, of course, no expert, but it seemed to me then that her condition agreed with her." Anna, being the oldest of five and experienced in the birthing of pigs and other farm animals, was, in fact, quite knowledgeable about pregnancy, but it did not seem appropriate to mention that to a professional midwife.

"Guardswoman, I know the Queen values you, so I will answer you. This change came on very suddenly, in the past sennight, and it worries me a great deal. It is not a usual pattern in these matters."

"Do you suspect any...any kind of influence here?" Anna could not bring herself to say *magic* to a midwife trusted by royalty.

The woman looked at Anna carefully. "I do not know, but the change was so sudden. I have supervised all of her meals and know that she has not eaten anything untoward. Of course, women have different responses to child bearing and problems within royal families are not unknown, but...."

Anna thought the expression on her face finished the sentence. The midwife did not dare to say the word "magic" either, and perhaps she did not even want to think it, but the idea still hung in the air. "Madame, I might know of someone who

209

could give you some advice, if the problem with Her Majesty is…unnatural."

Now the midwife looked scared. She made the religious gesture, took a deep breath, and said, "I would take any advice or action that might save the life of the Queen and her babe."

Anna realized as she left that she was as frightened as the midwife. She, too, would take whatever action was necessary to save the life of the Queen and the babe to come, but there was no question now that she must deal with this magical problem on her own, without any overt direction from anyone else. It was not the way she wanted to act, but the survival of the Queen—and the Realm—seemed to leave her no choice.

Though perhaps she could ask for guidance from her sister Berthe, who was, after all, a midwife herself. Perhaps her skill would be enough. And she would not frighten the others the way the witch would.

But what if her skill was not enough? Her father had said they thought of calling in the witch, but had not, because Berthe's healing had been sufficient. That implied that her sister could handle most routine accidents and illnesses, but that even she asked for help when the situation proved more dire. Even if Her Majesty was only suffering from a normal malady of pregnancy, her symptoms indicated it was a far from routine one. And if it were brought on by uncanny means, it would take power equal to that of the one who had done it to repair the damage, if it could be done at all.

As best Anna knew, Berthe was simply a good midwife and healer. She might have some minor magics, but she herself would consult the witch when faced with things beyond her ken. This whole situation reeked of high-level magic, and someone of minor skill would be out of her league. It would be like sending Susanne to command an army.

For the Good of the Realm

You are afraid of the witch and of getting too close to the uncanny, Anna scolded herself. But you have no choice. There is no one else to do it.

Chapter 23

WITH RESPONSIBILITY WEIGHING heavily on her, Anna made her way to the Maudite. Her own wine was better than theirs, but spending time with Asamir, Roland, and Jean-Paul might ease her soul, and perhaps the atmosphere of the tavern, however raucous, would provide some relief from her convoluted thoughts. She hoped her friends were still there, since she was arriving somewhat later than the appointed hour.

The sounds she heard as she approached the Maudite confirmed her expectation of rowdiness. A drunken chorus was butchering a popular drinking song, with the taunts of listeners frequently drowning them out. Anna paused at the entrance, wondering whether she did, in fact, wish to enter. As she stood there, she heard footsteps behind her and turned to find Roland. "Madame," he said, "our friends have already abandoned us for their usual pursuits. The crowd inside is unrelenting. Let us go somewhere quieter and converse. My rooms are not far."

He had never invited her to his rooms before. Their dalliances had always been in hers. "So long as you have decent drink, Monsieur, that is an excellent offer."

"Madame," he replied in a tone of mock hurt pride, "even in the leanest of times, my wine is always better than that served at the Maudite." He offered an arm, and she took it.

Roland's rooms turned out to be about half of the size of Anna's, which perhaps explained why he had never invited her to them before. They sat on simple stools at a table that appeared to do second duty as a desk; a quill pen, a penknife, and a small

bottle of ink sat in one corner next to two bound books. As Roland
fetched wine and glasses, Anna picked up the books. Gold letter-
ing on the smaller proclaimed it to be a collection of poems by
Eleanor d'Oc. The larger was unmarked. Anna, suspecting that it
might be a diary or commonplace book, did not open it.

Roland returned with bread and cheese as well as the wine,
which was, as promised, quite good. "What do you think of d'Oc's
poems?" Anna asked.

"They are fine meditations for a member of the Guard,"
he said. "She was captain of the Andrean Guard before the
reunification."

Anna nodded. "I met her once. My mother served under her
and had naught but good words for her leadership. But my mother is not one for written words, so I had to discover her writing on
my own. I agree with you about the value of such poems for those
who spend their lives in the fighting services. Though I know of
few guards who spend their time reading."

"Alas, 'tis my experience as well. While I find the reflective
life to be a good balance for the way of a warrior, reading and
study are not a common practice among my fellows. But still, I
hope that one day my own words will move some future guard
members."

"Is that what the other book contains? Your own verse?"

He nodded, but as he did not appear to be disposed to share
his work, Anna did not press him further. Perhaps he would, in
time, let her read some of it.

"I have heard that Her Majesty is ill," he said.

Anna nodded. "Yes. The midwife is concerned, as are her
closest ladies-in-waiting. However, Her Majesty continues to insist on being consulted in matters of state."

"Her Majesty is a woman who knows her duty in all things.
But how serious is this matter?" He hesitated, and lowered his
voice. "Does it have anything to do with the suggestions made by
the witch we met on the road?"

"I fear that it might, but hope that it is nothing more than the vagaries of pregnancy. Some women have more difficulty than others." Anna did not want to tell him that she was planning to seek out the witch. The fewer people who were involved in uncanny matters, the better.

"I, too, hope that it is nothing more and that she will soon be put to rights. But it seems to have had a chilling effect on the capital."

"Perhaps some of the discomfort we feel around us is also due to the anger of Her Eminence," Anna said. "She has been foiled in her attempts to use the Foraoise Realm to stir up trouble here and must be unhappy over the death of the former governor and, for that matter, the replacement of him by someone not in her camp of followers."

"That is possible, though I suspect it is primarily the failure of her efforts to use Foraoise to cause internal strife that is her biggest concern. Your suggestion earlier that Greybonne did not expect any help from her strikes me as sound. Still, my captain has warned me to avoid Hierofante's guards as I can. They have filed a complaint about my killing of the man, but the captain has chosen to reject it. He tells me both he and His Majesty have full confidence in me and my actions."

"I would say you have Her Majesty's confidence as well. But a powerful person thwarted can still strike out. We cannot let ourselves be guided by the fact that some will hate us for doing our duty to the Realm."

"Our many duties," Roland said. "Not just to the Realm, but mine to the King and yours to the Queen. And the other responsibilities. Our duties to our families and our fellows in the guard. And to the good of the people of the Realm, who should not have to suffer because of the ill deeds of the powerful."

"Heady thoughts, for a guardsman. Is that what you write in your poems? Such meditations might be too powerful to be published in wider form."

He blushed so deeply that even his dark skin looked rosy. "My words on such things are not yet well formed."

"Do you write of other topics, the glory of battle, perhaps?"

"And the blood of it. And the difficulties of keeping one's honor when hacking about with a sword." He paused, sipped more wine, and reached out for her hand. "Sometimes I write of love."

"Surely you must share those works. I am convinced they would have seductive powers."

"Someday I will show them to you, when I am certain they are finished. For now, I will rely on simpler methods of seduction." He kissed her hand, and then, standing up, brought her to her feet. "My bed is more comfortable than these stools."

A night in the arms of a good and willing lover provided the balm to her mind that Anna most needed, but on awakening just before dawn the next morning, she found herself once again worried about the uncanny matters into which she had stumbled.

She began to make plans to seek out the witch.

In the afternoon, she again visited the Queen and joined in her meeting with the foreign minister. Anna repeated her concerns about Her Eminence and the further difficulties she could cause. But the Queen was very tired. After fifteen minutes, the midwife entered the room to shoo them out. "I will speak more with the guardswoman," the minister told the Queen as they left, "and we will think on what to do."

But once they had removed themselves to the minister's rooms, the woman sighed and told Anna, "While I am concerned about the actions you report" — even in private and even with her rank, she did not mention the Hierofante by name or title — "I am even more worried about Her Majesty's health. If something should happen to her, and particularly should she leave no heir, we could see a return of the great divide, especially if there were an attempt by the Meloran faction to proclaim His Majesty ruler over the entire Realm. This time it could devolve into all-out civil war. I speak frankly to you, for I know that you come from an Andrean family, as do I. The survival of Her Majesty is vital to true reunification."

Anna said—with great care—"My lady, you know that I am country-raised. I know of someone who might be willing to advise the midwife on these matters, and the midwife has said she would be grateful of such advice. But that assistance requires more financial resources than I have available. I am certain that Her Majesty would finance such a venture, but I do not like to ask her in her current condition. Is there a way you could help?"

The minister looked at her closely. Anna knew she was treading on the edges of heresy—the word country hinted at old faiths, and the minister was of the Church. The silence grew. Finally, the minister said, "It seems someone"—and her voice showed she suspected who that someone might be—"is willing to risk their immortal soul. Why should I be more circumspect? If it will save the Queen, I will shower you in gold."

"It is she whose assistance I seek who will desire the shower, particularly since she will become visible if she undertakes such action. Her greed will outweigh her fear, or at least I hope it will. But I do not think I can prevail on her to act solely for the good of the Realm."

"There are few who will do such things. I will send some funds to you by the hand of the Queen's page before the day is over."

Anna went to the guard barracks to beg leave of the Captain. In the interest of protecting others, she used the health of her father as a reason for the leave. "Given the severity of his injuries, I should make certain he is healing well."

The Captain was not fooled. "I will note your leave as such and let others believe it so. That is likely for the best. But given the uncertain times, I know you are traveling on royal business. Do you need anyone to travel with you?"

"No," Anna said, abandoning pretense. "This is not a matter for anyone but myself."

Asamir proved as prescient as the captain. "You are going to seek out the witch," she said. "You will need help."

"Even were that true, 'tis best to limit the number of people who have such dealings. And other matters may arise here from the actions of Her Eminence. Best you be available should that happen. Only a few of us know the whole truth and the Captain will need your assistance should anything occur."

Asamir had to admit that was true. "But the Captain knows the facts. She will be able to call on others."

"But likely she will be unable, or perhaps unwilling, to tell them all that she knows. We are dealing in matters that frighten most, and with people who can be very dangerous. We must take care with whom we share what we know. I will feel safer if you are on hand to assist the Captain. Best that there be someone who knows the truth but is not tainted by direct dealings with ma... with the old ways." She amended her words just in time to keep Asamir from making the gesture.

"I will take on that duty," Asamir said. Her response had the air of an oath.

Cecile arrived with the promised funds just before Anna set out to meet Roland at the Maudite. "I am certain that you are undertaking another adventure," the girl said. "Please take me with you."

"Child, you must stay and attend Her Majesty. She will have need of you."

"I am one of many who attend her, and I lack all healing skills. I would not be missed."

"Her Majesty is fond of you. I am certain that you lighten her days. There will be plenty of time for adventure in your life in the years to come."

"Not if my father succeeds in finding me a husband," Cecile said.

"If that looks imminent, I will help you avoid such a fate," Anna said, and Cecile had to be content with that.

Roland had preceded her to the Maudite. They took dinner there, the hour being somewhat earlier and the inn less rowdy than usual, and then took themselves back to Roland's rooms, where they did not tarry overlong over wine before retiring.

Chapter 24

IN THE HOUR before dawn, Roland slept deeply, on his side, his face so relaxed that Anna could see what he must have looked like as a child. Almost, she curled around him, for another hour of comfort. But duty called. She had told him before they fell asleep that she was leaving early on a mission for her Captain, but she had not provided details and he had not asked. Once again she slipped past the landlord. By dawn she was astride her favorite mount on the road north. Although she had last seen the old witch farther to the east, she assumed that the best place to find her would be at her cottage near her family's homestead.

The river remained too high for fording, despite the fact that the weeks leading to final harvest had been dry, meaning that she must either take the main road or one of the lesser ones where a ferry across could be had for a price. Despite the worries in the Capital, which had spread out of the city, harvest time was too important to be ignored, and all roads were well-traveled. Should anyone be interested in her movements, she had no doubt they would be reported. Accordingly, she took the main road openly and made her way to the inn at Querville, which was not in the direction of the witch's home. Given her previous expenditures there—and despite the loosing of horses on her earlier trip that must have caused the innkeeper some grief—she was welcomed warmly. She made a point of being visible and somewhat voluble about her itinerary, which led, at this telling, to the provincial seat in the far northwest.

Her actions might be for naught—she saw no one who looked to be in the Hierofante's pay—but if anyone should come asking after her, they might be fooled.

The next day she set out again on the main road and only veered onto her real course when she was certain no one was behind her. Despite all her care, she could not shake the feeling that someone was following her. She heard nothing and saw no one, but the feeling remained. It might be Asamir, who could certainly track undetected and might have decided that she should have company on this venture whether she wanted it or no. But Anna also feared it might be someone with uncanny powers, sent to thwart her. Since she did not feel anything unnatural, but rather the merest hint that she was not alone, she decided to believe that the follower was simply a good tracker.

For all that she was in a hurry to obtain help for the Queen, it was equally important that she not lead whoever might be following her to the witch, particularly if they were in the Hierofante's pay. She turned at a crossroads in the wrong direction, moving toward the south. As the sun began to disappear, she set up a campsite not far off the path—clearly visible should anyone be following—and then looped back a short distance on the path and climbed a likely tree.

It was not long ere she saw a rider on the path, clearly one skilled in tracking, for the path itself was slight. As the person drew closer, she recognized the horse, the hat, and finally the face of Roland de Barthes. He stopped under her tree, sniffed the air, and turned his horse in the direction of her camp. Had he noticed her? Was he intending to join her at the camp? From his open way of riding, it seemed he might be.

She climbed down the tree and followed, watching him dismount and look around her site, as if he thought she might have stepped away for more wood. He did not call out while he looked around. Anna came up behind him. "Sir, what do you here?"

He jumped at her words, then turned. "I came to help you find the witch. You are searching for her, are you not?" He looked down at her hand, which rested on the hilt of her sword. "You have no need of that. I am not your enemy."

"Then why did you not catch me up on the road and travel with me openly rather than skulking along behind me? Your methods do not give me comfort, sir."

"I did not think it was wise for us to be seen together. Better for those who are our enemies to think we are about separate business on the main road."

"And so we are. My business is none of your affair, and yours should be none of mine. Though since yours appears to be to follow and see what I might do, it may require my response."

Roland opened his arms wide, his hands well away from his own sword. "Madame. My word as a guard and a gentleman and a servant of the Realm. No, my word as the man who recently spent two wonderful nights in your arms. I am here to help you, not to report on you, not to hinder you, not to spy on you for anyone. I am certain that you have taken on the responsibility of addressing the uncanny side of affairs, and I do not think you should deal in those matters alone."

The directness of his response cooled her anger. "But that is why I did not seek your help, nor anyone else's. These are dangerous matters, and 'twould be best if no one were involved who did not have to be."

"'Twould be best if no one had to act at all, but since the well-being of the Realm is at risk, something must be done. But comrades in arms—and we have become that, in more ways than one—help each other with dangerous affairs. I will not leave you to do this alone."

Anna sighed. It was clear that she had lost the argument. "Very well. I trust you were not followed."

"Do you think me a fool?"

"No. But our absence from the city will be noted."

"And with luck they will think we have left for romantic reasons."

"That will not keep them from seeking us out, if only to seek revenge upon you."

"That is true, but better they seek us out for the wrong reasons than they seek you out for the right ones."

She had to acknowledge the truth of that. They settled into her campsite, and enjoyed a merry evening despite the meagreness of their fare. As the nights were growing cool with the fading of summer, sharing a blanket provided additional comfort.

On the morrow, after circling around to be certain no one else had followed them, they set out for the witch's home. It was not far from the place where they had camped even though Anna had set her path in the opposite direction because of the presence of Roland behind her. Had she not been wary of followers, she would have gone straight there the previous day.

Roland noticed the change in direction, though he did not comment on it directly. "It seems you know where this woman lives," he said as they followed a tiny trail up a hill. "Either you have been given very good directions, or you have been here before."

"Perhaps I am just following indications in the woods," Anna said. She was not going to tell him of the earlier visit nor of the fact that it seemed that whenever the witch was willing to be found, it was easy to do so.

He shook his head. She knew he did not believe her.

It was not long before they arrived at the clearing and the old woman's cottage. It looked different with rays of sunshine poking through the trees now shedding their leaves than it had during the downpour of Anna's previous visit, when she had been scarcely aware of her surroundings. This time she noticed a small garden of herbs and vegetables, some now gone to seed, and could hear cackling from a coop of chickens. A place of comfort, for all that it was a good ways from the town.

They knocked at the door. This time, the witch answered quickly. "Ah, Guardswoman, Guardsman. I have been expecting a visit from you. Please, enter, and I will make you some tea."

The friendliness of her manner startled Anna. She had expected the rudeness of the previous visit or the oblique observations from their meeting on the road.

"Expecting us, Madame?" Roland said.

"There is trouble in the Capital, is there not?" She set a kettle on the hearth.

"Her Majesty is very ill. And since she is with child, this presents many concerns for the Realm."

"She is a fool," the woman said in a voice so quiet that Anna could barely make out the words. "Dabbling in things she does not understand so she can control all that happens in the world, instead of using her authority and talents to lead and advise as she should."

Anna did not think the witch meant the Queen when she said "she." Who then?

"So you think someone might have used sorcerous means to attack the Queen?" Roland said, using words much blunter than Anna would have employed.

"You certainly believe so, or you would not have sought me out," the woman said. "You are braver than your friends when it comes to the old ways, but both of you are still unsettled by them."

"Unsettled, but resolved nonetheless. Will you help us?" Anna said.

The woman stood up and put a teapot and some cups on the table. She got a jar from her cupboard and measured some of the contents into the pot. Roland started to say something else, but Anna put a hand on his arm.

"Seat yourselves at the table."

There were stools, and they each took one. The woman brought the kettle over and poured the hot water into the pot.

"This is not a matter I can handle from so far away. I will have to see the Queen and determine the true cause of her illness. Do you still wish my help?"

"The midwife—a woman of much experience—is confounded. She would take your assistance and be grateful."

"So long as she does not know exactly what I do."

"It is true, Madame, that the people we are asking you to help would rather not know the manner of your aid, but they are desperate for a solution. And they will reward you for your services."

"Oh, that," the woman said. "Yes, of course, I will want to be paid. I have a livelihood to earn, the same as any other. But this will be a dangerous task, not only for myself, but for yourselves and the royals as well. The ban on what is called "sorcerous means" blinds all to the dangers posed by someone so powerful that they believe they can avoid the consequences of defying it. Those dangers are magnified when the person wielding those powers has never received proper training in the crafts of magic. And that is what we are up against, and the person who is harming Her Majesty."

"So will you come and fight this evil, despite the risk?"

"Oh, yes. I will come. I must come. The loss of the Queen, or even the loss of her child to come, would cause harm to the Realm, and while the Realm does not take care of the likes of me, the chaos that would result would bring harm to my people. And this untrained woman could bring about far more evil than she intends, or even knows, and that would involve me and all the others with powers who hide throughout this Realm. Had you not come to fetch me, I would have found it necessary to come to the Capital without an invitation, though that would have made my task even more perilous.

"Still, know ye that some may condemn you for consorting with a witch should my efforts fail, or even should I succeed. Protect yourselves, Guardswoman. Guardsman." She poured the tea into cups.

They sipped tea in silence. "I gather," Anna said, after a few minutes, "that you know who in the Capital is following the path of sorcery."

"Indeed. Have you not divined it yourself, Guardswoman?"

"I have not. We thought at first it might be that...someone powerful"—even here she did not want to mention the Hierofante by name—"received assistance from a known sorcerer from Foraoise. But reports indicate the Foraoisian man is no longer a factor, and yet the sorcery continues."

"Yet you know who benefits. And I have said it is a woman."

"Do you suggest..." said Anna at the same time that Roland said, "No. It cannot be."

"Believe what you wish."

No wonder the woman was warning them of the dangers. "But the Church condemns it," Anna said.

"Which is why it should have been clear from the beginning to even those like you who lack powers that it was the woman herself and not someone in her employ, because no one would dare tell her they had power, and she would not put herself at risk of blackmail from such a person even if they did. It is also why she has no training, for she could not tell anyone when she came into her power. But I am sure she fancies herself quite the sorcerer. She must have learned that term in Foraoise, where they use it with pride. So pompous of them. They are witches just like me, but men and nobles always want to pretend they are something more lordly."

They sat in silence, considering what this might mean. "Even should you succeed in saving the Queen on this occasion, this person is likely to try again, using different uncanny means," Anna said after a few minutes. She had noticed that the witch never spoke of the Hierofante directly, and she followed that lead.

"Yes."

"Can you stop that as well? We will find a way to pay you."

"It will be difficult to do, because it will be nigh impossible for me to get close enough to her. But there is a way, should you be willing to help."

"I have come this far," Anna said, though she felt her stomach turn.

The old woman smiled at her. "You are indeed a brave woman. We will see what transpires in the Capital. This person needs to be stopped, if we can do it. Untrained witches are always dangerous, even if their intention is to do good. And even people who believe themselves of high moral character often do great harm when they think they are doing good, particularly when they have decided that, in their case, it is acceptable to ignore all concerns of ethical and decent behavior. Now we should be off. There is no time to spare."

"Madame," said Anna, "I should know your name so that I can introduce you in the proper manner to Her Majesty's midwife." Her sister Berthe had told her the woman's name, but she felt it best to ask directly.

"Ah, yes. I can see that it might cause problems if you were to refer to me as the old witch from the woods. I am called Martine Herboriste."

Madame Herboriste fetched a saddlebag and filled it with packets of herbs and other items. Before another ten minutes had passed, they were on the trail away from the cottage, all astride horses, for Madame had whistled when she went outside and a sorrel mare had responded.

By nightfall they had almost reached the main road. "We should camp for the night and then turn south toward the river on the morrow," the witch said.

"I had thought to take the main road, since we were not followed."

"As you wish, Guardswoman. I know that the two of you are renowned for your fighting skills. Perhaps you will indeed be able to defeat the dozen Hierofante's Guards who are waiting for you at the bridge. Though even should you be successful, such a victory would trumpet my presence."

"Are you certain?" Roland asked.

"Nothing in life is certain, except the end of it. But I fear crossing the bridge may be the end of both our lives and our mission. And there is a boat landing, known to the people of this province, though not to many others, that we can use to cross. Much more discreet. And we do wish to be discreet, do we not?"

"The river is passable there, then?" Anna asked.

"Oh, yes. It is only in times of heavy rainfall, such as you experienced on your expedition earlier this year, that crossing by means other than the main bridge becomes dangerous."

Roland looked at Anna. She did not meet his gaze.

"Ah, yes. It was he who waited for you on the bridge that time, was it not? But not with so many as the Hierofante's Guard has sent. And not on an expedition so crucial, for all that it must have seemed vitally important to you at the time."

So on the morrow, they did as the witch instructed. Indeed, there were several small craft moored at the landing. They took one across, leading their swimming horses, and then cut across pasture land to a back road into the Capital. Whether due to luck or some action by the witch, they did not encounter any opposition.

Chapter 25

W<small>HEN THEY ARRIVED</small> in the Capital, Roland took his leave from them. "It would be inappropriate for me to accompany you to any meeting with Her Majesty, and I know you will go there forthwith." To Anna he added, "I will hope to see you this evening at the Maudite, should you be able to come."

Anna stopped at the barracks and sent a messenger to the Queen's midwife, the foreign minister, and Cecile, then took Madame Herboriste to her own lodgings so they could repair the ravages of the road and present themselves decently to Her Majesty. Within an hour, Asamir arrived at Anna's rooms to let her know that she was expected at the palace.

"I will go with you to the palace. Madame should have a proper escort," Asamir said in a tone of frosty politeness that brooked no argument.

Anna could tell how angry she was. Madame Herboriste was more amused. "I welcome the additional company, Guardswoman, but hope that you will refrain from that movement you make because you hope it will protect you from things that frighten you. It will draw attention to the underlying matters everyone is aware of but no one wishes to acknowledge."

Asamir bristled at "frighten," but gave a curt nod of agreement.

Anna noticed that the witch had changed her speech so that she sounded more like a city dweller. And she had put on the same sort of simple dress and head covering favored by the Queen's midwife, which, while unlike the fancy attire of the courtiers, conveyed a professionalism that would soothe the fears of those who knew more than they wanted to know.

As they walked up the boulevard to the entrance to the Queen's rooms, Anna spied the girl Cecile had rescued exercising one of the horses in company of several other grooms from the stables. So she had decided to trust Cecile and come to take the position.

The witch also saw her. "That girl," she said. "I have need of her."

It was an odd request, but Anna had come to trust the old woman and was not moved to question it. She walked over to the girl. "Miss, I am escorting a healer to see the Queen, and that healer has requested your assistance."

The girl stared at her. "My assistance?"

Anna shrugged. "I do not know her purpose, but she does. Come with us. I will make it right with the head groomsman." She took the reins of the horse, pointed the child toward Madame Herboriste, and led the horse to one of the other grooms. "The girl is needed to serve Her Majesty," she said, and the groom took the horse without argument.

As she returned to the group, she heard the witch ask the girl her name.

"Joylene," she said.

"Well, Joylene, you will be my assistant in these matters, and I will show you how to do many things."

Cecile met them at the door and escorted the group to the midwife. Anna performed the introductions, saying that Madame was a healer and herbalist well known and respected in her province and one who had much experience with difficulties in childbirth. "The girl here is her assistant." Cecile looked puzzled at Joylene's presence, but the midwife had not seen the girl before and did not know that she had not traveled with them. The midwife responded politely to the introduction, though Anna noticed that she did not take Madame Herboriste's hand.

Madame said, "I will need a place to work with my herbs, and some water, both cold and boiling. My assistant needs a place to wash as well. Once I have my materials ready, I should like to see Her Majesty."

"Of course," said the midwife. "I will prepare Her Majesty for your visit." She turned to a servant who accompanied her. "Please take Madame and her assistant to my quarters and get her all that she needs."

"Madame," said Anna, "Do you need us to stay with you?"

"No, no, Guardswomen. You have done your part in this matter. Now it is the time of the healers, not the fighters."

"I will leave you to your duties," Anna said, hoping that her voice did not betray her relief. "Should you need me, send the page Cecile."

Both healers nodded. Anna and Asamir walked back to their barracks to wait and hope.

———

The Capital felt as if everyone had decided to hold their breath. People in the streets went about their business with the exaggerated steps and loud whispers used by those who walk by a performance or lecture and want to convey that they do not mean to interrupt it. No one spoke unnecessarily. The very air seemed to weigh on the city.

Anger radiated from Asamir as they walked. Her voice was low out of respect to the oppressive atmosphere, but she did not mince her words. "You took Roland with you in place of me. I know you find him handsome and honorable, and I am sure he kept you warm at night, but we have been friends and comrades for most of our lives. How dare you make such a choice on a matter of such import!"

"I did not. He followed me."

"Bah. No one can follow you. You have eyes in the back of your head."

"He is very good. Also, he made a good guess as to my destination. My only choices once I was discovered were to ally with him or kill him. And as I believed his intentions were pure, I did not wish to do the latter."

"Hmph," Asamir said, though she seemed a little mollified. "Was he helpful, then?"

"I could have accomplished the mission without him. And, of course, I could not take him with us to Her Majesty." Anna did not add that she had enjoyed having Roland's company.

"Things were very tiresome while you were gone. Everyone was so worried about the Queen that no one wished to duel or have fun of any kind."

"Even Jean-Paul?"

"He had duty most of the time. Very annoying."

"Not all are worried over Her Majesty. I fear some wish the Queen ill."

Asamir raised her hand as if to make the gesture, but forbore at the last moment, perhaps remembering that she had aligned herself with one side of the forces of magic against the other. "The ones of that persuasion were not looking for duels either."

Some people at barracks appeared to be trying to train, but most sat around, talking, or worrying, or even praying. "We can do nothing here," Asamir said. "Let us go have dinner and a drink."

"Not go pray?"

"I can pray and drink at the same time."

So they set out for the Maudite, for all that sunset was two hours off.

It was so quiet in the tavern that Anna's head began to ache from the absence of noise. Very few people were there, and those who were conversed in hushed tones. Asamir bespoke pies and wine for both of them, and they sat in a corner. Despite their desire for distraction, they, too, avoided conversation.

Within the half-hour, Roland and Jean-Paul walked in. "There's a chill in the air," Roland said, as Jean-Paul and Asamir began their bickering, though in quieter tones than usual."

"Odd. It felt almost like midsummer when we arrived," Anna said. "Unusually warm for a day so close to final harvest."

"We felt the wind blow in as we walked. A winter chill, not the nip of autumn more common this time of year."

The two men also ordered food and drink, but the conversation was far from merry. When Anna went out to use the latrine, she confirmed Roland's weather report. The sky was also growing quite dark, though by the clock the sun should just be disappearing.

She returned to find Roland alone. "Our two children went to find some place more amusing. Though I do not think such a place exists this night."

"All of the amusement tonight will be provided by the storm brewing. We should leave here before we are forced to spend the night. I believe it might snow."

"Snow? This early?"

"This is no natural storm," Anna said softly. "Let us proceed to my lodgings. I need to be available should anyone send for me."

A cold rain started before they reached Anna's rooms, but they made it inside before it turned to sleet. Fortunately, the landlady had provided enough wood for the hearth even though cold weather was not yet due. Anna got the fire going, and the two of them stripped off their wet outer clothes and huddled under a blanket in front of the fire, waiting for the room to warm up. But though they held each other closely, they did not proceed to more romantic behavior. They felt chilled by more than the weather.

After a time, Anna got up to add more wood to the fire. She looked out the window again. The sleet had turned to heavy snow, and a sudden flash of lightning showed that the alleyway was well-covered. The following crash of thunder startled Roland, who had almost dozed off.

"Snow in autumn. Now a thunderstorm accompanying the snow, which I have never heard of in my life. Will there be a plague of locusts next?" he said. The tone of his voice belied the jocular words. "Is this the work of your witch?"

"Our witch. You came with me, do you not remember? Perhaps it is the work of—" she closed her eyes—"Her Eminence."

"You believe the witch, then, that the person dabbling in dangerous magics here is she who is charged with leading the Church."

"If it is not she, it is someone doing her bidding. But given that anyone who admitted to skill in the old ways would be excommunicated at the very least, it seems unlikely that our Hierofante could have found a witch here in the Realm, for who would admit such to her? And if she herself has powers, who would discover that, except for another witch? She is unlikely to have told anyone or done anything that would be obvious to those not thinking of uncanny possibilities. None of her inquisitors would be likely to suspect Her Eminence of engaging in such behavior, even were they wise enough to suspect that anyone was engaging in sorcerous actions."

"Untrained, the witch also said. Does the Hierofante know what she does with this storm?"

Anna shivered, and not from the cold. "For all we know, our witch brought on this storm. Or perhaps it is the result of the two of them warring with each other." Another bolt of lightning lit up the room, and the crack of thunder was deafening. "We can only hope that Madame Herboriste knows what she's doing and that her powers are enough to defeat the Hierofante, save the Queen, and protect us all." She climbed back under the blanket with Roland, and they lay together on the floor, never quite sleeping.

The night seemed to extend on and on. The wind blew fiercely, whistling around the buildings and shaking all the trees. If the clock in the tower at the cathedral chimed the hour, as it ordinarily did, they had not heard it, and so did not know if in fact less than an hour had passed or if the sound had simply been drowned out by the sounds of weather.

Anna got up again to put wood on the fire, which was getting very low. Roland followed her, putting on his almost-dry leggings and undershirt, and wrapping the blanket around him. "I cannot sleep."

"Nor I," said Anna. She put on a shift and leggings from her chest and added a robe, then fetched some wine and cups from her store. They sat at the table for a time, sipping the wine, saying very little. Outside the wind blew, thunder crashed, and snow continued to fall. They finished the wine, though neither seemed drunk, and Anna got out some more. After they finished the second round, Roland brought pillows and the other blanket from the bed, and the two of them curled up again by the fire.

But again they did not sleep, and not only because the floor was harder than the bed would have been. Anna got up to get the kettle. There was enough water left in her barrel for some tea, with a little left over for washing. A glance out the window showed the snow still coming down in sheets. It was too dark to tell how deep it might be, but at least the lightning had stopped. She added another log from the dwindling pile to the fire and hung the kettle to boil. From the amount of wood they had used, it should be morning, but dawn still seemed far off. She poured the water over herbs for encouraging sleep, but even though they drank it all, neither slept. The next time the fire burned low, they waited until it was almost extinguished before adding another log. Even though the fire blazed back up, the room felt no warmer. They shivered and held each other tightly. It was as if the entire world had gone wrong. They did not sleep.

But they must have slept, because Anna woke just as dawn broke to the insistent singing of birds perched in the chestnut tree that grew next to the back wall of the building. She sat up, confused. Birds, singing in a heavy snow?

She managed to stand up, stiff from lying on the floor, and walked over to the window. A first ray of sunlight hit the thick leaded glass. She opened it for a better view and saw a perfect autumn morning. There was a hint of chill, but none of the bitter cold of the night before. Nor did any snow lie on the ground. As far as she could see, there was no sign at all that precipitation of any kind had fallen the previous night. The cathedral bell rang seven times.

"God in Heaven," she said. She, a person who lacked all faith, could barely restrain the desire to make the religious gesture.

Her exclamation woke Roland. "What moves you to pray? Or were you cursing?"

"Both, I think. The storm that should not have been is not only no longer with us, but the world is as if it never existed."

He came to stand beside her and shook his head when he looked out the window. "Did we dream all that?"

"We did not. The fire has died down, but we burned all that wood to stay warm. And our tunics are still damp. Something happened, but what it was I do not know. Still, I think the dawn bodes well."

It was yet too early to go out in search of breakfast, so Anna brewed more tea with the last of the water while Roland went out to the pump and brought back enough for washing. They sat at her table and talked of inconsequential things. The appearance of Cecile at the window seemed almost an afterthought.

"Good morning, Madame, Monsieur," the child said, bowing politely and refraining from commenting further on Roland's presence. "Madame, Her Majesty would like to see you forthwith."

"Her Majesty? Herself?"

"Yes. And by all forces holy and otherwise, she is truly herself this morning."

Anna let out the breath that she had not known she was holding.

"Others want to see you as well. The midwife and the foreign minister and the woman you brought to us yesterday. The witch—she is a witch, is she not?"

"Hush, child. The less said of anything like that the better."

"I thought she might be. And mayhap that girl I rescued is one as well, for she sat up with the wi—with Madame Herboriste—all night long."

They went out the front, and Roland took his leave. He might be involved, but matters at Her Majesty's were not the affair of a King's guardsman. Anna and Cecile walked to the palace.

Her Majesty was still in bed, but she was sitting up and eating a breakfast of eggs and fruit-filled pastry when Anna was admitted.

"Guardswoman. I understand that you found Madame Herboriste and brought her to us. She and my midwife worked all night to find a treatment for my illness, and now I feel renewed. Look, I am even being allowed real food again, and they assure me that the baby-to-be is doing as well as I am. I hope I have not brought you out too early, but I wanted to express my thanks as soon as possible."

"Your Majesty, I am delighted to see you in such improved health and very pleased that Madame Herboriste was able to provide assistance."

"But how did you find this woman? I gather she lives in the depths of the woods, though of course we will provide her with a home here in the Capital, so that we can avail ourselves of her services."

"I met her on some of my travels for the Realm," Anna said. "And, since I am country-raised, I recognized that she was a woman skilled in her knowledge of herbs and healing. When Your Majesty became so ill, I thought of her again, and was given permission to seek her out." She wondered if the Queen had any suspicion of the extent of Madame Herboriste's skills. Her manner did not indicate any discomfort.

But the midwife looked more uncertain. "Do not tire yourself, Your Majesty."

"Yes, yes. I must obey the healers. My undying gratitude, Guardswoman."

Anna bowed and left. The foreign minister was waiting in the anteroom. "Guardswoman, we are all very grateful to you. I did not dare to hope that Her Majesty would recover so quickly, but it appears that Madame's tisanes and potions were almost miraculous in their potency."

Anna thought she detected emphasis on "miraculous." She wondered what the foreign minister had seen or felt through the long night before. "I am glad Madame was able to help. It is truly wonderful to see Her Majesty so alert and healthy this morning."

"Yes. Once she is completely well, we will want to meet with you again to discuss the matters in Foraoise. And I suspect Her Majesty will want your opinion on the growing discord with Alhambra."

"I have no friends among the ministers of that country," Anna said.

"It is not just your connections, but your ability to analyze a situation that both Her Majesty and I find so valuable, Guardswoman. I did not speak lightly when I said you would be of value in a diplomatic career. And your willingness to take risks of every kind for the good of the Realm is yet another asset."

That was definitely a reference to her fetching of Madame Herboriste and a hint that the minister might hope that Anna would continue to cross that line between the accepted way and the more perilous path of magic. The words were complimentary, but the underlying assumption that she would take a particular kind of risk disturbed her. She had hoped to be quit of magical matters. At the same time, though, she found appealing the idea that she might be consulted on matters of state. The minister, daughter to a duke as well as an important member of the Realm authority, was treating her as almost an equal rather than as an inferior sent to clean up a mess.

The midwife came out of the Queen's bedchamber. "A few minutes only," she said to the defense minister, who nodded, bowed briefly to Anna, and went in. The healer turned to Anna. "My great thanks, guardswoman. It was a difficult night, but the change in Her Majesty is more than I could have hoped for. A day ago, I despaired of keeping her with us long enough to give birth, and now it appears we may have both a healthy ruler and a healthy heir."

Once again Anna murmured that she was glad to have been of service.

"A great service to both the woman and the Realm," the midwife said. It was obvious that the phrase "a difficult night" was as close as she was going to come to acknowledging what had actually happened.

Outside in the palace courtyard she found Madame Herboriste sitting under a tree. The child Joylene was asleep on the ground. Madame looked as if she wished she could lie down as well.

"So you were successful," Anna said.

"It seems so, for now. A long night."

"Felt by many across the capital."

"I would have preferred to be less obvious, but found it necessary to draw on very deep powers. It is my good fortune that there are few such as you who are attuned to the old ways even though you lack any talent. Most will forget the strangeness of the night and only celebrate Her Majesty's return to health."

Anna shook her head. "I do not think I will ever forget it, unless you should make it so, as you did when I was a child."

"And I will not, for you are no longer a child, and the Realm and I both have need of a woman of your ability and courage. That woman has veered very far into the blackest of arts. She is very powerful. It is our good fortune that she does not truly know how to use what she has, or I might not have been able to stand against her. She was stunned last night. It will take her some time to recover, and that will give us time to take action to protect ourselves and the Realm from her next foray."

Anna did not want to know more. "It seems the Queen wants to keep you with us here in the Capital."

The witch made a face. "I needs must stay for now, at least until the child is born, to make certain that no further evil occurs. After that, I will visit occasionally, so long as I am in good odor with Her Majesty."

"And this girl? Why did you need her?"

"She is like me, though she did not know it, and barely knows it now. I made use of her to keep myself grounded throughout the night. If she is willing, I will provide her with training."

"How does it happen, that someone has this talent?"

Madame shook her head. "I do not know. It seems to occur at random. In our Realm, those who have it do not know what to do with their talent, while in places like Foraoise or Alhambra, established witches watch for it and make certain the person receives training. I had good fortune in my mentor and hope I can do as much for this one. It is a shame that our enemy did not have such a one to teach her. Perhaps she would have been a different woman."

"Perhaps."

"But for now she remains dangerous. And I cannot get close enough to her to defang her. Her wards are too strong, and she knows who I am and where I may be found, at least here in the Capital."

"Is there aught we can do?"

"Yes, though it will be dangerous. She will come after you. You have defied her, and she knows it."

Anna shivered.

"She will seek a meeting with you."

"And I should avoid that meeting?"

"No. You must go. But I must prepare you for that meeting. Not now, for I am too exhausted, and we have some time. But soon."

"Are all my duties to this Realm to involve matters uncanny?" Anna said. But even though she was frightened, she said it quietly so that only the witch could hear.

"Duties are difficult matters for us all, Guardswoman. Ah, here is my escort come to take us to lodgings. I need sleep. We shall talk again."

Would that were not true, Anna thought as she took her leave. She liked the woman, but she would be content to finish her life without another foray into the world of witches.

Chapter 26

BUT NOTHING THAT so much as hinted at the uncanny happened for one fortnight, and then for most of another. The Queen was seen to walk in the park with the King. There were vague rumors of disquiet on the southwestern border with Alhambra, but no more than usual. The resumption of diplomatic relations with Foraoise relieved the various Guard troops of the need for additional training. Even the weather cooperated: a string of sunny days lasting just long enough for the farmers to get in the last of the hay and wheat, and then several thorough but gentle rains that came during the night. Life settled into a pleasant routine, and Anna began to believe she might never again be forced to deal with witches or other magic.

Her relationship with Roland deepened. One evening as they relaxed in his lodgings, he brought out his book and showed her a poem he had finished.

> When night is at its blackest hour
> And chaos storms through town and glade,
> She rises from our hidden bower
> And strides to battle unafraid.
>
> Another night we lie entwined.
> She tells me of her heart's desire
> And listens when I speak of mine.
> We share a moment far from fire.
>
> How have I come to find a love
> With heart so gentle and so brave?

A woman who will loose the dove
And yet fight on if more be saved.

She asks my help to seek the just.
May I be worthy of her trust.

She was as flattered by the trust as the sentiments. After that night, he took to reading her sections of his work in progress and asking her opinion. They were growing not just fonder of each other, but comfortable together.

Relations between the King's and Queen's Guards had become so friendly that there was scarcely a duel to be found, much to Asamir's dismay. Fortunately, the Hierofante's Guard did not share in this friendship, and despite the fact that they often enforced the dueling laws, it became clear that many of them could be persuaded to cross swords. Asamir made a point of taking advantage of this. Still, the Realm was as peaceful as a country of its time and place could ever hope to be.

And everyone was looking forward to the birth of an heir.

But even in this time of peace, conflict arose, for peace in a world of fractious human beings is but a time when disputes lead only to minor violence. While Her Eminence was not seen in public, had not sent out any pronouncements, and was rumored to be ailing, there were some among her people who harbored great resentment against Roland over the death of the former Andalucie governor Greybonne. They were led by Lieutenant Verlaine of the Hierofante's Guard, who, Anna had discovered, was cousin to the deposed governor. On one Sunday afternoon, when Roland and Anna were strolling in the Governor's Gardens, enjoying some time by themselves for no purpose, he walked up, blocked their path, and said, "Your time is coming."

Roland did not reply, but stood his ground, meeting the man's eyes until Verlaine turned on his heel and walked away.

"It was all I could do not to reach for my sword," Anna said after the man had gone.

"But you did not. Thank all the stars in alignment that I was with you and not Jean-Paul, who would certainly have drawn his. I do not want to play into that man's hands."

"I did suspect he wanted to goad you into challenging him."

"Or even into attacking him without the formality of the requisite words. I wonder if he has friends nearby."

And indeed, as they left the Gardens, they noticed several other guards wearing the Hierofante's white also leaving the area.

Several days later, they were dining at the Maudite with Asamir and Jean-Paul, when five Hierofante's Guards entered. They walked across the room abreast, forcing people to move out of their way, creating enough of a scene that by the time they reached Roland, the place had become as quiet as a tomb—something that rarely happened in that rowdy establishment.

"Monsieur de Barthes, we are here to arrest you."

Noise resumed, but of a different kind than before. The Maudite was crowded with members of the King's Guard, and not a few of the Queen's. There was a pushing back of stools from the table, a rustling of hands toward swords, a murmuring of curses and threats.

Roland moved his own stool back, as preparation for standing. Something about his movement indicated to Anna that he was going to surrender himself to prevent a riot; she was certain that there were others of the Hierofante's Guard nearby waiting for chaos to break out to give them an excuse to come in fighting. The man leading the five—not Verlaine, but one of his seconds—was known to her to be no fool. He had not come here to fight an unequal battle with King's guardsmen.

She put her hand on Roland's arm, shook her head at him, and stood up, her hands at chest level, away from her sword. "If you have come to make an arrest, you must show a warrant. No crime has been committed here to justify an arrest without an order from a judge or other person of authority."

"The charge is murder," the man said.

"Indeed. Then you certainly must show what gives you the right to make such a charge, for that is a major allegation and not one for which an arrest can be made without official action. Produce your documents."

Anna was quite certain that no legal proceedings had been begun against Roland, for his Captain had informants throughout the Capital and would have let him know if he were in any danger of official arrest. If he went off with these troops, they might well kill him; if he did not, he might be killed in the ensuing riot. If he survived, he would certainly be arrested for causing the outbreak of violence.

One of the Hierofante's troops said, "Look, a King's Guardsman hides behind a Guardswoman. Odd loyalties, those."

"She is his slut," said the leader, who then proceeded to describe what Roland and Anna must do in bed in terms so graphic and ugly that even Asamir, who was not easily shocked by matters sexual and who had her hands full keeping Jean-Paul from attacking the men, gasped.

"It must be true what one hears of the Hierofante's Guard, that they take the same vows as the priests. For it is clear they do not know what two people who love each other might do in private."

The leader bristled at Anna's words, but the sounds of amusement from the corners of the room told her that she had, in fact, lowered the tension.

"Show us your documents, your authority to arrest," Anna said again. "And if you cannot, leave now. Monsieur de Barthes is ever ready to respond to legitimate authority, but he must have proof of the legitimacy of any allegations."

A chant went up in the room. "Show the papers. Show the papers." People began to bang on the tables with their cups.

"Well?" said Anna. "Have you documents? Have you a warrant?"

"We have orders."

"Show your papers. Show your papers."

"You need proof of those orders. I suggest you go and fetch it."

He glowered at her. After staring at her for what felt like minutes, though it was likely only a few seconds, he said, "We will be back."

They left in more of a single file, for people did not scurry out of their way.

"Thank you," Roland said. "I did not want to go with them, but I was certain that they hoped to provoke a riot if I did not."

"They will be waiting for you outside. I doubt they have any official authority, but they are likely to have other tricks up their sleeves."

And so it came about that Roland left the bar in the guise of a member of the Queen's Guard. It was useful that he generally went clean-shaven, and the formal hat of the Guard, set over his shoulder length hair as arranged by Asamir, covered his face. None of his friends accompanied him, but he traveled in the company of five guardswomen. He leaned on the shoulder of one of them, looking as if he might have over-indulged in the Maudite's libations. Several Hierofante's guards standing in the street spared a glance for them, but did not stop them or ask any questions.

Anna and Asamir left with Jean-Paul, in part to constrain him from starting any fights on his own. They were questioned closely by the Hierofante's guards as to the whereabouts of Roland but allowed to leave when they refused to reply. The guardswoman who had lent Roland her tunic left as part of a rowdy band of guardsmen, all singing off key. They were not noticed.

Anna returned home to find Roland awaiting her. "Your friends escorted me here, and I climbed up the back. But perhaps we should go somewhere else, for they might search for me here as well."

"I do not think they will try anything else tonight," Anna said. "Invading a private residence is likely beyond their orders. Let us go to bed."

And while neither of them slept well, they did spend the night unmolested.

As they sat over morning tea, Anna said, "I think you need to leave the Capital for a time."

"My captain suggested as much yesterday, but I do not like to run away from trouble."

"I understand that, but in this case the trouble will not exist if you are not around. They are not even pursuing me, Asamir, or Jean-Paul, though they could. I suspect your captain will find it easier to work on your behalf if you are not present, for as long as you can be found, Verlaine and those he commands will continue to look for opportunities to attack you. With you gone, the tension will subside."

Roland nodded. "I know it would not help matters if I were to kill him, though I confess my desire to do so grows stronger every day. So where shall we go?"

"A large assumption, that 'we.' But as it happens, I do have an idea for an expedition for us both, one that will also be of use to both your captain and mine. It is end of the term at Saint Demetrius, and the Queen's Guard has been invited to watch the students' final demonstrations. My captain and I discussed yesterday whether she should send someone, for it is always of value to know the skills of those who will soon be looking for positions in Guard units. Perhaps your captain would also like to have the students evaluated. We could travel there together."

Roland agreed, and they went out to seek the blessings of their commanders and to make their plans for travel. Given their concern that Verlaine had deputized a number of Hierofante's Guards under his watch to seek Roland out, Anna gave him a plain tunic to wear. She went out the front door, and, indeed, found several Hierofante's Guards loitering in her street. She engaged them in banter, knowing that Roland was leaving by the back. Sooner or later the Hierofante's Guard would find that handy tree, but on this day they continued to assume that there were no other exits.

They met up at a prearranged point, and Anna made sure that Roland got to his own barracks without incident before heading for hers. She returned the borrowed Queen's Guard tunic and sent Roland's to his barracks via a messenger. The Guard members at barracks were all talking about the incident in the Maudite, as was the Captain when Anna met with her.

"An excellent job of avoiding trouble last night," she said by way of greeting. "I wish all my guardswomen had your talent for using words to avoid duels."

"I fear it might have grown to more than a duel. Some from the Hierofante's Guards have targeted Monsieur de Barthes despite the fact that no legal body has taken any action against him. They are looking to either harm him or cause trouble that can be blamed on him. And for once, our Guard and the King's are aligned together against them."

"That is a matter of politics and will have to be resolved that way. Monsieur de Barthes had best lie low until it is, however."

"It had occurred to me that he and I might both go to see the students at Saint Demetrius. I have some skill at leaving the Capital without being tracked. And no one is likely to be at the school from the Hierofante's Guard; they recruit all their troops from the religious school. Saint Demetrius officials would not have invited them in any case, as the head is noted for her opinion that religious orders should not keep their own troops."

"And I am certain that you and the gentleman would enjoy spending time together," the Captain said.

"The plan has more than one advantage," Anna replied. She had decided that admitting she enjoyed Roland's company was the only defense against the constant teasing.

Roland's captain approved the plan, while assuring him that he would take all steps to end the abuse and harassment by Verlaine and the others of Hierofante's Guard. "It is possible that we will need a Royal edict that approves your action; I will see if that can be obtained. But be careful as you travel. I cannot protect you from attacks while on the road."

They left on horseback early in the morning on the next day, with Roland once again attired as a member of the Queen's Guard. Several other guardswomen accompanied them. They passed the Hierofante's guards on several occasions, but were neither approached nor followed. The others rode with them until they were across the great bridge over the Adabarean River. Once they were traveling alone, they left the main road for a trail through the forest, and both changed their tunics for the plain brown favored by country folk. They rejoined the main road on the outskirts of Querville and once again put up at the inn there.

"Ah, Madame," the innkeeper greeted them. "Are you traveling on personal business?" She had noticed the ordinary dress.

"This is more practical for travel," Anna said. "But we would prefer to avoid company, if you could accommodate us with a private room."

"That can certainly be arranged. Though you must not disturb the horses this time, Madame." The innkeeper wagged a finger at her, though the smile on her face suggested that Anna's payment for that inconvenience had been sufficient.

"Madame, I cannot afford to do so again," Anna said, and they both laughed.

Roland stared at her. "You did that on purpose?"

"As, Monsieur," said the innkeeper. "You were in the opposite company on that occasion, as I recall. But now you know how Madame keeps her reputation as one of the smartest of her Guard."

Her amusement seemed to make up for the fact that Anna's payment was not quite so generous as before, since she had only her own and Roland's funds to draw upon, not the largesse of Her Majesty. They were given a comfortable room with a view of the road. A good fire burned on the hearth, and the innkeeper provided excellent wine and dinner. To their relief, the only other travelers who stopped at the inn that night were merchants and farmers headed to the Capital for the autumn fairs. They two avoided the common room, so as not give rise to gossip.

They left after the others in the morning and headed west to Saint Demetrius. The school lay less than a day's ride beyond the town, so they traveled at a leisurely pace, wandering off the road to picnic by a stream at midday.

"What was it like, going to a soldier's school?" Roland asked as they lingered over bread and sausage.

"Quite a change from living on a farm. Though the hours and workload were much the same: up at dawn and always something that must be done. My mother had given me a good base of training in the sword, but the lessons in strategy and history expanded my skills greatly. And I would not have learned poetry at home."

"You enjoyed it, then?"

"It was exhilarating and convinced me that the way of the sword, not the way of the plow, was my destiny."

"I think I would have enjoyed it," Roland said. "I was tutored at home, with my sister. I think our lessons in literature and history were quite good, and we did get decent sword instruction. But strategy was not in our curriculum, and far too much time was spent on court etiquette. Our studies ended abruptly when our father was usurped. I had to pick up the rest of a soldier's skills on my own, catch as catch can."

"And yet you are as fine a soldier as any in the Realm. There are many paths to learning the skills one needs in life."

"And many ways to live it. Even tragedies may have their positive side. Had my family not lost our estate, I would never have become a guardsman and had the pleasure of your company."

Susanne was thrilled to see Anna and to meet Roland, whose reputation had preceded him to Saint Demetrius. While the school had managed throughout the years of the Great Divide to stay on good terms with both the Andrean and Meloran factions—no easy feat, and one that had left quite a few of its alumni at odds with each other—it had never aligned itself with the religious factions. Some of the students and teachers had family ties in Andalucie and shared the rampant dislike of the now-dead governor, making Roland a hero in their eyes. In fact, Anna realized when talking with her history teacher, a man she had always both respected and adored, Greybonne's sins had been well-known everywhere but in the Capital.

"It is often true that when the power of a realm is established in one place the abuses that occur in the less elite places are overlooked," he told her. "It was even true during the Great Divide. Both the Andrean and Meloran royals were unaware of poor leadership in the provinces, those of their own as well as those of the other faction. They were far too focused on their own struggles to notice those of their subjects who were not close at hand. It would behoove those of you who have access to the royal ears to keep them apprised of the goings on in the provinces."

Anna protested that she did not have much influence, and her teacher gave her a smile. "You are being modest or discreet, or else you are misjudging your own influence. Monsieur de Barthes is not the only one whose reputation is much bruited among the students and the faculty."

Susanne was allowed to join them at meals—making her the envy of all the other students—though she was unable to spend much time with them due to her preparations for demonstrations and the written exams that would follow.

On the morning of the demonstrations, the head asked Anna and Roland to begin things with a sword match. They had no time to prepare—perhaps the head had considered that, for she introduced them with the admonition to the students that guardsmen and women must be prepared to fight at any moment. Taking it in their stride, they began with a formal bow, and then proceeded to demonstrate a variety of basic sword moves. Anna struck toward Roland's head, and he responded with a simple block, then struck toward hers, giving her the opportunity to show a second one. They went on through strikes to the neck and knee and stabs toward the body as if they had set out to conduct a class, though they were using live blades.

Roland came in with an overhead strike somewhat faster than before. Anna stepped to the side at the last moment and brought her sword up under Roland's wrist. He raised his sword and stepped back just in time. The overall speed of the contest increased. They continued at an almost all-out pace, finding that balance between giving a worthy opponent the respect they deserved by not pulling the attacks, but still bearing in mind that they did not want to kill, or even injure, each other. Anna felt exhilarated and relaxed in a way that she had not known in some time.

They reached a point where both were crouched deep, with Roland's sword held down under Anna's, and both holding their blades with two hands on the hilt for added strength. If she raised her sword, she could easily strike his open neck, but once she released his sword, Roland could cut up through her groin. Mutual destruction.

Instead, Anna let go of her sword with her right hand, continuing to hold it in place with her left, which was not strong enough to keep Roland's blade blocked. She reached her right out toward him. And he, too, let go with his right, letting his sword hang loosely in his left, and grabbed her hand. They came to standing together and bowed to the crowd, which went wild with applause.

"As your head informed you, guard members must be prepared to fight at any time. But fighters must be prepared to save lives as well as take them," Anna said, after the applause had quieted down.

"Killing is sometimes necessary, but remember to keep yourself open to other possibilities at all times," Roland added.

Susanne demonstrated great skill in the group presentations of training forms, empty-handed as well as those with sword and staff. Anna noted with approval that she was excellent at staying at the group's pace—an aspect of training that some students found difficult. Roland agreed. "Very useful in battle, that awareness of the others around you," he said.

Anna's sister also acquitted herself well during the tournament portion of the demonstrations, ranking among the top students in archery as well as empty-hand and staff fighting. Both Anna and Roland made note of several other students who showed promise.

The sword matches were the featured event, for the teachers and students of Saint Demetrius shared the Realm's passion for blades and duels. A competition was held for each class year, with the students who won the top honors for the top two years vying for all-school fall champion. The students used padded weapons. Susanne, a member of the most senior class, made short work of her first opponent, knocking his sword aside and landing a quick blow to the head. The second gave her more trouble, but she won that match on points. In the finals for the senior class, she met a young man of equal skill. They began their match by each taking a strong stance and moving carefully around each other, looking for an opening. Susanne showed great patience, finally moving in a way that hinted at an opening. The young man fell for it, moving with a stab toward the center of her body only to find that she had moved at the last possible moment, and struck him on the head.

The all-school final was less of a challenge. The younger student was too eager to score on Susanne, who made short work of her. Anna, though she had seen many a tournament and knew that luck played a part, found herself very proud of her sister. It honored their family legacy.

Over dinner, Susanne told Anna and Roland that she had considered ending the senior match as they had ended theirs, with a yield to friendship. "But I know that boy, all too well. He would have responded to my opening with a strike, not a handshake."

"You made the right call," Roland told her, matching her seriousness.

On their way home two days later, Roland said, "Your sister has the makings of an excellent guardswoman. Do you plan to recommend her to your captain?"

"I would like to, but is it honorable of me to promote the virtues of my sister? Many of the other students also show promise."

He shook his head. "I think you must be the only person within the Realm who would even consider that. Have you not noticed that everyone seeks favor for their own interests whenever they can? Verlaine, after all, is using his authority to get revenge on me for Greybonne's death."

"And is that not wrong?"

"Perhaps. But you are not in so morally compromised a position. Your sister is a strong candidate on her own and, in fact, by demurring too much, you would deprive the Queen's Guard of a fine member. If you do not recommend her to your captain, I will recommend her to mine."

"Since when does the King's Guard take women members?"

"Why should they not? They no longer confine themselves to Melorans, and your guard is not restricted to Andreans. Why continue the artificial divide by gender?"

It was a good question, and Anna did not have an answer. Other guard units were mixed, the Hierofante's most notably. But it occurred to her that she liked things as they were.

"Perhaps at some point," Roland continued, "we will have only a Royal Guard, with men and women pledged to both King and Queen. One assumes the heir to come will not share authority with a spouse."

"That will be after our time, if all goes well," said Anna. "We will let those in charge then determine what sort of guards we will have. Meanwhile, I will take your advice and recommend Susanne. You are right: she is the caliber of guardswoman we want."

Chapter 27

ON THEIR RETURN, they were met at the bridge over the Adabarean by a large group of King's and Queen's Guards, as arranged in advance, and escorted into the Capital with no incident. Few Hierofante's Guards were seen in the streets. Roland's captain assured him that Verlaine had been called to account and that it was more unlikely than ever that any legal proceedings would take place.

But just as Anna had begun to believe that all might be well—she had not even seen the witch since their return—Roland informed her that he had been ordered to meet with the King the next day. He had not been told what it concerned.

"Do you think he might take action against me over the death of the governor?" he asked Anna.

"Not unless Her Eminence has regained his ear."

"Which could have happened, since you told me that the Hierofante was only stunned, not completely defeated, in her battle with the witch. And she might have reined in Verlaine and the others to give her an easier passage to His Majesty."

"Perhaps he wants to honor you for doing your duty."

"Perhaps." He did not sound satisfied.

The poem he shared that night dealt with the vagaries of lords.

> Some curry favor with their lords
> With fawning words and lavish praise
> And once assured of favor there
> Seek power far beyond their due.

Those who give astute advice
In words less politic or nice
Are often shoved aside, ignored,
Or even cast beyond the court.

And worse, the flatterers then use
Their ill-gained powers to attack
Those they hate for reasons old, and
Those whose wealth and means they crave.

Beware of lords who are bespelled
By flattery and unmeant praise.
Such lords will not be fit to lead
In times of peril or distress.

Anna liked it, but cautioned him to destroy it. "'Twould be dangerous if His Majesty were to see it."

Roland agreed, though she was not certain he would take her advice. They made plans to meet on the morrow, after his audience.

⌇

Anna spent the morning on the training ground, working a group of junior guards hard to keep her own mind occupied. Her rendezvous with Roland was not until early afternoon, and despite her reassuring words to him, she could imagine all kinds of scenarios by which their lives would be upended. As she dismissed the exhausted troop, Cecile arrived for her training session. Anna threw herself into that as well, doing exercises alongside the child and sparring with her until both were soaked through with sweat. The girl brought no message from Her Majesty, though she reported that all appeared to be well at the palace. The Queen had breakfasted with one set of advisors, held a post-meal meeting with a second group, and had been setting off on a walk with a group of courtiers—the King being engaged—when Cecile had left to meet Anna.

The two of them were repairing their appearance in the lounge when the guard from the front gate came in search of Anna. "Excuse me, Madame, but there is a messenger here for you." Cecile walked with her to the gate.

The messenger, barely more than a girl, wore the white tunic of the Hierofante's Guard. "I am to wait for your reply," she told Anna as she handed her a card.

The document asked her to attend upon Her Eminence on the following morning at ten peals of the cathedral bell. Anna's stomach clutched. But she did not show her fear to the messenger. "Inform Her Eminence that I will be there." She did not add false assertions of pleasure. The Hierofante would know them for a lie, regardless, and she saw no point in pretending their relationship was anything but adversarial.

She stared after the Hierofante's guard as she left. Less than a month of life without the peril of the uncanny. Was that the best she might ever hope for? Cecile shifted impatiently, obviously wanting to ask what had occurred, and the gate guard gave Anna a look of concern. "Should I call the captain, Madame? Is there trouble with the Hierofante's Guard?"

"No. It is not a matter for the Captain. 'Tis my own affair." Or rather, the affair of royalty who relied on her but could not protect her from dangers they did not want to believe existed and of witches—both friend and foe—who wanted to use her for their own ends. She wondered if the Hierofante would only try to harm her, or whether she would attempt to bring her into her fold. She was not sure which she dreaded more.

Anna turned to Cecile. "Might you be able to inform Madame Herboriste that I would like to call upon her before the sun sets? If she would prefer another time or place, she should send a messenger to me, but I must meet with her before the morning. 'Tis urgent."

"Of course, Madame," Cecile said. In a whisper, she said, "Her Eminence?"

Anna nodded.

"I will return myself if Madame sets a different hour."

Anna joined her comrades for a brief luncheon of soup and bread. The conversation around her was lively, with bets being placed on when Her Majesty would give birth. Dates at the beginning of February seemed most popular. A winter baby, always worrisome, but those who were country-raised pointed out that all signs indicated the season might be milder than usual. Anna did not join the betting pool, though she managed to smile enough at appropriate times to prevent anyone from asking what troubled her. Cecile did not return.

After lunch she set out for the Governor's Gardens where she had agreed to meet Roland, walking briskly to keep anxiety at bay. Due to the pace, she arrived early. She forced herself to walk through the park, to look at the trees—some still gold, others already denuded of leaves—at the small animals scurrying along with their winter stores, at the few birds who wintered in the Capital flitting from place to place in search of grain or insects.

The church bell rang twice, but Roland did not appear. Did that mean he was detained, or was it the usual vagaries of royal privilege? The bell was sounding the half hour when she saw him walking toward her. Even from a hundred paces away, she saw that he was smiling. He began to run when he saw her.

"Their Majesties have restored my family's lands and our title," he shouted as he neared her. Then he recovered his manners and kissed her hand.

"It is only your due," Anna said. "But as you wrote, the doings of lords..."

"Are not always for our betterment. You are right. I must destroy that one. It may be true—my happiness does not give me illusions—but I should not seem ungrateful."

"I have never seen you so happy."

"I have been this happy in your arms, Madame. But this means my mother will have a comfortable old age. My family

will no longer have to rely on my sister's husband for the necessities of life. And my father's honor—the honor of our whole
family—is restored."

"Will you or your sister take the title? Or is there another
sibling of whom you have not told me?"

"There are no others, and I am the elder. I shall be the Baron
de Barthes. Though I regret that my father is not with us to enjoy
more years of what was so unjustly taken from him."

"Will you find it necessary to spend a good deal of time in
your barony, then? I am given to understand that titles come with
responsibilities and duties."

"Many of those, alas. And the seat of the barony is in the
south. I will miss the Guard, though since we are on the southern
border, it is our duty to the Realm—as His Majesty reminded
me—to keep our own guard and assist the governor with patrols.
There are always rumblings with Alhambra."

"You will do well by it all."

"Come and help me celebrate."

"I must see Madame Herboriste this afternoon, but perhaps I
can join you for some mild celebration tonight. Tomorrow I meet
with Her Eminence."

Roland's face fell. "I had hoped that would not occur."

"And so had I."

"Go and speak with Madame. Perhaps she can give you more
protection. I will be at the Maudite, and I fear the celebration
there may become rowdy, but I still want to spend a little time
with you." He kissed her hand once more.

Madame Herboriste was at home in the lodgings at the edge
of the palace grounds that Her Majesty had provided. Joylene
greeted Anna at the door.

"Are you staying here as well?" Anna asked the girl.

"Yes. Madame has been very good to me. I liked the horses,
but the work with Madame is better. She says she will take me
back to the woods with her and teach me the arts of healing and

herbs. She will even help me find a place for my mother and brothers, who are not happy in the city."

Anna noted that the child had already learned that she must be circumspect in how she described her trade. Though perhaps she did not yet fully understand it herself.

"Bring the Guardswoman in, girl."

Joylene showed Anna into the front room, where Madame sat by the fire with a purring tortoiseshell cat on her lap. "I fear I shall have to take this creature to the forest as well. I do not know what my wolf will make of her, but the cat will not be pleased if she is left behind. But sit, Guardswoman."

"I have come, Madame, because I have been summoned by Her Eminence, as you predicted I would be. I would appreciate any advice you can give me on this audience and fear I might also need your protection." The last was hard to say, for Anna's training in the way of the warrior had left her unaccustomed to asking others for assistance.

"I have prepared something that will protect you should she try to turn your mind or will by spells. Girl, go and fetch it." Joylene disappeared into the back room. "And I have some instructions for you, for I have thought of a way to further limit that woman's powers, if you are able to convince her to do and say certain things."

"I lack all skills in the uncanny, Madame," Anna said, trying not to show the fear she felt at the very idea that she might have to deal with magics.

"I am well aware of that, Guardswoman. I will handle the magics; you will only be my mouthpiece, since you can get close to the woman, and I cannot."

Joylene returned and handed the witch what appeared to be a simple shift of undyed wool. "Here is the protection I have made for you."

"I am certain that it will keep me warm, and the days do grow more chill, but...."

"Do not joke with me, Madame. This is a matter of urgency. I knitted this garment myself and have incorporated spells and materials that will prevent any witch—even myself—from taking over your will or mind."

Anna wondered if she could truly trust that Madame had protected her even against herself, but prudently decided not to pursue that point.

The witch gave her the shift and took up a wide wristband. "And this band will provide a link between us, so that when you say the words I set and act as I will tell you, my power will come through you."

Anna took the band with more trepidation than she had taking the shift. It had been woven, rather than knitted, and although it too was made of undyed wool, it looked as if had elements of metal worked into the weave. It was laced on the underside with braided yarn.

The old woman raised her arm, showing a similar band. "They are linked to each other. While we both wear them, I will be aware of your every move and able to act on those around you. So do not wear it when you go to bed with your handsome baron, or you will tempt me into doing things I should not." She laughed.

Anna did not take comfort in those words, but she tied the band in place. The laces were long enough to hang loosely.

"You should return the band to me after your meeting," the witch added. "I may have need for it again with someone besides yourself. But keep the shift, for it will protect you in other dealings with those who follow the old religion. Yes, truly, even from me." She laughed again, clearly enjoying Anna's discomfort. "As for your instructions. First, you must make certain to touch that woman with the hand that wears the band both when you first arrive and just as you leave. This should be relatively simple. Religious leaders do like to have their supplicants kiss their ring of office, do they not?"

Anna nodded. "Though I have usually avoided so doing."

"You will have to let go of your principles in this matter and do so. Second, during the course of your conversation, you must get her to say the words, 'I am bound.' It does not matter what words come after that. She will not feel the effect of those words until after you touch her the second time, so the order of these actions is important. Do you understand?"

"Yes. Or rather, I know what I am supposed to do. Understanding the whole is beyond my ken."

"Guardswoman, you continue to demonstrate that you are wise. You do not need to understand more, and given that you lack any talent for the old ways, you are better off not knowing."

"But how shall I handle Her Eminence? What should I say to her requests or threats or whatever else she may choose to try on me?"

The witch waved her hand in dismissal. "Whatever you like, my dear. I have noticed that you are often very quick in complicated conversations. My contribution is to protect you from dangers no person without magic can handle, and to bind that woman's power. I am certain you will handle the politics of the matter in your usual competent way."

Anna noted that, once again, the old woman never called the Hierofante by title or name. She did not know if it was for reason of contempt or because she thought such words conveyed power. "I would prefer it that all the matters I deal with could be resolved with a sword."

"You are noted for your abilities with your sword, Guardswoman, but if you will think back on your actions over the last few months, you will realize that you are also quite talented at resolving conflict in other ways. Rely on your wits, guardswoman. They are your best asset, and they will not decline as you grow older. And remember: if you touch her twice and she says the words I set for you, she will not trouble this Realm for some time to come."

"Not forever?"

"Nothing is forever, Guardswoman. Nothing is forever."

———

Roland was holding court in the Maudite when she arrived, buying drinks for a crowd of fellow guardsmen as well as for Asamir and a few others from the Queen's company. He leapt up to kiss her hand and hand her a cup, and she obliged him with a toast to Baron de Barthes, draining her wine.

Someone refilled her cup. She sipped at it, nursing it. Drunken parties were the order of the day when celebrating good fortune, but she did not feel able indulge in such behavior this night. The life of a soldier always carries the risk that tomorrow one might die. Many used that awareness to excuse bawdy living in the rest of their lives, and while she had never been one given to excess, she had always before been able to enjoy herself at such gatherings. But for all that tomorrow she might well die, she could not deal with that awareness in the carefree manner common to guards. The many months of treading on the edges of the uncanny had changed her. Things went on in this world, things just beyond her ken, and far beyond that of the guards in this crowd. Those things could change lives in a moment, yet few were aware they existed and even fewer understood their import.

She finished her wine, gave Roland a peck on the cheek— to wild applause and lurid commentary—and slipped away. She would need her wits about her on the morrow.

But someone was following her. She turned, and Roland stood there. "Let me walk you home, Madame."

"They will miss you in there."

"They are far enough along to being drunk that they no longer care whose health they drink. I will return to pay my bill and take a final bow, but I would have your company for a while longer."

They walked quietly, companionably, down the streets. Since the return of the Queen's health, the capital had resumed its lively ways. Boisterous sounds came from other taverns, and crowds of people wandered the streets.

"The Realm is happy today," Roland said. "You caused that to happen."

"With your help, sir. With your help."

"Aye. We have both done our duty to King and Queen and to the Realm. And by our doing so, I am now able to do my duty to my family. It comes to me that perhaps I might think of myself, for once."

"That would be a pleasant thought, would it not," Anna said. "Should I survive my meeting on the morrow, perhaps I will consider thinking beyond my duty as well."

"Then let me give you something to consider, Madame." He took her left hand in his. "Would you do me the honor of becoming my wife?"

She had not expected this, for all that their once casual romance had become something deeper. "Sir, you do me great honor in the asking. You are now a lord restored to his title, while I remain what I have always been, the daughter of a pig farmer."

"And the foremost member of the Queen's Guard. Come now, do not be modest. Everyone has heard of the valiant Anna D'Gart."

"And a guardswoman who has always tried to live up to her duties, yes. But there is no noble blood in my veins. Surely your family will want you to make a marriage that can bring your family more position and honor."

"I have done sufficient duty to my family by restoring the title. And in any case, my sister married well. Surely I am entitled to marry for my own purposes."

"But will your family agree?"

"I am the baron." He laughed at his own arrogance. "They are not so proper as all that, and our name and lands are not so far removed from farming that we should look down on it. You would be welcome in my family."

"We would live in the south."

"But come to the Capital as often as we can. And you could manage the guard for the border. It would be simple work after all you have done here, but you would be a swordswoman, not simply a baroness. There is always disquiet on the Alhambra border; we are ancient enemies. You could do much good there." He hesitated. "I do not want to tame you, Madame. I only want to spend my life with you."

Almost, she said yes. She did love him, and, at the moment, the idea of a simpler life held many attractions. But something held her back. "Sir, I cannot answer you until after my appointment with Her Eminence. Whatever might transpire there could change both our lives for good or ill. I will give you my answer on the morrow."

"A fair response." They walked the rest of the way to her lodgings in silence. At her stoop, he took her hand. "I must return to my drunken friends, Madame. But I will expect you to call on me when you finish with your duty to Her Eminence."

"My duty there is to the Realm, once again," Anna said. "Or so Madame Herboriste has charged me."

He kissed her hand and took his leave.

Chapter 28

ANNA ARRIVED IN advance of the hour set for her meeting with the Hierofante. The guards who let her in first through the gate of the Cathedral grounds, then through the door that led to the audience chamber, were unknown to her and seemed to bear her no specific ill will, though their manner said that anyone not of the Hierofante's Guard was unworthy of their respect. She was greeted in the anteroom by a man in the robes of the church who was well-pleased with himself.

"Her Eminence is engaged. She will see you when she has a moment." His voice implied that she was a supplicant seeking favors.

The insult was deliberate, and she thought of walking out. But her duty to the Realm required this meeting. She gave him the no-nonsense look reserved for bureaucrats and troublemakers. "Please let Her Eminence know that I am here at the time she appointed. I remain at her service."

The man gave her a curt nod, but did, in fact, go into the other room. Anna doubted that Her Eminence was engaged in anything but strategic annoyance.

The cathedral bell rang the hour and a lesser bell within the compound the quarter hour before Anna was admitted to the august presence.

The Hierofante stood in the center of the room. "Guardswoman," she said, holding out the hand that held her ring of office.

"Your Eminence." Anna bowed, though she did not kneel despite the fact that the Hierofante was shorter than she. Following the witch's instructions, she took the Hierofante's hand in a way that allowed the band and its laces to touch the woman's fingers. She brought her lips close to the ring, though she did not let them touch it.

The Hierofante allowed the corners of her mouth to turn up slightly, perhaps assuming that Anna's gesture of obeisance meant that she controlled this conversation. She stepped up onto a platform, which made up for her lack of height, and sat in a large chair carved with religious imagery and coated with gold—one that evoked the thrones occupied by Their Majesties when they handled official matters of state. A wave of her hand indicated that Anna should sit in a modest wooden chair. Anna considered continuing to stand, but decided that defiance at this point in the meeting would be poor strategy.

Though the Hierofante was not a young woman—she was, Anna guessed, about the age of her own father—she remained handsome. Her once blonde hair was turning silver with age, but that enhanced her appearance rather than detracted from it. Her skin was as pale and pink as that of her nephew the King.

"It seems we are at odds, Guardswoman."

"It has not been my intention to be so, Your Eminence."

"Yet you have had fractious exchanges with members of my guard."

"Only in pursuit of my duty to Her Majesty and to the Realm, not out of any enmity toward them or yourself."

"But I, of course, give my duty to the Realm as well, within the confines of my duty to God. And my guards act in performance of that duty. There should be no conflict between your duties and theirs."

Anna wondered if she would have believed that statement even when she was young and starry-eyed with dreams of the honorable pursuit of a guardswoman's life. Likely not; her mother had known of the woman when she was but a bishop, long before reunification, and had conveyed her distrust of the Hierofante along with lessons in the sword. "We perhaps have different understandings of our duties, Your Eminence. My intention is only to follow mine."

"I have given my duty to this Realm and to God since long before you were born, Guardswoman. My role in the Church has not kept me from being aware of what was important to the Realm, especially as the interests of the two are allied. I advised my brother during the years in which he ruled, and I now advise my nephew as well. My interests are not my own, however much you may believe differently."

Dealing with the Hierofante gave her the same uneasy feeling she had in dealing with the witch. Both women seemed to answer her unspoken doubts in a way that made her think they were reading her mind. But perhaps in this case the Hierofante was only reading her body language and commenting upon Anna's actions in opposition to her own.

And perhaps Her Eminence truly believed she was acting in the best interests of the Realm. Anna had always thought of the Hierofante as one who meddled in matters that were not properly her concern, and learning of the woman's talents in the ways of magic had caused that idea to solidify in her mind. It had never before occurred to her to wonder why the Hierofante meddled so much; she had merely assumed the woman did it to cause trouble. But what if she did it because she truly believed her vision of what the Realm should do was the correct one? That did not change the danger posed by her forays into black magic, especially those that were aimed at Her Majesty, but it did affect how Anna should deal with her. Did the Hierofante truly believe that reunification was the wrong choice and that the Queen was doing damage to the Realm? Well, she had implied that her brother had ruled the whole of the Realm, when he had only ruled the Meloran half. Did that explain her actions?

"I do not doubt your devotion to your duty, Your Eminence." Politic words seemed like the right response. Anna felt warmth from the shift she wore under her tunic. Did that mean the

Hierofante was trying something uncanny? The witch had not warned her of this. She wondered if the Hierofante knew the shift was there and what it did. Dealing with matters of magic meant that one constantly worried about things unseen. Anna was tired of it.

"I am glad to hear it. And despite our differences, it seems I have offered you safe conduct in the past."

"You are known for your care for the subjects of the Realm, Your Eminence. I am certain that you were aware of the strenuous tasks I was undertaking to assist in the avoidance of war and wished to provide ease in my work."

Anna could tell Her Eminence had not expected that response. The shift was getting warmer, though it was not yet uncomfortable. Was the Hierofante merely buying time in the hope of doing something uncanny to her, or did she have other purposes in mind?

"Ah, yes, you are the woman who has put in a great deal of effort to obtain peace with the people of Foraoise," she said. "A good thing, peace. I suppose. Perhaps if you and I worked in concert we could do even more to improve the Realm's relations with its neighbors."

"Are you inviting me to take a position with the Church, Your Eminence? Or offering me a commission with your Guard?"

"No, no, Guardswoman. Nothing so official. You are well placed to aid me and the Church from where you currently serve. Our relationship would be an informal one."

"I am not suited for such a role, Your Eminence. I am bound to Her Majesty and the Realm; there is no room in my life for a duty beyond those. I take my vows seriously and endeavor never to make any promises beyond what I know I can do."

"Yes, yes," she said. "But sometimes duty to the greater good calls us to go beyond our official roles. You are one who understands that there is more to the Realm than what one sees on the surface. To do one's duty can at times require measures that might seem less than honorable to an outsider. I know that all speak of the honor of Anna D'Gart, but it appears you have done some things of late in furtherance of what you think is your duty that counter that reputation."

Was that an attempt to blackmail her? "I have done nothing save serve the interests of my Queen and our Realm, Your Eminence. I fear that dealing with measures that could entail dishonorable behavior would be too complicated for me. Perhaps you find it easy to be bound by your duty and yet act in ways for the greater good that others might find contradictory or worse, but I am a simple farmer's daughter and cannot imagine such a path."

"There is nothing simple about you, Guardswoman."

"I shall take that as a compliment. But I am bound by my duty to Queen and Realm, just as you are to God and Realm. You are so bound, are you not?"

"Of course. I am bound by my duty...." She hesitated a moment... "By my duty to God and the Realm. And I will continue to do it."

Her Eminence had said the words. Now all Anna needed to do was to touch her once more with the wristband. "Is there anything further, Your Eminence?"

"You would be well advised to cease your efforts to thwart me, Guardswoman. I would hate to find it necessary to excommunicate you, but if you continue as you have begun...." She left the sentence unfinished.

"I have no intention of thwarting you, Your Eminence, so long as I am not required to do so by my duty to Her Majesty and the Realm. But I know that you are aware that status within the Church is not a requirement for service in the Queen's Guard."

"Perhaps not, but the Church will not countenance the marriage of someone who has fallen from its favor. And I doubt the Famile de Barthes would want an excommunicated baroness in their midst."

How had she known of her conversation with Roland? This was not a simple threat to her, who cared little for the Church; this was a promise that the Hierofante intended to continue to interfere in both her life and Roland's. If the witch's spell worked, Her Eminence might not be able to cause havoc in their lives magically, but that was far from her only power. And while Roland's family was now restored, they could once again lose everything to the whim of their superiors. "You must do your duty as you see fit, Your Eminence. As I will do mine. One hopes that will not put us at odds."

Anna stood and, as it seemed the Hierofante would remain seated, walked over to the woman's chair and bowed deeply. "Your Eminence, I bid you good morning," she said.

The Hierofante reached out her hand in a careless manner, and Anna took it, bent over the ring once again, and made certain that the wristband pressed against the other woman. This time she felt a jolt and, from the surprised look on the Hierofante's face, it seemed that the other had felt it, too.

The Hierofante opened her mouth, and Anna expected another threat. But all the woman said was, "Good morning, Guardswoman."

Anna turned and left.

The captain of the Hierofante's Guard met her at the gate, standing so that she must get past him to leave. "You should not behave as if Her Eminence is your enemy." His voice was cold, but his hand was not on the hilt of his sword.

"When has she ever shown herself to be my friend? A word to you and your fellow guards: Do not try to come between me and my duty to our Queen and our Realm. I will not allow it." She walked straight toward him, and he yielded.

⤙⫟

Anna walked through the streets of the capital with no destination in mind. It was easier to think while walking. The Hierofante had always been her enemy, but in the general way in which she was enemy to all of the Queen's Guard and to all those who had followed the Andrean line. Now, though, Her Eminence was very aware of her personally, and perhaps had even guessed that Anna knew of her secret dealings in the sorcerous world. It was to be hoped that the witch's spell had limited the Hierofante's ability to use the uncanny, but the power she wielded as head of the Church and aunt to the King was still quite dangerous.

But Anna had made her choice and did not regret it. She had declared for the Queen and the Realm, and opposed her who would undermine both. Such a choice was perhaps not safe, but changing sides would not make her any safer. And it would besmirch her honor. The Hierofante's observation that Anna was not the simple person she professed to be echoed earlier remarks from the foreign minister and, for that matter, the witch. Anna was beginning to recognize the truth of it. She had become a person with some power in the Realm, and she had achieved that by adhering to her duty, rather than by subverting it, which in itself was gratifying. But her success, and thus her power, had come from thinking strategically and from following her well-honed intuition on what risks to take, not from following orders.

Anna realized with a burst of clarity that she liked being a person with power, even if it required her to deal with matters uncanny and to make dangerous decisions on her own. She would not give up that power lightly.

As she strolled into the Governor's Gardens, she met Madame Herboriste. "Guardswoman, you have done well today. The woman is crippled."

"She has other powers besides uncanny ones. She will find ways to cause more trouble."

"The world is never safe from such as she, the ones who never doubt that they are right, who never question themselves. We must take our victories where we find them."

"Yes, I suppose we must." Anna sighed.

"Are you troubled, Guardswoman?"

"I am more puzzled. I had determined in my mind that the woman, as you call her, was acting out of some evil purpose. But now that I have met with her, I believe that in fact she does what she does out of the belief that it is what is needed by the Realm. And as I have done the same, I begin to wonder what is the difference between her and me."

"Your asking that question is the difference, Guardswoman. That woman has never questioned whether her idea of the right action for the Realm was indeed the proper one, any more than she questioned whether she should pursue the dark arts despite her Church's objection to magic. I think this is a curse of the nobility. People such as ourselves, who were not born to power, do not make such assumptions. Though living here close to the center of things, I might find myself beginning to believe that my way is the only way. That is why I will leave and return to my home in the forest as soon as the babe is born. And why you must continue to be the honorable Anna d'Gart, even if tempted beyond it.

"I suggest you visit me in the forest from time to time and perhaps spend more time with your family and their pigs, for all that you will never be a farmer again. You are an important person in the Realm, but you do not want to forget that you are someone else as well."

Anna nodded. It was the sort of advice she needed to hear. She bade the woman good day and continued on her walk. As she approached the barracks, she found that her mind had cleared. She knew what she believed and what she must do.

In the early evening, Anna called at Roland's lodgings. He greeted her formally at the door, with his customary kiss of her hand, but once he drew her into his rooms, he kissed her mouth passionately, urgently. She responded in kind.

He poured wine for them both, and they sat at his table across from one another. "How went your meeting with Her Eminence?"

"We parted enemies. But it appears that Madame Herboriste's scheme succeeded. The Hierofante's uncanny power is crippled, at least for the present. She was unable to harm me and should be unable to attack the Queen again. However, her power in the Realm is not diminished. She will continue to plague us all in the ordinary fashion."

Roland sighed with relief. "That is a power we understand, at least. So we have both ventured among the powerful and survived."

"Even prospered, in your case."

"Indeed. Though knowing from my history that what His Majesty gives can be taken away, I do not rest completely easy."

They sat quietly for a few minutes, sipping wine, touching hands. Roland at last broke the silence. "Have you considered my offer?"

"I have, sir. Deeply and completely. And I regret to say that I cannot marry you."

He frowned, but did not pull away his hand.

"It is not that I do not love you or want to be with you. It is not even that I am completely unsuited to the life of a baroness, though that is an important fact that must be considered. And, yes, I trust that you would not try to make a courtier of me, but I would have duties should I marry you, duties that I would execute badly, I fear.

"But Her Eminence threatened me today with excommunication, something that remains within her power. I am not religious, except by convention, and the Queen's Guard does not judge its troops on their religious fealty. My own family does not follow the faith in a serious fashion, so it would cause no difficulties for them.

"But the Church would not recognize a marriage between us, should she do this thing. And while I know you have little in the way of religious feelings yourself, it would bring a stain on your family, one you can ill-afford when your title has been so recently restored."

"I care not for any of that. I want to spend my life with you." It was the bluster of a noble, a man who, at his core, believes he can have all that he wants.

"If you are taking up the title of baron in duty to your family, then you must pay attention to such matters. The Hierofante cannot harm us as guards or for performing our duties, but she can always use the might of the Church against us."

Roland shook his head. "She can try, but even Her Eminence must provide reasons for what she does. Besides, I have also been told by some among the Hierofante's Guard that she is considering excommunicating me directly unless I do penance for the death of Greybonne, something I will not do. I did not act wrongly and I will not pretend I did. If she tries to take action against either of us, we will find a solution. Do not let the Hierofante block our happiness." He took her hand in his and brought it to his lips.

Anna gently pulled it back. She had not wanted to tell him the whole truth, had hoped that the Hierofante's threat would provide enough excuse. She sighed.

"There is more, is there not?" Roland asked.

She nodded, but could not yet bring herself to speak.

"If you do not love me enough, please say so quickly. You will break my heart, 'tis true, but I am a grown man and know I will survive that."

"It is not that I do not love you enough. I am not like Asamir, always flitting from lover to lover, never taking any of them seriously. My affections are given deeply or not at all, and I have given them all to you. Were you not now the Baron, with estates to run and duties far away and in need of a wife to help you manage those duties, I would marry you tomorrow.

"But marrying you would mean changing what I do. That is the price of nobility in our day and age. And I find that I very much do not want to change that."

"I know," he said quietly, "that you take your duty very seriously."

"This is about more than my duty or my honor. I have become a person of some power within the Realm. I am consulted by Her Majesty. I know great secrets, and I deal with persons of great power. It is possible that when my captain decides to retire, I may succeed her. I may be offered other important work, but even if am not, I will still be in a pivotal position, able to influence the goings-on in the Realm.

"I like having that power. This is not my duty; this is, in fact, my ambition, the very ambition I denied having when I spoke with the Hierofante. But in fact, she is right about me. I have become a person of power and I do not want to give up my influence. And I cannot wield it from so far away as your barony, cannot wield it by operating a small guard to help protect our borders. I need to be here, where the decisions are made.

"All my life I have done my duty to others as I understood it. Today I know that I must do my duty to myself as well. I might pretend to others that this is for the good of the Realm, and indeed I think that the advice I have to give in high places is for the good of the Realm, but I will not lie to you and pretend this is only duty."

He sat there, saying nothing. Anna could not read his face. She stood up. "I will continue to love you, sir, and to cherish the times we have shared. I wish you well as you go to rebuild your family's fortune." She picked up her things and walked out the door. He did not call her back.

Tears welled in her eyes as she walked through the streets back to her own lodgings. Anna did not doubt her decision, but even so, the loss of their relationship brought deep pain. She found she could not even wish that Roland's title had not been restored, for all that her own life would have been perfect had he remained a simple member of the guard. It was justice that he take his title, no matter the cost to her. "Defeat even in victory," she whispered to herself as she entered her rooms and poured herself some wine.

It took her some hours to go to sleep, but she eventually managed it only to be awakened in the wee hours of the morning by the sound of someone at her window. "Damn and blast," she said as she rose to open it, having shut and locked it against the night chill. She had not expected a summons from Her Majesty at this point.

But it was not Cecile at her window; it was Roland. "I did not want to disturb your landlady by knocking at the door."

She stepped back to let him crawl in. He stood in front of her, then reached for her hands.

"After you left, I at first railed at you, that you would put your worldly desire over our love. And then I realized that I was doing the same. I want to rebuild my family's estates and name, and if the Hierofante tries to interfere, I will do what I can to stop her. It might be more politic if I were to yield to my sister, who does not have my enemies, but it is important to me to be the one who restores the family."

"I would not ask you to make such a choice."

"No. You did not. But I asked such a thing of you. And worse, I asked you to give up not just something that you wish to do, but a position where you do good for the Realm. It was unfair and selfish of me, and I am sorry."

She did not know what to say. Whatever she had expected, it had not included this.

"I accept that you cannot marry me, cannot take up the responsibilities that come with marrying into a title. But would you be willing to continue as we have begun? I will have to spend much time in the south, but I will also need to travel to the Capital often, if only to remind His Majesty of my loyalty and to protect my estates from actions by Her Eminence. And perhaps you could travel south now and again, for Their Majesties would benefit from your review of the border with Alhambra."

"But you must have a wife and heirs," she said, and then wondered for a moment if he were proposing to both marry someone else and continue their relationship.

He shook his head. "My mother is still in good health and can deal with official matters. It will please her no end to do so. And my niece—my sister's eldest—is a formidable young woman. She will make an excellent baroness once she is old enough. I need neither a wife nor additional heirs. But I do need you in my life."

He pulled her to him, and she did not resist.

Epilog

A fortnight beyond the winter solstice, on a day that was unseasonably warm for winter, Her Majesty gave birth to a healthy daughter. Holiday was declared throughout the Realm, and there was much rejoicing in the streets—and taverns—of the Capital.

Madame Herboriste told both the midwife and the Queen that all portents were in the child's favor. She and her new apprentice took leave of the city after assuring Her Majesty that they would return from time to time. The midwife, so Anna heard, was pleased to see them leave, for all that she was grateful for their help.

Nothing of importance had been heard from Her Eminence, though no one—and certainly not Anna nor Her Majesty—took that as a sign that she would not try some new tactic in the future. Still, matters in the Realm were as quiet as anyone could desire.

On a day not long thereafter, Anna sat waiting—with resignation rather than patience—while Asamir primped after training.

"What shall we do with the evening?" Asamir said.

"Roland remains in the south. Jean-Paul is on duty in the west. I fear we must entertain ourselves."

"Our credit should be good at the Cafe Maudite."

"Indeed. But if you intend to provoke anyone into a duel, we had best take Nicole or one of the other young women spoiling for a fight along with us, for I will not second you. I seek a quiet winter sitting around the fire, not the strife we have had for the past year."

"The peace will not last," Asamir said.

"No. It will not. But I shall enjoy it while we have it."

About the Author

Nancy Jane Moore started making up stories about women with swords when she figured out at the age of nine that, under the rules of Spanish, she could change "Zorro" to "Zorra." With the help of her sister, she acted out sword fights and other adventures in the back yard. Eventually she moved on to writing the stories down.

Her other books include the science fiction novel *The Weave* and the novella *Changeling*, both from Aqueduct, and the collection *Conscientious Inconsistencies* from PS Publishing. Her short fiction has appeared in numerous anthologies and in magazines ranging from L*ady Churchill's Rosebud Wristlet* to the *National Law Journal*.

She practiced law for fifteen years, specializing in cooperative organizations, and then worked as a legal journalist. In addition to writing and law, she has studied martial arts since 1979 and holds a fourth degree black belt in Aikido. She teaches, speaks on, and writes about empowerment self-defense.

A native Anglo Texan, she lived for many years in Washington, DC, and now resides in Oakland, CA, with her sweetheart and two cats.

And yes, she owns a sword.

Website: http://nancyjanemoore.com/

Blog: https://treehousewriters.com/

Follow her on twitter at @WriterNancyJane

Pronouns: she/her